The Sister Jane series

Outfoxed

Hotspur

Full Cry

The Hunt Ball

The Hounds and the Fury

The Tell-Tale Horse

Hounded to Death

Fox Tracks

Let Sleeping Dogs Lie

Crazy Like a Fox

Homeward Hound

Scarlet Fever

Out of Hounds

Thrill of the Hunt

Lost & Hound

Time Will Tell

Books by Rita Mae Brown with Sneaky Pie Brown

Wish You Were Here

Rest in Pieces

Murder at Monticello

Pay Dirt

Murder, She Meowed

Murder on the Prowl

Cat on the Scent

Sneaky Pie's Cookbook for Mystery Lovers

Pawing Through the Past

Claws and Effect

Catch as Cat Can

The Tail of the Tip-Off

Whisker of Evil

Cat's Eyewitness

Sour Puss

Puss 'n Cahoots

The Purrfect Murder

Santa Clawed

Cat of the Century

Hiss of Death

The Big Cat Nap

Sneaky Pie for President

The Litter of the Law

Nine Lives to Die

Tail Gate

Tall Tail

A Hiss Before Dying

Probable Claws

Whiskers in the Dark

Furmidable Foes

Claws for Alarm

Hiss & Tell

Feline Fatale

The Nevada series

A Nose for Justice

Murder Unleashed

Books by Rita Mae Brown

Animal Magnetism: My Life with Creatures Great and Small

The Hand That Cradles the Rock

Songs to a Handsome Woman

The Plain Brown Rapper

Rubyfruit Jungle

In Her Day

Six of One

Southern Discomfort

Sudden Death

High Hearts

Started from Scratch: A Different Kind of Writer's Manual

Bingo

Venus Envy

Dolley: A Novel of Dolley Madison in Love and War

Riding Shotgun

Rita Will: Memoir of a Literary Rabble-Rouser

Loose Lips

Alma Mater

The Sand Castle

Cakewalk

TIME WILL TELL

TIME
WILL TELL

A NOVEL

RITA MAE BROWN

ILLUSTRATED BY LEE GILDEA

BANTAM

NEW YORK

Copyright © 2024 by American Artists, Inc.

Illustrations copyright © 2024 by Lee Gildea, Jr.

Published in the United States by Bantam Books, an imprint of Random House, a division of Penguin Random House LLC, New York.

BANTAM & B colophon is a registered trademark of Penguin Random House LLC.

LIBRARY OF CONGRESS CATALOGING-IN-PUBLICATION DATA
Names: Brown, Rita Mae, author. | Gildea, Lee, Jr., illustrator.
Title: Time will tell: a novel / Rita Mae Brown; illustrated by Lee Gildea.
Description: First edition. | New York: Bantam, 2024. |
Identifiers: LCCN 2024037729 (print) | LCCN 2024037730 (ebook) |
ISBN 9780593873823 (Hardback) | ISBN 9780593873830 (Ebook)
Subjects: LCGFT: Detective and mystery fiction. | Novels.
Classification: LCC PS3552.R698 T56 2024 (print) |
LCC PS3552.R698 (ebook) | DDC 813/.54—dc23/eng/20240816
LC record available at https://lccn.loc.gov/2024037729
LC ebook record available at https://lccn.loc.gov/2024037730

Printed in Canada on acid-free paper

randomhousebooks.com

2 4 6 8 9 7 5 3 1

First Edition

TO GULLIVER
Always in my heart

CAST OF CHARACTERS

Jane Arnold, MFH, "Sister," has been a Master of Foxhounds for the Jefferson Hunt since her late thirties. Now in her middle seventies she is still going strong. Hunting three days a week during the Season keeps her fit mentally and physically. She is married to Gray Lorillard, choosing not to take his last name, which is fine with him.

Gray Lorillard isn't cautious on the hunt field but he is prudent off of it. Now retired, he was a partner in one of Washington, D.C.'s most prestigious accounting firms. Often called back for consulting, he knows how "creative" accounting really works. Handsome, kind, and smart, he has dealt with decades of racism. Doesn't stop him.

Betty Franklin has whipped-in for Jefferson Hunt for decades. Her task is to assist the Huntsman, which she ably does. In her mid-fifties and Sister's best friend, she can be bold on the field and sometimes off. Everyone loves Betty.

Bobby Franklin especially loves Betty; he's her husband. They own a small printing press, work they enjoy. Bobby is a good businessman. He leads Second Flight, those people who don't jump but might clear a log or two.

Sam Lorillard is Gray's younger brother. A natural horseman, he works for Crawford Howard, who has a farmer pack of hounds. After hitting the skids he finally overcame his alcoholism with Gray's help. He is a bright man and a good one.

Daniella Laprade is Gray and Sam's aunt. Somewhere in her nineties, she can be outrageous. Stunningly beautiful, she even now looks good, considering her years. No one in Jefferson Hunt has known life without her. Having three rich husbands helped her live comfortably. As to her numerous affairs, she was discreet.

Wesley Blackford, "Weevil," hunts hounds for Sister. He loves his work; and being young, is learning, soaking up everything. Aunt Daniella had an affair with his grandfather, whom he greatly resembles. He is in love with Anne Harris.

Anne Harris, "Tootie," is another natural horseman. She whips-in to Weevil. Betty is her idol, as Betty exhibits incredible instincts in the hunt field. Tootie left Princeton to hunt with Jefferson Hunt. She is almost finished at the University of Virginia. She looks very much like her famous mother.

Yvonne Harris was one of the first Black models. She and her detested ex-husband built a Black media empire. Divorcing him, she moved to Albemarle County to be near Tootie in hopes of repairing that relationship. She wasn't a bad mother, but was unwittingly neglectful. She can't understand that Tootie has little interest in racial politics. Tootie is the product of her parents' success. She has no idea about earlier struggles.

Crawford Howard is best described by Aunt Daniella, who commented, "There's a lot to be said about being noveau riche and Crawford means to say it all." Given his ego, large as a blimp, he learned about Virginia and hunting the hard way. He made his first fortune in Indiana. They may have been irritated by him but the

Hoosiers were used to him. He is restoring Old Paradise, a great estate built with funds stolen from the British during the War of 1812.

Marty Howard, married to Crawford, patiently guides him to less bombast. She has a passion for environmental projects and the funds to pursue them.

Walter Lungrun, MD, jt-MFH, practices cardiology. He has hunted with Sister since his childhood. He is the late Raymond Arnold's outside son. His father accepted his wife's indiscretion, raising Walter as his own. It wasn't discussed and still isn't. He and Sister have a warm relationship.

Ronnie Haslip is the hunt's treasurer, indefatigable in raising funds. He was RayRay's best friend, Sister's late son. He is a good rider, loved by his chihuahua, Atlas.

Raymond Arnold, Jr., "RayRay," died in a farm accident in 1974. Loved and remembered by Sister, Ronnie, and those who knew him, sometimes they feel his spirit. He was a good athlete and a good kid.

Kasmir Barbhaiya, born and raised in India, was educated in England like so many upper-class Indians. He foxhunts with gusto and rides well. When his wife died he left India to come to Virginia to be near an Oxford classmate and his wife. He fit right in. He is a man with broad vision, knowing the world in different ways than an American.

Alida Dalzell brought Kasmir back to life and happiness. They met on the hunt field. She adored him but never made a move out of respect for his late wife. Ultimately, Kasmir realized his beloved wife would have wanted him to be happy. These two are made for each other.

Edward and Tedi Bancroft are stalwarts of the hunt. After All, their property, abuts Roughneck Farm, Sister and Gray's farm. Now in their eighties, the Bancrofts are slowing down a bit but fighting it every step of the way.

Ben Sidell is the county sheriff. He got the job after coming from Columbus, Ohio, good training, as that is a university town. In Virginia, towns and rural areas have separate political structures, so Ben is not responsible for policing the university. There's enough to do in the county. He rides Nonni, a saint. Sister found the mare for him and told him to learn to hunt. It's the easiest way to understand Virginia, which is not like Ohio.

Veronica Sherwood moved to Madison County, Virginia, a year and a half ago, give or take. She manufactures special design cardboard boxes. With her sister, Sheila, she buys houses, restoring them with special teams of women workers. She rides with Bull Run Hunt.

Sheila Sherwood, her sister's business partner, takes women from halfway houses, rehabilitation centers, to teach them construction skills in the hopes they don't relapse. A good salary is a start to stability. She also is a member of Bull Run Hunt.

Adrianna Waddy, MFH of Bull Run, is friends with Sister Jane. She owns a successful realty company, has a sense of the land. Her work helps her as a Master of Foxhounds. She and Sister Jane greatly enjoy each other's company. Magnum is her retired foxhound.

Lynn Pirozzoli has had a big career, winding up becoming the White House liaison at the Environmental Protection Agency. Now retired and running The Black Horse Inn with her husband, her degree in Environmental Science and career have given her an understanding of foxhunting as an environmental bulwark. Her Jack Russell, Baxter, has a high opinion of himself.

Mike Long is also an MFH at Bull Run, along with James Moore, Jr. With 38,000 acres on which this remarkable hunt has permission to hunt, a master works nonstop. Mike's knowledge of the battle of Cedar Mountain is astonishing. He literally knows where the bodies are buried.

Birdie Goodall, recently retired from running Walter Lungrun's MD office, suffers a devastating loss when her grandson, Trevor, is murdered. It's fair to say Trevor did not live up to his potential, but did he deserve to die for it?

Mary Willard-Brooks is an Albemarle County firefighter. Fearless, she has no occasion to demonstrate this ability in this volume. She checks old chimneys between fire breakouts. Her qualities will be highlighted in the future when fire is a weapon.

Cynthia "Skiff" Cane hunts Crawford's pack. She gets along with him. He went through three huntsmen before her. She also gets along with Jefferson Hunt.

Shaker Crown hunted Jefferson hounds for decades. A bad accident ended his hard riding. He fell for Skiff, and helping her helped him, as he was lost without the horn. Hunting hounds was his life and he loved it.

Freddie Thomas hunts First Flight. She rarely talks about her profession, which is accounting. She, Gray, and Ronnie are all accountants, which sometimes amuses them. She is Alida Dalzell's best friend.

Kathleen Sixt Dunbar owns the 1780 House, a high-end antiques store. Her husband left it to her even though they rarely saw each other, living hundreds of miles apart. They never bothered to get divorced. She drives Aunt Daniella around to follow the hunt. She absorbs so much about the hunt, plus everything else. Aunt Daniella is a font of information.

Rev. Sally Taliaferro is an Episcopal priest who hunts. She is always there if a parishioner needs her or if anyone else needs her.

Father Mancusco is the priest at St. Mary's. He's fairly new, having been there three years. He and Sally get along, both more than happy to give people prayers in the hunt field.

THE AMERICAN FOXHOUNDS

Lighter than the English foxhound, with a somewhat slimmer head, they have formidable powers of endurance and remarkable noses.

Cora is the head female. What she says goes.

Asa is the oldest hunting male hound, and he is wise.

Diana is steady, in the prime of her life, and brilliant. There's no other word for her but *brilliant*.

Dasher, Diana's littermate, is often overshadowed by his sister, but he sticks to business and is coming into his own.

Dragon is also a littermate of the above "D" hounds. He is arrogant, can lose his concentration, and tries to lord his intelligence over other hounds.

Dreamboat is of the same breeding as Diana, Dasher, and Dragon, but a few years younger.

Hounds take the first initial of their mother's name. Following are hounds ordered from older to younger. No unentered hounds are included in this list. An unentered hound is not yet on the Master of Foxhounds stud books and not yet hunting with the pack. They are in essence kindergartners. **Trinity, Tinsel, Trident, Ardent, Thimble, Twist, Tootsie, Trooper, Taz, Tattoo, Parker, Pickens, Zane, Zorro, Zandy, Giorgio, Pookah, Pansy, Audrey, Aero, Angle,** and **Aces** are young but entered. The "B" line and the "J" line have just been entered, and are just learning the ropes.

THE HORSES

Keepsake, TB/QH, Bay; **Lafayette,** TB, gray; **Rickyroo,** TB, Bay; **Aztec,** TB, Chestnut; **Matador,** TB, Flea-bitten gray. All are Sister's geldings.

Showboat, Hojo, Gunpowder, and **Kilowatt,** all TBs, are Weevil's horses.

Outlaw, QH, Buckskin, and **Magellan,** TB, Dark Bay (which is really black), are Betty's horses.

Wolsey, TB, Flaming Chestnut, is Gray's horse. His red coat gave him his name, for Cardinal Wolsey.

Iota, TB, Bay, is Tootie's horse.

Matchplay and **Midshipman** are young Thoroughbreds of Sister's that are being brought along. It takes good time to make a solid foxhunter. Sister never hurries a horse or a hound in its schooling.

Trocadero is young and smart, being trained by Sam Lorillard.

Old Buster has become a babysitter. Like **Trocadero,** he is owned by Crawford Howard. Sam uses him for Yvonne Harris.

THE FOXES
Reds

Aunt Netty, older, lives at Pattypan Forge. She is overly tidy and likes to give orders.

Uncle Yancy is Aunt Netty's husband but he can't stand her anymore. He lives at the Lorillard farm, has all manner of dens and cubbyholes, as well as a place in the mudroom.

Charlene lives at After All Farm. She comes and goes.

Target (a gray) is Charlene's mate but he stays at After All. The food supply is steady and he likes the other animals.

Earl has the restored stone stables at Old Paradise all to himself. He has a den in a stall but also makes use of the tack room. He likes the smell of the leather.

Sarge is young. He found a den in big boulders at Old Paradise thanks to help from a doe. It's cozy with straw, old clothing bits, and even a few toys.

James lives behind the mill at Mill Ruins. He is not very social but from time to time will give the hounds a good run.

Ewald is a youngster who was directed to a den in an outbuilding during a hunt. Poor fellow didn't know where he was. The out-building at Mill Ruins will be a wonderful home as long as he steers clear of James.

   Mr. Nash, young, lives at Close Shave, a farm about six miles from Chapel Cross. Given the housing possibilities and the good food, he is drawn to Old Paradise, which is being restored by Crawford Howard.

Grays

Comet knows everybody and everything. He lives in the old stone foundation part of the rebuilt log-and-frame cottage at Roughneck Farm.

   Inky is so dark she's black and she lives in the apple orchard across from the above cottage. She knows the hunt schedule and rarely gives hounds a run. They can just chase someone else.

   Georgia moved to the old schoolhouse at Foxglove Farm.

   Grenville lives at Mill Ruins, in the back in a big storage shed. This part of the estate is called Shootrough.

   Gris lives at Tollbooth Farm in the Chapel Cross area. He's very clever and can slip hounds in the batting of an eye.

   Hortensia also lives at Mill Ruins. She's in another outbuilding. All are well constructed and all but the big hay sheds have doors that close, which is wonderful in bad weather.

   Vi, young, is the mate of Gris, also young. They live at Tollbooth Farm in pleasant circumstances.

THE BIRDS

Athena, the great horned owl, is two and a half feet tall with a four-foot wingspan. She has many places where she will hole up but her true nest is in Pattypan Forge. It really beats being in a tree hollow. She's gotten spoiled.

Bitsy is eight and a half inches tall with a twenty-inch wingspan. Her considerable lungs make up for her tiny size as she is a screech owl, aptly named. Like Athena, she'll never live in a tree again, because she's living in the rafters of Sister's stable. Mice come in to eat the fallen grain. Bitsy feels like she's living in a supermarket.

St. Just, a foot and a half in height with a surprising wingspan of three feet, is a jet-black crow. He hates foxes but is usually sociable with other birds.

SISTER'S HOUSE PETS

Raleigh, a sleek, highly intelligent Doberman, likes to be with Sister. He gets along with the hounds, walks out with them. He tries to get along with the cat, but she's such a snob.

Rooster is a Harrier bequeathed to Sister by a dear friend. He likes riding in the car, walking out with hounds, watching everybody and everything. The cat drives him crazy.

Golliwog, or "Golly," is a long-haired calico. All other creatures are lower life-forms. She knows Sister does her best, but still. Golly is Queen of All She Surveys.

Atlas, a chihuahua, stays with Sister when Ronnie Haslip, his owner, is injured.

J. Edgar, a young box turtle with a beautiful shell, has landed at Roughneck Farm. Golliwog, the cat, is appalled.

USEFUL TERMS

Away. A fox has gone away when he has left the covert. Hounds are away when they have left the covert on the line of the fox.

Brush. The fox's tail.

Burning scent. Scent so strong or hot that hounds pursue the line without hesitation.

Bye day. A day not regularly on the fixture card.

Cap. The fee nonmembers pay to hunt for that day's sport.

Carry a good head. When hounds run well together to a good scent, a scent spread wide enough for the whole pack to feel it.

Carry a line. When hounds follow the scent. This is also called working a line.

Cast. Hounds spread out in search of scent. They may cast themselves or be cast by the huntsman.

Charlie. A term for a fox. A fox may also be called **Reynard**.

Check. When hounds lose the scent and stop. The field must wait quietly while the hounds search for the scent.

Colors. A distinguishing color, usually worn on the collar but sometimes on the facings of a coat, that identifies a hunt. Colors can be awarded only by the Master and can be worn only in the field.

Coop. A jump resembling a chicken coop.

Couple straps. Two-strap hound collars connected by a swivel link. Some members of staff will carry these on the right rear of the saddle. Since the days of the pharaohs in ancient Egypt, hounds have been brought to the meets coupled. Hounds are always spoken of and counted in couples. Today, hounds walk or are driven to the meets. Rarely, if ever, are they coupled, but a whipper-in still carries couple straps should a hound need assistance.

Covert. A patch of woods or bushes where a fox might hide. Pronounced "cover."

Cry. How one hound tells another what is happening. The sound will differ according to the various stages of the chase. It's also called giving tongue and should occur when a hound is working a line.

Cub hunting. The informal hunting of young foxes in the late summer and early fall, before formal hunting. The main purpose is to enter young hounds into the pack. Until recently only the most knowledgeable members were invited to cub hunt, since they would not interfere with young hounds.

Dog fox. The male fox.

Dog hound. The male hound.

Double. A series of short, sharp notes blown on the horn to alert all that a fox is afoot. The gone away series of notes is a form of doubling the horn.

Draft. To acquire hounds from another hunt is to accept a draft.

Draw. The plan by which a fox is hunted or searched for in a certain area, such as a covert.

Draw over the fox. Hounds go through a covert where the fox is but cannot pick up its scent. The only creature that understands how this is possible is the fox.

Drive. The desire to push the fox, to get up with the line. It's a very desirable trait in hounds, so long as they remain obedient.

Dually. A one-ton pickup truck with double wheels in back.

Dwell. To hunt without getting forward. A hound that dwells is a bit of a putterer.

Enter. Hounds are entered into the pack when they first hunt, usually during cubbing season.

Field. The group of people riding to hounds, exclusive of the Master and hunt staff.

Field Master. The person appointed by the Master to control the field. Often it is the Master him- or herself.

Fixture. A card sent to all dues-paying members, stating when and where the hounds will meet. A fixture card properly received is an invitation to hunt. This means the card would be mailed or handed to a member by the Master.

Flea-bitten. A gray horse with spots or ticking that can be black or chestnut.

Gone away. The call on the horn when the fox leaves the covert.

Gone to ground. A fox that has ducked into its den, or some other refuge, has gone to ground.

Good night. The traditional farewell to the Master after the hunt, regardless of the time of day.

Gyp. The female hound.

Hilltopper. A rider who follows the hunt but does not jump. Hilltoppers are also called the Second Flight. The jumpers are called the First Flight.

Hoick. The huntsman's cheer to the hounds. It is derived from the Latin *hic haec hoc,* which means "here."

Hold hard. To stop immediately.

Huntsman. The person in charge of the hounds, in the field and in the kennel.

Kennelman. A hunt staff member who feeds the hounds and cleans the kennels. In wealthy hunts, there may be a number of kennelmen. In hunts with a modest budget, the huntsman or even the Master cleans the kennels and feeds the hounds.

Lark. To jump fences unnecessarily when hounds aren't running. Masters frown on this, since it is often an invitation to an accident.

Lieu in. Norman term for "go in."

Lift. To take the hounds from a lost scent in the hopes of finding a better scent farther on.

Line. The scent trail of the fox.

Livery. The uniform worn by the professional members of the hunt staff. Usually it is scarlet, but blue, yellow, brown, and gray are also used. The recent dominance of scarlet has to do with people buying coats off the rack as opposed to having tailors cut them. (When anything is mass-produced, the choices usually dwindle, and such is the case with livery.)

Mask. The fox's head.

Meet. The site where the day's hunting begins.

MFH. The Master of Foxhounds; the individual in charge of the hunt: hiring, firing, landowner relations, opening territory (in large hunts this is the job of the hunt secretary), developing the pack of hounds, and determining the first cast of each meet. As in any leadership position, the Master is also the lightning rod for criticism. The Master may hunt the hounds, although this is usually done by a professional huntsman, who is also responsible for the hounds in the field and at the kennels. A long relationship between a Master and a huntsman allows the hunt to develop and grow.

Nose. The scenting ability of a hound.

Override. To press hounds too closely.

Overrun. When hounds shoot past the line of a scent. Often the scent has been diverted or foiled by a clever fox.

Ratcatcher. Informal dress worn during cubbing season and bye days.

Stern. A hound's tail.

Stiff-necked fox. One that runs in a straight line.

Strike hounds. Those hounds that, through keenness, nose, and often higher intelligence, find the scent first and press it.

Tail hounds. Those hounds running at the rear of the pack. This is not necessarily because they aren't keen; they may be older hounds.

Tally-ho. The cheer when the fox is viewed. Derived from the Norman *ty a hillaut,* thus coming into the English language in 1066.

Tongue. To vocally pursue a fox.

View halloo (halloa). The cry given by a staff member who sees a fox. Staff may also say tally-ho or, should the fox turn back, tally-back. One reason a different cry may be used by staff, especially in territory where the huntsman can't see the staff, is that the field in their enthusiasm may cheer something other than a fox.

Vixen. The female fox.

Walk. Puppies are walked out in the summer and fall of their first year. It's part of their education and a delight for both puppies and staff.

Whippers-in. Also called whips, these are the staff members who assist the huntsman, who make sure the hounds "do right."

TIME WILL TELL

CHAPTER 1

November 2, 2023, Thursday

Sunset brushed the west side of Cedar Mountain with gold. As twilight embraced the trees, the bush turned to scarlet, lavender, and finally the color of a dove's wing. Daylight birds and mammals tucked up. Night creatures began to move. The bats spoke as they flew, but most of the night animals remained silent.

If one believes in ghosts, this is when the fallen at the battle of Cedar Mountain appear. Even if one doesn't believe in spirits, being at a place of extreme emotion casts an eerie spell. One would have to be half-dead not to feel it.

Two women watched the colors as the day quietly ended. November 2, Thursday, was a hunt day for Bull Run Hunt. One of the masters, Adrianna Waddy, stood next to Jane Arnold, Sister Jane, the master of the Jefferson Hunt. The two hunts, an hour away from each other as the crow flies, took a good hour and a half to travel to one or the other from each hunt's kennels. Heavy traffic clogging roads, thanks to the unchecked growth of Charlottesville, Virginia, might make it two hours, if you wanted to show up on time for the first cast of the hounds.

Sister Jane, about thirty years older than Adrianna, had come up to visit and hunt. Her best friend, Betty Franklin, and another hunt member, Alida Dalzell, drove the big trailer with everyone's horses. They brought Sister's horse back to Roughneck Farm, took care of the big boy. As anyone who has ever worked with horses knows, this is a great kindness. Sister wanted to stay behind to talk with Adrianna. Masters share many similar problems, regardless of the hunt. Bull Run was enjoying an expansion, plus the regrooming of the various fixtures, never an easy task.

Sister shivered for a moment.

"Cold?" Adrianna asked.

"It felt as though a cold hand brushed my face." Sister smiled, adding, "Time of year. We're on the cusp of fall turning into winter; I always feel it so strongly."

Adrianna nodded. "If I don't feel it, my feet do."

"There is that. The leaves have fallen, so one can really see the land. Makes hunting easier."

"Well, I love the color of cubbing." Adrianna mentioned the season before formal hunting when the attire changes as well as a few rules of foxhunting. "But it's so much easier when you can see and this is such an odd fixture. It's not super steep but it's steep enough, the footing so variable. I have to keep my wits about me."

"Oh, Adrianna, you always have your wits about you."

A rueful smile crossed her lips. "Not always."

They both climbed back into the ATV, big enough to be called a mule, with a small wagon behind it. "That's how we learn."

Adrianna fired up the motor, her retired foxhound, Magnum, sat in the backseat, observing all. A hound never knew when a whiff of his quarry might present itself, so he turned his head from side to side then lifted his nose straight up.

"He never stops, does he?"

Adrianna laughed. "He doesn't realize he is retired and I wish you had known him in his prime. The most beautiful voice I have ever heard."

"Well, I wish you had known me in my prime," Sister fired back.

"You can still outride most of us."

"You flatter me. You, Lynn Pirozzoli, tough girls. And let us not forget, from my area, Carolyn Chapmen, Jennifer Nesbitt, Lynne Gebhard. All dazzling as ever."

"How about your young whipper-in? What's her name?"

"Tootie, Anne Harris. So bright."

"Good rider. There are fewer and fewer young people who can really ride. Even when I was young, there weren't as many distractions, but now, well, now I guess most parents are taxi drivers, ferrying those kids from one activity to another."

Still looking to the west, Sister agreed, then said, "It's, well, a feeling. We're on the site of an early battle. Who knows what's underfoot? Stop for a minute," Sister requested. "Is that lovely farm to the east a fixture?"

"Constance Hall, an old one. Two sisters bought it last year. So far so good. They let us hunt through. The younger one hunts, the older one occasionally goes out," Adrianna said.

"Sounds good. Are these like maiden aunts?" Sister raised an eyebrow.

"No. Forties. Both had endured divorces, took the money, and here they are."

"Is there such a thing as a good divorce?" Sister sounded rhetorical.

"People say there is. I'd be more worried about living with a sister, but they get along."

"You're right. I didn't think of that. Your sister or brother knows when you stole cookies out of the cookie jar."

They laughed. Adrianna lifted her foot off the brake.

Magnum informed them, *"Deer nearby."*

"Are you being chatty?" Adrianna asked.

"Giving a report. They'll cross the path behind you. You won't know they're here." The impressive foxhound dearly loved Adrianna but knew she couldn't smell a thing.

"Are you getting a lot of new people? The area, thanks to Richmond's growth, Charlottesville, too, has become desirable."

Adrianna slowed for a small pothole. "We are. Interesting people, like the two Sherwood sisters. They've taken in some young women from the women's center, or older teens at risk, to teach them skills."

"Good for them."

"What's unusual is the sisters teach them construction skills. Those jobs pay better than so many female-heavy jobs. Veronica and Sheila buy houses, restore them, and flip them. They use their own workforce."

"Anyone that can build or repair stuff will do okay. And have you ever noticed your stove goes out before you have guests for dinner? The furnace heat dies on the coldest night? Never fails."

"That's for sure."

As they slowly drove down the dirt path, rock-hard thanks to a drought, minks scurried into their dens for the night.

"Magnum, don't get any ideas," Adrianna instructed her dog.

"He won't. He already has a fur coat."

They laughed as they reached the bottom, Adrianna driving to the clubhouse where Sister's car was parked. She had followed the horse trailer with her new Bronco Sport. She went through a car about every three years, thanks to the hard country, the miles, and the changeable weather.

Getting out, Adrianna hugged Sister. "So glad you could hunt."

"Me too. Going over the problems of leading helps. I wish Lynn could have gone up the mountain with us. Her mining background had to give her a sharp eye for topography."

"I forget you taught Geology at Mary Baldwin."

"Loved it. Speaking of women's colleges, did you see where Sweet Briar has a new president? Mary Pope Maybach Hutson? She's the first alumna to hold that spot. Pretty fabulous."

"Did. You go down there and hunt with Bedford, don't you?"

"I do. The growth of Sweet Briar after early closing is a testimony to what happens when people put their heads, hearts, and wallets together. We need more of it."

"We do. In some ways that's our job."

Sister opened the door to her SUV. "Is. Trying to keep the land, our country, is our biggest challenge. I used to think it was animal rights groups who accused us of killing foxes while showing footage from England, years old, not from here. I mean, with AI, Adrianna, you can falsify anything. Anyways, it's development. Even with high mortgages, the banks chickening out, well, that's my opinion, but I don't have an answer unless we could create syndicates to buy up raw land, old properties."

"We've made some progress with our landowners. Most everyone is an environmentalist."

"I can't say the same." Sister sighed. "Some are. Some not. Well, let me get back to the farm. I could talk to you all day and almost have." She laughed.

"Joint meet?"

"You bet. Let me check the calendar."

With that, Sister drove into the rapidly darkening sky, toward home.

"Honey, I'm home." Sister opened the door from the mudroom into the kitchen.

A deep voice answered from the back of the house. "About time."

Her Doberman, Raleigh; the Harrier, Rooster; and the cat, Golly, all greeted her. J. Edgar, the box turtle, stirred in his large living quarters complete with dirt so he could dig if he felt like it.

Gray, her husband, paper in hand, walked into the kitchen, gave her a kiss on the cheek. "How was it?"

"Dry. Got a bit of something, but this Season so far has been a whistling bitch." She never minded swearing with her husband or best friends.

"Has."

"The fixture was stunning. They have terrific territory. Wonderfully open, wide paths where needs be and lovely jumps. Perfect, really, and Adrianna and Lynn kept me up front with them. Nice hound work despite the dryness. Enthusiastic young huntsman. Sooner or later we have to get some rain."

"Glad you were able to just go and enjoy hunting." He saw her juggle problems every day.

"You know what was so interesting? Adrianna took me up Cedar Mountain after hunting and the breakfast. The sun was setting. Just beautiful, but eerie. Don't know how to describe it. Chilly. Yes, the sun was setting, but I don't know. A place of sorrow."

He put water on for tea. "August 9, 1862. Had to be hateful hot. It was an early battle in the war that gave a hint as to the future number of losses, heavy losses. Armaments had changed. Wasn't Napoleonic anymore."

"I guess that would add to destruction."

"For the North, 314 killed, 1,445 wounded, and 594 missing."

"How do you remember those numbers?"

He grinned at her as the water began to boil. "I'm an accountant, remember?"

She grinned back. "Of course."

"For the South, 231 killed, 1,107 wounded. No number for the missing, but I expect it had to be close to the Union number. And less than one year later, the casualties at Gettysburg were 51,000."

"Dear God," she exclaimed. "I was never as good of a history student as you, but 51,000."

"Changed everything. The fact that we could kill so many so quickly. But what shocks me is that the Europeans sent observers over here to study our fighting. Otto von Bismarck was one; he was young, on the rise. They went home and World War I blows up. Right? A lot of those military men were still alive, as they came over here as young officers sent by their countries. World War I had more deaths than anyone could have imagined, even though the British, the Germans, the Austrians, you name it, had observers here. Is it stupidity, or insanity, or not giving a damn about human life?"

"Maybe all three. But now that you mention the losses, maybe there's leftover anguish. A feeling. Spirits. I know I sound woo-woo," Sister said.

"No, I believe there are all kinds of energies on this earth. You know what else is important about Cedar Mountain?"

"I don't, but I bet you do." She smiled as he brought a pot of hot tea to the table then returned with two mugs.

"It was Clara Barton's first nursing event, first being at a battlefield. She nursed both sides. Neither one had nurses. It was all too new. Florence Nightingale started battlefield nursing, but that was during the Crimean War. We had nothing, but Miss Barton believed in herself and nursing. She eventually organized women to take care of the wounded and she started that in Madison County."

"You think the local women came out to help?"

"They did. Had to be dreadful for them. Who had ever seen anything like a man blown apart by a cannonball? I give those women credit. They took the wounded back to their homes, churches, wherever there was space to house them. The women took both blue and gray. And in the heat."

"There are all kinds of heroes, aren't there?"

"Yes." He poured them both strong tea. "But only the winners get much credit and women nothing until recently."

"Gray, I think you're a better feminist than I am."

"I've spent my life negotiating institutionalized oppression. Haven't done a bad job." He laughed.

Gray was Black. Had worked his way up to being partner at a powerful accounting firm in D.C. Speaking of a different kind of warfare, he knew where all the bodies were buried. Gray had become a powerful man, rich through his efforts, or at least wildly comfortable, depending on your standard of what is rich. Steady, cool under pressure, and able to root out fiscal corruption, he could send terror into a congressman's office by simply walking into the room.

"I can't say the same for myself; I never was political. Just wanted to do what I wanted to do. I think I missed a lot. Loved teaching, but I probably could have done more. Well, it's too late now."

"Never too late. You deal with politics all the time being a master."

"Oh, territory disputes, personality clashes. I don't think that's political."

"Honey, anytime there are people together, it's political."

"Yeah, I guess you're right." She sipped her tea as Raleigh came up, putting his head under her free hand.

"Brownnoser," Golly half hissed.

"If there's a treat to be had, you are worse than we are," Rooster the Harrier responded.

"I'm just more successful." The beautiful long-haired calico cat preened, to the dogs' disgust.

"Know what I thought?" Sister put her mug down.

"Can't wait."

"I bet many of those wounded boys fell in love with their nurses. Including the Yankees."

He laughed. "I bet you're right. Maybe those relationships helped once the war was over. Surely some married."

"Isn't it incredible what people do, go through? We were taught battles in school, peace treaties, etc. We were never taught what people lived through. It's the individual who truly teaches you. Like your family. Free Blacks since the seventeenth century. Lorillards and Laprades. Who fell in love with whom and when and how did they all manage to survive the wars?"

"Yes, well, individual lives aren't tidy. Historians and politicians want tidiness. I know my great-great-grandmothers nursed. That's what Mother and Aunt Daniella said."

Aunt Daniella, his aunt, still alive at ninety-six, really older but she finally moved off ninety-four last year, admitting to ninety-six, was a rich repository of the family history.

"Your aunt forgets nothing. Your mother had a good memory as well. She was such a sweet soul, Graziella. Everyone loved her."

He smiled, remembering his mother, for it was true. "You know what they did say? That the women in our family have always been good-looking, so I don't doubt that some of those fellows fell in love with them. Chantal, one of my great-grandmothers, did indeed marry a Yankee and moved to Maine, of all places. We have some family up there; I'll have to ask Aunt Dan. He was a timber baron. Lots of money. Here I am nattering on. Are you hungry?"

"Actually, I am. Let me warm up last night's leftovers."

"I can help. I bet you're tired from hunting. Their territory is a lot more open than ours, undulating. Long runs."

"Beautiful, really. Okay. You make a salad and I'll warm up the beef soup. It's full of vegetables."

"You can make more meat," Raleigh added hopefully.

"Tuna," Golly suggested.

"All right, all right." Sister opened the cabinet, putting special crunchy treats in everyone's bowls.

"Not from the table but it's good." Rooster eagerly rushed to his bowl.

As the humans puttered in the kitchen, happy to be catching up, fixing things, pleased to be together, they chattered on.

"Falling in love, well, it adds a new dimension to history." Sister stirred the soup.

"Aunt Dan swears that love is the wild card of existence."

"She's right."

"The past is never the past. It's here." Gray tore the butter lettuce into tinier pieces.

CHAPTER 2

November 4, 2023, Saturday

A stiff wind brought tears to Sister's eyes. Hounds roared ahead of her. A stone wall, some of it crumbling, lay straight ahead. Lafayette, her Thoroughbred, dappled gray, easily soared over, as the part he selected was perhaps three feet. The footing, soft, helped. A light rain Thursday night, late, took some of the edge off the brick-hard ground.

Betty Franklin, on Sister's right, rode ahead of her as the pack was pulling away from the field of riders. Being a whipper-in, Betty had to stay on the shoulder of the pack. She rode on the right, Tootie Harris on the left, while the Huntsman, Wesley "Weevil" Blackford, flew right behind them, the hounds.

Saturday hunts brought people out, given that no one was working; although Ben Sidell, the sheriff, who rode with Jefferson Hunt, had some working weekends.

This Saturday, Ben rode in Second Flight. This meant he took a few low jumps but stopped to open fences for those who didn't want to take the big jumps. Bobby Franklin, Betty's husband, led Second

Flight today. He knew the territory inside and out, which proved a good thing, as Close Shave, today's fixture, was tricky.

As the pack pulled away, Sister urged on Lafayette. He needed little prodding. Being a Thoroughbred, he had blinding speed. Many of the riders following Sister in First Flight rode Warmbloods; Appendix horses, which were Thoroughbreds mixed with Quarter horses; Appaloosas; even a draft horse or two. They couldn't keep up with the well-conditioned gray fellow.

Sister had to stay behind the hounds. As her field began to fragment into two sections, those also riding Thoroughbreds kept up with the Master. Riders on other breeds of horses soon constituted a second First Flight. Her joint master, Dr. Walter Lungrun, on a terrific fellow, Clemson, but not the fastest, now led that group.

A steep hill, part of a long chain of low hills, loomed ahead. The wind blew stronger. Sister ducked her head, holding on as the big fellow, long stride, reached out to climb the hill. He slipped at one greasy spot. She grabbed the martingale.

"Dammit," she cursed.

Once on the hill, all was silent. Horse and rider stopped to catch their breath. Kasmir Barbhaiya, Ronnie Haslip, Alida Dalzell, Freddie Thomas, and Sam Lorillard, along with Tootie's mother, Yvonne Harris, thundered up behind her. All stopped behind their Master, grateful for the respite. The wind now had to be puffing twenty-mile-an-hour gusts.

Gray, who usually rode up with his wife, stayed back to help Bobby. The speed was too much for some of the people in Second Flight. Most could ride well but didn't want to take the big jumps. A few people were coming along, and the pace wore them out. Legs can tire more quickly than one realizes.

Sister took her cap off, the wind tossing her silver hair about. Listening intently, she looked around to her crew, for she knew them all well. She shrugged.

Sam, Gray's brother, also removed his cap to listen. Not a peep.

She rode toward the group, maybe ten yards behind, only a few steps. "This wind makes it impossible to hear. I'm going down to the bottom to see if I can hear anything. I can understand if anyone wants to turn back. The temperature is dropping and the wind makes it colder. However, if hounds are running, I'm running, too."

Everyone smiled. No one was turning back. Getting to the bottom of the hill would at least get them out of the gusts.

Lafayette carefully picked his way down. A thin stream trickled at the bottom through old pastures slowly being rehabilitated.

As the group reached a somewhat protected spot, Walter came into view at the top of the hill. Sister waved for him to come down. The back half of First Flight made their way down, everyone relieved to be out of what was turning into difficult weather.

All sat there. Nothing.

A streak caught the Master's eye. A healthy, gorgeous red fox ran right for them on the other side of the little stream. He stopped, viewed the assembled, then took off at a faster clip.

They waited. Hounds could now be heard, the cry was faint. Where in the devil had this fellow taken them?

Finally, hounds charged into view, the whole pack tight together. The stream intensified the scent, which water usually does, and the handsome fellow ran right alongside of it. Hounds were singing at a high decibel level. The entire pack flew right by them on the opposite side of the stream. Sister didn't move. Best to wait for her Huntsman.

Finally, he galloped up, Betty on one side, Tootie on the other. Their horses were beginning to lather. They had been out two hours. Stop and go, but the go was galloping.

As the Huntsman passed, Sister turned, following on her side of the stream. Then back up the hill, only to nearly slide down the other side, as she needed to veer right, cross the stream on that side, and try to keep up. Second Flight waited, then they, too, crossed.

Someone, or a few someones, must have parted company with

their mounts for Bobby to be so far behind. Sister didn't envy him, believing leading Second Flight was much harder than leading First.

Again, she ran flat out. She lost her sense of time, concentrating as she was on keeping behind her hounds and Huntsman.

They headed back toward the outbuildings of this fixture, avoiding old farm equipment standing out in the elements. Then the silence was pierced by one anguished howl.

This complaint was followed by others.

The fox slipped into his den under one of the old timber cabins. The hounds, too big to even dig at the opening, since it was under the cabin itself, created a din.

Weevil dismounted, reins falling to the ground. Showboat, his horse today, ground tied, so he stood there a picture of obedience.

Blowing "Gone to Ground," Weevil lavishly praised his hounds and patted them on their heads. He then mounted Showboat from the ground, easy for a man in his early thirties, and sat looking down at hounds he loved.

Betty was on one side of him while Tootie waited behind the cabin, just in case the fellow might come out. He did not.

Dasher, a hound with great drive, walked next to his sister Diana. *"Tough going on the other side of the hill."*

"Was but scent held. At least he didn't bolt out of the territory or worse, go up the Blue Ridge."

The area in which they hunted today, Chapel Cross, rolled up smack against the Blue Ridge Mountains. Any fox going straight up would eventually lose the pack. However, there were many ways to lose them staying in the pastures that comprised this beautiful area of central Virginia.

Named Chapel Crossroads since 1776, the area encompassed miles dotted with a few old estates, most built right after the Revolutionary War when what was then the Wild West could safely be settled. As the soil, fertile, enticed people, most of the early farmers made a decent living. No tobacco, soil and temperature not right for that, but they could grow any grass crops with ease, as well as corn, lots of corn.

Over time, the residents of Chapel Crossroads, or just Chapel Cross, increased their productivity and wealth. The War of 1812 didn't slow down their efforts. A few sortie parties of Brits rode through, but they were fairly easily scattered.

Some of the early settlers had money enough to buy people to work their land. Many didn't, but whoever you were, chances were you were outside more than inside. After yet another war, the enslaved were freed. Many left but some did not. This meant old families still lived here, and best to figure out who was who. Newcomers often assumed a Black family was perhaps not educated or well off, when in reality they usually had more money than the newcomers. This could, and did, create interesting collisions.

One of those rich people was Gray Lorillard. Sam was not, thanks to alcoholism, which he finally beat. Close Shave, the fixture they now hunted, was owned by people new to the area. In time they settled in and all was well.

Riding up to Weevil, Sister turned her face partially away from the wind. Still blew her words away, so she rode right up next to her gifted Huntsman.

"Lift them. It's been a good day for a change, and the weather is turning against us."

"Yes, Master." He nodded his head, turning to his hounds. "Come along."

As everyone now followed the pack back to the trailers maybe two miles away, they chatted. One is not to speak during hunting, one is not to do anything that will bring up hounds' noses. Now they could review the day, marvel at the saucy fox who literally walked right by them.

"The pastures in the back look good," Freddie Thomas remarked to Alida, a dear friend.

"Never ends. The thing about Close Shave is all the outbuild-ings. They've restored the ones by the house but the rest of them, cabins, storage, well, what a job."

"What an expense."

Both women agreed on that as their horses, happy to be head-ing back to the trailers, dreamed of cookies and some fresh water. The real food would be back at their respective stables.

Trailers, parking organized by Walter, had been lined up to foil the wind.

It helped.

The point of the way he had people park their trailers was, they could have a breakfast on the inside, the outside blocking the cold wind. While not exactly warm, at least those miserable gusts would be less effective.

People set up two long tables, brought out potluck dishes.

Some riders removed their hunt coats to switch to down coats, scarves, and lumberjack caps. Everyone crowded around hot tea and coffee poured by Alida and Freddie, who acted as hostesses for this weekend's breakfast.

Folding chairs now sat in the space between the trailers and the food. Everyone had that or upturned buckets to sit on.

Ronnie, the club treasurer, had been Sister's deceased son's best friend. Raymond Jr. at fourteen died in a farming accident. Sis-ter and Ronnie remained close. She loved Ronnie for that, as well as for himself.

"What's happening across the road?" Ronnie asked.

Kasmir, who lived at the crossroads, itself in a wonderful place, Tattenhall Station, the old train station, remarked, "A lot of work-men. I thought Crawford would know," he mentioned Crawford Howard, who owned Old Paradise, also at the crossroads, on the other side, "but he doesn't. Rumor is, it's being rehabbed. The house needs a new furnace, kitchen, stuff, as you know."

"I hope it can be restored. It was once so beautiful," the Rev. Sally Taliaferro remarked.

She was the young Episcopal priest. Sister thought of her as one of her divines. The other was Father Mancusco, the priest at St. Mary's. As they hunted together, over the years they became friends, bubbling with high spirits and amusing dogma questions for each other. Father Mancusco, perhaps early fifties, was a bit older than Sally. They were dearly loved and had helped club members through the wounds and losses of life, as well as celebrating children and grandchildren.

"I would think Crawford would buy it. He's bought up so much," Ronnie said. "He's worked a miracle at Old Paradise."

"Maybe restoring that is enough. Five thousand acres, plus that extraordinary house with the Corinthian columns, all the stone buildings as well as frame ones. It's a lifetime's work."

Freddie appreciated what Crawford and his wife, Marty, had accomplished.

"Whoever has bought Wolverhampton, we'll know," Yvonne added quietly. "Nothing stays a secret at Chapel Cross for long."

She owned Beveridge Hundred on South Chapel Road.

"True." Sister laughed.

"True, but there are so many new people coming into the area. COVID plus state taxes elsewhere have people looking for better places. Virginia is one of those better places," Betty piped up.

"Florida, Texas," Ronnie interjected. "Their taxes are better there."

"But there you have political turmoil. We're a purple state," Alida spoke. "Are there progressives here? Sure. Are there right-wing people here? Sure. But in the main, Virginians are practical. Ideology doesn't seem to be so compelling. One governor is tagged as conservative. The next will probably be a liberal. But have you ever noticed they say what the edges of their party want to hear, especially at the primaries, then once elected they come back to the center?"

"Well, they have to throw red meat to their followers, the party pimps, as I think of it," Sam, who attended Harvard, simply stated.

"Well, that's everyone since BC." Kasmir, educated at Oxford, smiled.

"And nobody learns a thing." Sister ate a deviled egg, her favorite.

"Well, what could happen that would upend Chapel Cross? Really," Freddie wondered.

"Newcomers not allowing hunting over their property." Sister half smiled. "But what if someone wanted to put in a wind farm? Oh yes, there would be an uproar because of the birds. Maybe someone else would want to put in a high-end spa. If you think about it, any number of things could create havoc out here."

"In other words, don't leave the nineteenth century." Gray said this with humor.

A silence followed.

Then Yvonne, herself a newcomer of five years, replied, "What's wrong with the nineteenth century?"

"Mom, you wouldn't have had a modeling career." Her daughter pointed this out.

"Lillian Russell," her mother replied.

"Mom, she was fat."

"Now, now," Yvonne started, laughing at her daughter.

"In those days, that was being well padded, like upholstery. Some men loved it. Jim Brady sure did."

This got everyone off on body types, desirable and undesirable, over the centuries.

"Why are we talking about women's bodies?" Sister slightly raised her voice. "Let's talk about conformation. Take my Lafayette, for example."

After that, they became sillier, looser, and generally a group of people who rode hard, helped one another, and lived life at a brisk gallop.

What could possibly go wrong?

CHAPTER 3

November 6, 2023, Monday

"I hate this hill." Betty Franklin grimaced as she started up the steep hill to the hanging-tree pasture at the top.

"You bought new sneakers. Shouldn't be too bad," Weevil teased her.

"Did you know shoes are made from cow skins?" Diana nudged Aces, a youngster walking next to her.

"I had no idea." His eyes widened.

"Look at their feet. If they ever have their shoes off. Useless feet." Trinity cocked an ear.

"The real problem is, they walk on two legs. They can't help it, of course." Giorgio liked the Jefferson Hunt humans.

"That's why they ride horses. So slow. Oh, they are just so slow," Ardent, also young, announced.

"Look at it this way," Cora, an older hound, advised. *"Thanks to those bad feet and two legs we go out, they are on horseback and we fly. Fly. What could be better?"*

The hounds being walked discussed treats. Some thought greenies would be better; others, a juicy bone; and still others, a nap in the warm sun. Everyone threw around an opinion. Weevil, Tootie, Sister, and Betty trudging up the hill were oblivious to the pack's discussion.

The top of Hangman's Ridge, where the huge old hangman's tree loomed, was always windy and not a little foreboding. The criminals of the late eighteenth century were indeed hanged on that tree. Sometimes the hounds heard whispers or spied a spirit. The humans felt something but dismissed it.

Finally, up on the high meadow, Weevil allowed the hounds to play while the people took a breather.

Jolly, a first-year hound starting to hunt, obeyed the older hounds, as did the others of the J line, the litter now ready to hunt. All were learning.

Jingle tagged after her brother, who peered over the north side of the long flat meadow.

"Clytemnestra," he barked.

This giant cow, owned by Cindy Chandler of Foxglove Farm, had no business being halfway up the north side of the hill. Worse, right behind the imperious, mean animal, followed her enormous son, Orestes.

All the hounds rushed over. Weevil, thinking this was the beginning of disobedience, blew the hunt horn. The pack came back but so did Clytemnestra and her idiot son. As Jefferson Hunt hunted Foxglove at least once a month during the Season, those two bovines knew the hound calls as well as the hounds and horses.

"Dear God!" Betty exclaimed.

Sister, thankful that the mother and son stopped to simply stare at them, quietly said, "Why don't we turn around and tiptoe down the hill."

As they tried this, Tootie, looking over her shoulder, said, "They're following us."

"If that horrible cow pushes me, I'll be tossed into next week." Betty unfurled her whip just in case.

"Weevil, stop a minute," Sister commanded. "If we walk down to the farm, they'll follow, and if Clytemnestra has one of her temper tantrums, who knows what she'll destroy?"

The others considered this a real possibility, for the mother and son needed a six-plank fence to corral them, and even then if Big Momma had a mood, she'd crash right through it, followed by her adored son.

"What should we do?" Betty feared those two.

"Weevil, you and Betty walk the hounds back to the kennel. Give me your horn. Tootie and I can walk to Cindy's. I think Cly will follow the horn. Then you all can come pick us up."

"And what if she just runs wherever she pleases?" Betty huffed.

"Nothing I can do about that, but I think they might follow. We'll have to cross Soldier Road, but after that I'm pretty sure she'll go across the wildflowers and up to her pasture. Betty, call Cindy and tell her what we're doing, because she can come out with a bucket of grain and rattle it. These two will never refuse food."

"That's the truth." Betty shook her head, as they were huge, gargantuan.

"Have you got your cellphone, Tootie?" Weevil asked his whipper-in and girlfriend.

"I do."

"If anything goes wrong, call me," Betty told her. "After we get hounds in the kennels, one of us will pick you up."

"Sounds like a plan." Sister walked past the two cows, blew a tootle, and sure enough, Clytemnestra followed, as did Orestes.

As Master and young whipper-in now headed down the north side of Hangman's Ridge, Betty dialed Cindy on her cellphone.

"Hey. Sister and Tootie are walking toward you from the ridge.

Clytemnestra and Orestes, we hope, are following her. They came up here as we were walking hounds."

"Let me throw on a coat and see if I can help."

"The best thing to do is get a bucket of grain. Once they are all across Soldier Road, shout and rattle it from your farm road."

"Okay. Catch up with you later." Cindy hurried to her front hall, grabbed her own hunt whip, then walked outside, upset, realized she forgot her coat so she ran back in, went to the back of the house to the fancy mudroom; everyone in these parts called a room with raincoats, umbrellas, Wellies, etc. a mudroom even if it was perfectly laid out, painted, etc.

Once outside again, driving her ATV she roared down the farm road. As she passed the cows' pasture, she could see where Clytemnestra, either in a fit of boredom or sheer meanness, smashed her fence. Well, that would be a job.

Once at the crossing to Soldier Road, when Cindy was above it she could see the two humans followed by naughty cows.

"If that elephant slips, she'll take us both out." Sister laughed.

Tootie, giving up on avoiding the hitchhikers sticking to her jacket, replied, "Those two could put a dent in a tank."

"That they could." Sister thrashed at the path with her old knob-end crop, for it needed to be cleared. The club hadn't gotten to it. Brush and thorns made the journey unpleasant. The cows added to it. The thorns didn't bother the two big oafs. The good thing was, having walked up the hill, Clytemnestra and Orestes did widen the path a bit.

"I see Cindy." Tootie could make out the club stalwart on the hill, waving her arms.

"Uh." Sister stumbled, lurched forward, nearly landing on her face.

"You okay?"

"Yes." The older woman brushed herself off and then noticed a glitter. "Wait a minute."

She knelt down, picked up a man's watch, a Rolex Submariner with a green dial.

"You all right?"

"Yes. Didn't mean to stop, as those two will walk over us. Just found a watch. We can worry about that later." She dumped it in her pocket.

The two women got the cows across the two-lane paved highway, an east-west highway. Fortunately, no traffic. Soldier Road zigzagged up the Blue Ridge, few people used it. It was old, rough. Route 250 proved much better, and the big interstate, I-64, was even better.

"Ready?" Sister asked the lovely young woman, whom she had known since Tootie was a student at Custis Hall, the girls' school in Staunton.

"We are getting our exercise." Tootie looked at yet another climb.

"Let's move to the far right of this little path. If these two hear that bucket before we do, they'll charge."

"That's an awful thought," Tootie rejoined.

As they neared the farm road, Cindy, a farm girl, knew exactly what her two terrible cows would do if she rattled the feed before Sister and Tootie could get safely out of the way.

Clytemnestra shook her head rhythmically as she walked. Nothing excessive, just her way of going. Orestes stared straight ahead.

Cindy called out, "Here goes."

The two hunt staff members stepped aside, giving the cows a wide berth.

"Oats, sweet feed, goodies." Cindy shook the bucket, hopped back on her ATV, because those two, mooing loudly, began to run. She hit second gear, then third, the two monsters closing in. Then she pulled a U-turn right in front of their special barn because they couldn't be with the horses, Clytemnestra was too sensitive. That was Cindy's explanation. She hurried into the barn, dumping half the bucket in one stall bucket, half in the other. Within minutes each cow barreled into his or her stall. Cindy shut the door as they munched, thrilled for an extra treat.

Back on her 450cc ATV, Cindy drove back as Sister and Tootie now waited on the driveway.

"Hop in."

The two squeezed behind Cindy. As all three women were fit, they could just do it. Cindy slowly drove to the house.

"Well, that was an adventure." Sister laughed. "We walked a good two miles."

"The terrain makes it seem longer." Cindy nodded.

"Come on in. Getting chilly."

"Weevil or Betty will pick us up. Soon."

"Tootie, they'll have to fight over who stays with hounds and who goes." Sister laughed.

"We can make a bet. Come on." Cindy opened the back door. "I bet one dollar Betty wins."

"I bet a dollar on Weevil." Tootie smiled.

"Oh, I bet on Betty. She can outtalk him." Sister laughed.

They removed their work jackets. No sooner than their nether regions hit the chairs, the sound of an old Bronco alerted them all.

"Betty!" Sister grinned.

Betty drove her old yellow Bronco. People tried to buy it. Everyone wanted to restore it to enter car shows. Betty refused. Ran great, plus she loved it. Who had the money for a new car?

"I've come to rescue you." Betty opened the back doors, as Tootie fished for a dollar in her pocket.

"You can rescue them after we all have a sherry, tea, or what?" Cindy said.

Betty threw off her coat. "Sherry. How civilized."

"Uh, tea," Tootie replied, putting the dollar on the table.

"Me too, but I'll have just a tiny jigger of sherry, tiny, Cindy." Betty stared at the dollar.

"I know." The hostess rose to get the drinks. "This was too easy." She pushed the dollar back to Tootie, who laughed.

"Throwing money around." Betty watched Tootie pick up the bill, fold it, stick it in her pants pocket.

"Cindy won a bet that you would outtalk Weevil to come pick us up."

"I bet on you, Betty, but I didn't pull out money." Sister rose.

"Where are you going?" Betty asked as Sister left the table.

"Forgot something."

She returned, placing the watch on the table.

"You didn't buy that, did you?" Betty had a prudent moment concerning finances.

"Tripped and found it."

Betty reached for it. "Heavy."

"Whatever could a watch be doing on the north side of Hangman's Ridge?" Cindy walked over, peering at it in Betty's palm.

"Looks new," Betty said.

Sister poured sherry while Cindy put a tea infusion in her ceramic teapot. Tootie looked at the watch.

"Big."

"Sport watches just get bigger and bigger. And the thing is, one shouldn't wear a sport watch except when sporting, so to speak." Cindy brought the pot over, following with cups and two sherry glasses.

"I only need a jigger," Sister reminded her.

"What if you change your mind? You never know." Cindy sat down. "Oh, I have some brownies."

Sister told her, "We aren't hungry."

Betty sighed. "Well."

"Okay, one of us is hungry."

"Betty, you know my kitchen as well as I do. Open the fridge. I have fresh brownies and also Brie and Gouda, take out whatever you want."

Betty did just that. She also brought out a cutting board, small plates, then she sat down to cut the Brie. She'd put out crackers. As everyone had known one another since the earth was cooling, this wasn't rude. Tootie, in her early twenties, marveled at the old friends, as a young woman, a child, she had never seen this kind of closeness.

Cindy studied the watch. "Twenty thousand? More? I don't know that much about men's watches."

"I'd say twelve thousand to forty-five depending on the exact model," Sister said. "Remember, my late first husband loved watches, cuff links, signet rings. If he had been a woman, he would have tried to buy some of Marie Antionette's jewelry."

"Bad luck," Betty predicted, shoving a cracker with a hunk of Brie on it in her mouth.

"At the end of her life, she showed great courage." Sister, although not as knowledgeable as Gray, liked history. "She had been reviled, lied to, bargained for like a horse when she was sent to France to marry the Dauphin. Judged constantly. No wonder she became frivolous. Built La Trianon. But in the end, she met her death, including her stay in prison, with dignity. And look what happened to those who killed her? It's the dynamic of revolutions. You kill your enemy or oppressor. You come to power and then you kill one another."

A solemn moment followed this.

"Do you think that could happen here?" Tootie asked as she, too, ate some Brie.

"Without a doubt," Sister said, then shrugged. "It's like the stages of cancer."

"Now, there's a comparison." Cindy sipped her sherry. "Back to the watch. It was just on the ground?"

"Yes. Took me a moment to process it. I stumbled, looked down, there it was." She held out her hand as Cindy dropped the watch in it. "Clytemnestra and Orestes are good for something."

"When you drive out, look at their paddock. How could a Rolex watch wind up where it did?" Cindy wondered.

"Maybe someone was killed and his watch fell off," Betty offered.

"Betty, you're watching too many murder mysteries."

"There wasn't a body." Sister drank her jigger of sherry, followed by a sip of deliciously hot tea.

"Could have been buried. Or maybe the vultures will show up tomorrow. You never know." Betty stuck to her murder theory.

"True," Cindy agreed. "But maybe a husband and wife had a fight. She took off his watch and threw it out the car window."

"If he was driving, she wouldn't have been able to reach it," Sister sensibly said. "But could it have been thrown out of a car? Yes. Who can imagine what would provoke that?"

"One helluva fight." Cindy smiled.

"Could it have slipped off someone's wrist when we hunted here two weeks ago?" Tootie wondered. "Given how expensive the watch is, surely he would have noticed. We'd be out looking for it."

"I make a prediction and don't give me a hard time about murder mysteries. Whatever this is about, it can't be good," Betty said.

CHAPTER 4

Later

"Don't do that." Gray, standing, placed the Rolex back on the kitchen table. "There's no way to identify the watch. Anyone can say it's theirs."

"I even called Rolex to see if they could identify the owner based on the serial number, but it belongs to someone whose name I've never heard before." Sister scrubbed the cat's food bowl. "Still. To lose such an expensive watch."

"I'm sure there's a good story behind it."

She smiled. "Drama. I was never that dramatic when young."

"Me neither. We're all made a little differently. Look at some of the blowups in hunt clubs. Clashing egos, dramas, money fights. People."

"The one real drama we had was when Crawford left in a huff because I didn't ask him to be a joint master. So he starts his own pack, knows nothing about hunting or hounds and blows through one huntsman after another until he finally finds Cynthia 'Skiff' Cane. That, and your brother slowly brought him around. But what a mess.

You can't just order people about in a hunt club. The rules when hunting are clear. It's the other stuff. Anyway, the watch bothers me."

"See. Betty made you wonder."

"Well, she did."

"Honey, she has never seen a murder mystery she didn't like. She drives herself crazy trying to figure it out. If she's right about the killer, hooray. If she's wrong, she has to go back and revisit the clues."

"She's super observant. One of the reasons she's a good whipper-in," Sister praised Betty.

He picked the watch up again. "When you think of it, how much jewelry can men wear without looking like a drug dealer or a rock star? Watches, rings, and maybe a necklace with a medal or a cross or some religious symbol. I have my signet ring as well as my wedding ring. My riding watch and my dress watch. That's about it. You have a lot more choices than I do."

"Well," she paused, "you can put a diamond stud in your nose. You can now wear earrings, but I was taught no big watches. Mother drummed that into my head. That and never wear major jewels before sundown." She grinned thinking of her mother, who had been determined to make her a lady.

"No matter what you wear, you look sensational."

She kissed him on the cheek. "Flatterer, but don't let that stop you."

They both laughed as she walked back to the sink, dried the bowl, opened the small kitchen bar, and poured him a single malt scotch. Then she put some Temptations in Golly's bowl.

"I thought you'd never get to it." The cat stuck her head into the treats.

"Here, honey." Sister handed Gray the drink. "It's getting cold outside."

"Oh, thanks. Remind me to buy more bourbon for Aunt Daniella. She impressed that upon me over the phone."

"Tomorrow after hunting, we can get some. Which reminds me, I'm going to ride Keepsake for Thanksgiving hunt. I assume you'll be on Cardinal Wolsey. You know, we should all get bourbon for Aunt Daniella for Thanksgiving."

"Right." He put the watch back, picked up his phone, and sat down.

"Good Lord." She leaned over his shoulder as he scrolled prices for a new Submariner. "So you really can go underwater with them? Forty-two thousand dollars."

"You can buy a used one for less. But this looks new enough." He put the phone down, picked up his drink.

"That's a lot of money to throw away."

"If it was thrown away. What are the chances of finding an expensive diving watch in the old path off Hangman's Ridge? People rarely hike over there. We ride through it from time to time. I guess there is a story with this, and who is to say Betty isn't right." He opened his eyes in mock horror. "Murder."

"Well, what do we do?"

"Keep it until we hear something, or just keep it in a drawer if we don't. No advertising a found watch."

"You aren't tempted to wear it?"

He studied it. "I like the green. Well, maybe I'm a little tempted."

"I'm not. I'd get a bigger left bicep if I wore that thing."

"Possibly. Well, back to whatever you were going to say about Thanksgiving hunt."

"How do you know I was going to say anything?" She sat down as Golly jumped into her lap, having eaten every crunchy morsel.

"I'm married to you."

"Oh." She brushed the calico's cheek. "Well, yes. We have to get our horses braided. Also, Tootie and Weevil's. They won't have any time before the hunt."

"One or two of Lynne Gebhard's students can do it. Just ask Lynne and offer one hundred dollars a horse. It's expensive."

"Everything is right now. But that's a good idea. Young people can always use the money and they have those wonderful nimble fingers. I might be able to braid Keepsake but it would take me hours. And it's usually cold Thanksgiving morning, even in the barn."

"Is. Which reminds me, Aunt Daniella also gave me a food list for Thanksgiving dinner. Yvonne is really going to do the cooking, most of it the night before. All Aunt Dan will have to do is turn on the oven, warm things up. But I'm glad she's our hostess. Does her good to be the center of attention."

"Honey, your aunt is always the center of attention."

He took a long sip. "So she is. I bet we could have talked Walter into hosting. After all, we're hunting from Mill Ruins." He named the estate rented by the joint master on a ninety-nine-year lease.

"Would be easier for everyone, but he would have to hire someone to cook. We all hunt Thanksgiving morning. Aunt Dan can stay home. And if she needs more help, we can find it. Yvonne will be hunting, too, her first Thanksgiving hunt."

"I have an idea." He reached over to pet Golly, reveling in the attention, especially since the dogs sat on the floor. "Why don't I wear the watch?"

"And?"

"See if anyone notices."

"I suppose. I'd have to tell Betty, Tootie, and Cindy, but who knows what it will scare up, if anything."

He frowned a moment. "Maybe I'll wait until Thanksgiving. Give more time for something or someone to turn up."

"Probably a good idea." She looked down. "He's chirping."

"Honey, that turtle has everything."

"Well, I'll just sit next to him for a minute." She left the chair, walked over to J. Edgar's large living quarters.

The box turtle walked about. He had dirt and leaves to dig in, anything he wanted to eat and did. A nice tiny pond if he wanted to bathe, plus drinking water changed every day. A small log rested in the corner.

"How about a treat?" Raleigh walked over to sit by J. Edgar.

"Do we need to do anything over at Mill Ruins before Thanksgiving hunting? Walter is good about taking care of it, but keeping the territory open is nonstop. Big territory."

"He hasn't said anything, so I think we're okay. We'll be at Mousehold Heath tomorrow. The Jardines will be at work." She mentioned the young owners of the fixture.

"I've got that meeting in Richmond. That drive is so boring. When I was a kid, the only way there from here was Route 250. The tension turnpike. That was boring, too." He smiled. "I've spent my working life in Washington, D.C., yet never learned to like cities."

"He chirped again. Sorry. I find J. Edgar fascinating. Cities. I don't know, New York is exciting for two days, and then the crush of people and the bad air, m-m-m, I like breathing."

"Me too." He laughed.

CHAPTER 5

November 7, 2023, Tuesday

"Dammit to hell," Betty cursed as she sweated to keep up with the hounds.

Mousehold Heath, on the other side of a low wooded ridge, really was two fixtures. The land near the small charming house rolled, green even in November. The grass wasn't growing, but it hadn't died yet.

As one headed west, this changed, rougher footing crossed with old ditches, small rocky hills next to them.

Betty cleared an old cultivation ditch. Outlaw, her beloved Quarter horse, easily shot over the two-foot-wide ditch. Two feet isn't problematic unless you looked straight down, which Betty did not. The pack, to her left, ran flat out. Scent improved with each hunt as the temperature cooled. It was still too dry but hounds could pick up a line and run it for maybe fifteen minutes. After that, it dissipated, for the fox was smart enough to understand conditions. He knew the territory better than the hounds.

Weevil, behind hounds, suddenly pulled up. Fallen trees

blocked everything. The owners hadn't gotten to clearing this. These trees lay out of eyesight.

Weevil, stymied, saw Betty but couldn't go that way, more debris.

A whistle alerted him to Tootie, whom he could see. She waved him on toward her.

By the time Weevil reached Tootie, he could barely hear his hounds. Both staff members galloped as fast as they could over increasingly difficult terrain. An old country road could be seen in the distance.

Sitting there were Aunt Daniella and Kathleen Sixt Dunbar, an antiques dealer, in Kathleen's station wagon. They acted as wheel whips today. The pack was heading straight for them.

"What should we do?" Kathleen was in her second year of being the last defense, a wheel whip.

"Get out. See if you can turn them back. The land on the other side of this fixture is closed now because of deer season."

Kathleen shut the motor, got out, and grabbed a whip, the long kangaroo cord rolled up, cracker at the end.

She stood by the side of the road, ready to try to be an obstacle.

The pack bore down on her. No fox in sight, but it seemed obvious he had crossed the road.

She lifted the crop, flung out. Then snapped her wrist. It sounded like a gunshot. "Hold hard."

Pookah, a second-year hound, wondered, *"What do I do?"*

Dreamboat, experienced with a great nose, slowed down. *"Better stop."*

"But the scent is heading right for the road," the youngster bewailed.

"I know." The older hound slowed to a trot.

Thimble, a few years older than Pookah, grumbled, *"Why? Why turn us off a hot line?"*

Trinity, his littermate, also slowed down.

Zane, another young hound, a few years under his belt, trotted then walked. *"Better to do what she says. I can hear hoofbeats."*

Kathleen cracked her whip again. The pack slowed, although one first-year entry, Barmaid, crossed the road.

Weevil and Tootie finally reached Kathleen as Aunt Daniella dropped her window down. "Good work."

Tootie crossed the road to turn back Barmaid. "Leave it."

The beautiful hound stopped, looked up at Tootie, her eyes sorrowful.

"Come on back, Barmaid," Trinity called to her.

Gunfire startled all of them. Then another shot.

Weevil called to his hounds, turning back. "Come along."

Frightened by the gunfire, the hounds readily followed him as Tootie veered off to ride on the shoulder of the pack.

Sister, hearing the shots, stopped, waiting for the pack to return.

Ronnie Haslip, riding up with her today, complained, "New people."

"Yes. They have been good about us hunting over there, but this inflation has people looking for more money. Renting to a deer hunting club has proved a godsend for some of our landowners."

"Cost me over one hundred dollars to fill up my Dually." He understood inflation.

She nodded. "Someone else mentioned that yesterday to me. I hope this passes soon, but I don't know. When it does, some other misery-producing event will take its place."

"Right," he ruefully agreed.

Hearing more gunfire, Weevil rode back to Mousehold Heath. Seeing the trailers up ahead, everyone breathed a sigh of relief. In all the history of foxhunting, no rider had been killed. However, no one in Jefferson Hunt wished to be the first.

Once back, untacking, throwing blankets over their horses, some being walked onto the trailer, others tied outside, hay bags hanging for them, the people set up two folding tables, everyone brought their chairs and some food and they all sat down, their backs to the wind.

"Does anyone know someone in that hunt club?" Alida asked, pulling a cashmere scarf tighter around her neck.

"No," Sister responded. "It's their first year. Let's see how it works out with the landowner. I'll ask to talk with them if the deer hunting will be back next year. As it is, deer hunters have until the first Saturday in January, so there's a lot of deer season left."

"You're right." Alida, feeling the chill, zipped up her heavy jacket, as she had changed in the tack room of her trailer. "Aren't you all cold?"

Some nodded in affirmation, others shrugged, just as Kathleen and Aunt Daniella pulled up. Aunt Daniella stayed in the car. She was not going to sit out in the cold. People waved to her.

Kathleen did join them. "What good hounds. All I had to do was crack my whip."

Weevil sat in a chair for a bit, as he needed a hot drink before heading back. "They are a good group. Walk them almost every day but Sunday and the days they hunt. Helps. Plus they get cookies for being good."

"Did you see that fox?" Father Mancusco asked.

"No. Given the cry, we weren't far behind, but the drought still hurts scent. I don't remember a drought in the late fall. July and August, but not now."

"Weevil, every now and then we'll get a parched fall, but not often," Bobby remarked.

Ben Sidell, the sheriff, sat next to Bobby. "I'm worried about fires."

"People can't be that stupid," Freddie declared.

"Want to bet?" Ronnie teased her, then turned to Ben. "Anything exciting happening? Haven't heard of much."

"A robbery here and there, but it's been relatively quiet. A few stolen cars."

"Do we have a lot of shoplifting problems?" Reverend Sally asked.

"More than we used to, but locking stuff up helps. It costs in other ways, as customers don't want to get a salesperson to unlock a case. More stores are hiring security."

"Good for them." Freddie posited, "If wrongdoing isn't punished, it grows. Actions need to have consequences."

"One hopes." Betty wiggled her toes, cold in her boots. "Ben, no reports of serious robberies? You know, someone rich?"

"No, but there's always time." He smiled.

"Anyone rob a jewelry store?" Betty continued.

"No." Ben ate an egg sandwich, made by Alida for the group.

"You need some earrings?" Sister smiled at Betty over her robbery questions.

"I'm just curious," Betty replied.

Sister hoped Betty would remember not to talk about the watch. She didn't.

Ben's cell rang. Looking at it, he took the call, as it was from one of his young deputies, Jude. He listened intently.

"Walter, will you take Clemson back and take care of him for me? I have to go." Ben stood up. "Sorry to leave you all."

Betty watched him go to Aunt Daniella.

"Kathleen, we need to take Ben to Rogers Corner." She named a small convenience store at a crossroads five miles away heading west. "Jude will pick him up there."

Betty perked up. "Bet we have a crime."

"If it's big enough, we'll hear about it." Sister grabbed another sandwich, hungry from hunting, plus she didn't eat breakfast before a hunt.

CHAPTER 6

November 8, 2023, Wednesday

Ben Sidell studied the young man on the slab. He knew him superficially, as his grandmother owned property behind Mill Ruins, plus she worked in Walter's medical office. Twenty-four, not much of a beard, he had been dumped by the side of I-64. A commuter on the way back from Richmond found the body. The driver's license in his pocket identified him as Trevor Goodall.

"What's your guess?" Ben asked the coroner, who had had time to examine the body.

"Shot in the head then pushed out the car door. Has scratches, injuries, consistent with rolling."

"Well, we have to send the body to Richmond."

"Yes. It's wise. They'll find out whatever is in his system. They have advanced equipment. Our state has not spared funding for our medical examiner's office. No matter what is in his system, the cause of death won't change."

"No." Ben noted the young man's thinness. "Given his size, not much on him, I'm willing to bet he was on something. That doesn't explain his murder."

"Years ago, before you arrived here, there was a well-organized gang of silver thieves. They'd hit up Farmington Country Club maybe once every four or five years. Locals informed on them. Made a few bucks. There are many ways to offend the wrong people. They left just enough time for people to not forget but to let their guard down. They covered the state. Worked over Richmond's west end, always made a haul at Virginia Beach. Wherever the money was, there they were. Northern Virginia proved a target. Maybe they even crossed the river and lifted silver from Georgetown. Don't really know."

"Ever get caught?"

"The gang? No. One member, yes. An ordinary-looking man, mid-forties. His car stalled as he was following what had to be others. The sheriff got him. Tried everything to wring a confession out of him. Guy wouldn't talk. He was sent up. Had no defense, as he was found with sacks of silver. You name it. Tiffany. Georg Jensen. Old silver from the early eighteenth century. Never, never talked. Served his prison term. Released and disappeared."

"A gang?" Ben looked at the immobile features of the corpse.

"Well, I've been reading about the shoplifting gangs."

"So far our shoplifting has been haphazard."

"Come on." Peter Bamberg, the coroner, motioned to his assistant to roll the corpse back into the cooler while he led Ben to his office. "A lot of gangs use people on drugs, paying them with drugs. We won't know for a while if Trevor was on drugs. But I'm willing to bet he made a bad decision about money. Sit down." Peter moved his desk chair next to Ben's.

The office, nicely furnished, had two comfortable chairs with a small coffee table between them, Peter's desk, and some book-shelves.

"When I pick up a young person committing a crime, I figure it's for money for drugs, for some kind of need they have. The kid's in too deep to get out. Some crimes are spur of the moment," Ben said.

"You know, opportunity makes a poet as well as a thief. And sometimes it's just to see what someone can get away with." Peter continued, "The Goodalls are an old county family. Good people. Skilled labor. Nothing requiring college degrees, but they're good people. Trevor is a bit of a black sheep. Nothing terrible, but endless scrapes. He'll have a file."

"I looked it up when you gave me his name. Stealing a car was the most daring thing he did, if you want to rank a kid who pinched other people's wallets, filled his car with gas numerous times and drove off without paying. A stolen credit card from time to time. Stuff like that. Nothing major, but a growing record," Ben replied. "Hard on the family. I see it was his grandmother who usually picked him up from jail."

"His father disowned him. Harrison Yoder was quite a righteous fellow." Peter lifted his eyebrows. "A strict Christian, but he couldn't or wouldn't forgive his son. Trevor took his grandparents' last name. Quiet revenge. At any rate, Yoder died of a heart attack maybe three years ago. Birdie does what she can. She's retired, you know."

"We went out there yesterday. Poor woman." Ben hated delivering this kind of news, as did all law enforcement people.

"Here's my hunch. Trevor had a one-way ticket down. He could be useful. In a sense, he had nothing to lose. No reputation to defend. Knowing him over the years, I think he got talked into something. Something where his youthful looks would cause others to overlook him."

Leaning back in the chair, Ben folded his hands together for a moment. "Sex? There are male prostitutes."

"Stealing a car gets my attention. I'd say he became involved with stealing on a whole new level. Somehow he endangered his boss or bosses."

"Thank you, Peter. You and Sister, plus the old guard at the Hunt Club, give me the backstories, as they say in Hollywood. Helps me. Saves time, too. I love what I do."

"I know that," Peter interrupted.

"But more and more, I see people falling by the wayside. Less concern for others, no sense of community responsibility, and not much of a long view. It's become 'I want it now' instead of 'let's work together.' "

"I'm a lot older than you, Ben. Sometimes I wake up and wonder, is this my country?"

Ben nodded. "Well, it is. I don't know if we can make any changes, two people who often see the worst of life, the sorrows, but maybe if we simply do a good job, we'll be helpful."

"I hope you're right."

Driving back to the station, Ben, puzzled by the murder, knew he had to start with Trevor's file again, and it occurred to him he might want to review the recent files of anyone brought in between the ages of eighteen and thirty. Might there be a pattern?

As Ben arrived at the station, Walter, driving, with Sister in the passenger seat, pulled to Birdie Goodall's house. They brought food.

Ben had notified Trevor's mother, then Birdie. Mother and grandmother had a falling out over a year ago concerning Trevor.

The first person Birdie called was Walter, her former boss. Walter called and texted others as he knew many people close to Birdie. Word got out quickly, but bad news always does.

Other cars were parked all along the driveway.

Parking stretched out on the old road, Walter looked at Sister as he turned off the motor. "Ready?"

"Yes." She looked at him.

The door opened before they knocked. A young lady with an older lady directed them to the living room while taking the casserole.

Birdie, sitting on the couch, exclaimed when they walked into the room. "Sister. Walter." Then she burst into tears.

Most everyone there knew one another, at least in passing. Birdie retired from Walter's medical office recently. Seeing him brought more tears.

Sister walked over, leaned down to hug her. Then Walter being tall got down on one knee as chairs were filled. This made Birdie even more emotional.

"Oh, please. Fred. Let Dr. Lungrun sit next to me."

Fred, hair and beard shockingly white, rose, and Sister sat on one side of Birdie while Walter sat on the other, holding her hand.

"He wasn't a bad boy," She spoke of her grandson. "He bounced around, Sister, you know. His own parents aren't here. I can't believe my daughter is so hard-hearted." She sobbed now.

Sister took her hand, squeezed it and kissed it.

"Birdie, you did everything you could. You loved him. He knew you loved him, but he struggled to find his way."

She nodded. "He did."

Walter, mute, now put his arm around Birdie's heaving shoulders. "You did everything possible. You couldn't make up for his other losses, but he had you."

She nodded. "Why Melinda ever married Harrison Yoder, I'll never know. I blame him."

"He certainly didn't help." Sister believed it best to agree with Birdie although in truth, Harrison had been way too rigid, cruel in a way.

The two Jefferson Hunt masters sat with Birdie as other people filed in.

"Birdie, so many people want to talk to you. Walter and I need to make way."

"One thing. We have our Thanksgiving hunt at Mill Ruins," Walter said. "Hounds could come your way. You have a fox up here that often gives us a go. We'll change it. You need peace and quiet."

She grabbed his hand. "No. No, I love seeing the hounds, and everyone dressed up. It will take my mind off this."

Sister rose, kissed her on the cheek. "Birdie, even in your distress you are kind."

Blurting it out, poor soul, overcome with emotion. "I want to live. I want to see things and people that make me happy."

"And so you shall," Walter soothingly replied as two other people came over taking their places.

Sister and Walter chatted with other mourners. After a half hour, they left.

Walter, always the gentleman, opened the door for Sister, whom he had known since he was a child.

She sighed. "No one seemed surprised."

"I don't know. Maybe some people are just born under a dark star." He drove toward Sister's farm.

She replied, "What's that line from Shakespeare? 'The fault, dear Brutus, is not in our stars. But in ourselves.'"

Julius Caesar." He turned down the farm road. Mill Ruins was about eight miles from Roughneck Farm. "Love Shakespeare."

"Come on in," Sister said.

He followed after her. Gray was in Richmond. The consulting job was heating up.

"I'll make you anything you want to drink and you know I have that wonderful bottle of port."

He plopped down in a kitchen chair. "You know, I'll take some port."

"Anything you want to do for the Thanksgiving hunt?"

"No. The usual."

Sister poured him port. "I didn't know Trevor well. You probably saw him more than most of us."

"Nice enough kid. Would come into the office. He'd usually ask her for money. Nice though he was, Trevor mooched off his grandmother. Occasionally after a long day, I stop at the Jolly Roger, the bar close to the hospital. Trevor tended bar there for maybe a year. As I said, I only stopped in from time to time, but he was pleasant enough. I'm not a regular. He treated me like one but then I'd see him at the office when he'd come to see Birdie. We miss her. Best office manager ever. Always knew where I was, if I was operating. She knew my schedule better than I did. Sorry, got off track. Trevor would come in to ask Birdie for money. He mooched off of her. She couldn't say no." Walter continued, "Why does one person turn out okay and another doesn't? If people knew how many others they hurt when they steal, beat people up, hang around unsavory characters, get girls pregnant, the list could go on."

"I don't think they care who they hurt." Sister's voice was decisive. "Whatever was that kid doing to get himself shot in the head and tossed out on 64?"

Walter shrugged. "I can't imagine." He stopped himself, then added, "Well, I can, but I don't want to. Know what I mean?"

"Maybe. All I can think of is, he jeopardized others. Bam."

"The amount of money made through crime. I've been reading about these shoplifting gangs. Kids hired by adults, some people say the Mafia, to smash and grab at expensive stores. They run out, give the goods to their contact, and get paid maybe two or three hundred dollars, which to them is a lot of money. The stuff goes on eBay. People are making a fortune." Walter tapped his glass.

"How can you know if what is being sold on eBay or any format is not stolen goods? He wasn't shoplifting. People here know him. Someone would have recognized him. Had to be something else."

"A sex ring? Or maybe sex trafficking."

"Walter?"

"There are men who want young bodies. He was a good-looking kid."

"I can't even think of that." She grimaced.

"He goes to bed with someone rich or a politician then he blackmails them. Could happen?"

"Well, I guess."

"You're not buying that one?"

"It really is possible but somehow if he did get involved in something well organized, I doubt it would be that."

"Betty." Raleigh heard the old Bronco coming down the farm drive.

Rooster barked, too.

Golly perked her ears.

The back door opened then closed then the mudroom door opened.

"Sit down. Walter's having port." Sister was glad to see Betty.

"How was it?" Betty walked to the stove and put on the kettle. "Bobby and I couldn't get out of our business meeting."

"Sad."

"I'll bet. Anyone want something hot?"

"I'll take tea. While you're there, bring out that shortbread I bought yesterday. It's in the fridge."

"Why the fridge?"

"I didn't know how long it would keep, but now that we are all going to eat it, I could have kept it at room temperature."

Shortbread on the table, everyone with their drinks, they talked about Trevor, Birdie, reviewed the hunt season so far, and hoped this would be the only upsetting thing to happen during the Season.

"Hey, I was thinking, since we will all be at Aunt Daniella's for Thanksgiving, we have to get bourbon. We've each got our food list, but what makes her happy?" Sister asked.

"Bourbon improves with age and Aunt Daniella improves with bourbon." Betty smiled.

CHAPTER 7

November 8, 2023, Wednesday Night

Baxter sat on Lynn Pirozzoli's lap and behaved himself. Being a Jack Russell, he was interested in everything.

Adrianna and Veronica sat across from Baxter and Lynn.

"This place is packed." Lynn looked around. "I had no idea Orange County had a nightlife."

Veronica laughed. "It's not nightlife yet. We're just here as people get off work. The cruises and bruises show up after eight."

"Thank you for agreeing to meet us. Lynn and I both drive from different directions. The bar was in the middle."

Lynn, sharp-eyed, watched the people at the bar. A few young men sat on stools, but most were middle-aged fellows who stopped by after work.

The waitresses, young, took orders from those at the tables.

The bartender, male, knew his customers, engaged in every conversation. A few women, young like the waitresses, sat at the bar, chatting up the men.

"People are having a good time."

"Lynn." Veronica grinned. "People always have a good time when work is over."

"True," Adrianna agreed. "Let me get to the point. We'd like to use your gorgeous farm for our spring hunter pace. Hunt season will have just ended. People's horses will still be fit. A hunter pace helps the club make money."

"Sarah." Veronica waved over a pretty girl. "Bring out taste tests and," she looked at Baxter, "a very small hamburger for the dog."

"Veronica." Lynn held up her hand.

Veronica knew the place well and they knew her.

"You'll pick at the food even if you're not hungry. And you know Bubba, is that his name?"

"Baxter."

"Baxter will be thrilled. How about a drink?"

"Long drive home. I'll have a Perrier with lime." Lynn looked up at Sarah.

"Uh, me, too. My drive isn't as long as Lynn's, but long enough," Adrianna replied.

Sarah, having the order, left.

"Sorry that I interrupted you but the place is filling up. Better to order now," Veronica apologized.

"It is filling up." Adrianna then returned to her subject. "You are east of Cedar Mountain, we'll get people from Deep Run, maybe Warrenton and Charlottesville. We'd like to build some new jumps and, as we get closer, organize a parking area so your fields don't get torn up."

"I think we can do that. My girl team can help with the jumps."

"Veronica, thank you. Do you find the women you are helping like construction work? Working with their hands?"

"They do. I find they are careful, plot out what to do before they start."

They discussed details while trying the foods. The service was fast.

Baxter was in heaven. Warm hamburger. His own plate and chair. He ate french fries off a small plate on Lynn's lap. She pretended not to notice.

Veronica, from time to time, chatted as someone stopped by. She introduced them to Adrianna and Lynn.

Lynn watched the pretty young women talk to the men at the bar.

"Those girls are perking up tired businessmen."

Veronica examined the bar. "They don't look so tired."

"I'm sure it's the booze," Adrianna added.

"You know, Constance Hall, your hunter pace site," Veronica added, "was once a makeshift hospital for battle victims?"

"I did know that," Adrianna answered. "Most of the homes around here were filled with wounded; both sides."

"Sheila buried herself in the research. My sister has to have all the details. It's remarkable, really. We were the same people. Somehow that makes the war worse." Veronica leaned forward. "Family feuds. Well, *feud* isn't the right word, but those fights are always the worst."

"Seems to be the case," Lynn agreed. "Think of it. Those women caring for the men, so many of them amputees. God, how awful."

"We had no nurses. Clara Barton started it right here." Adrianna, having hunted Cedar Mountain for years, knew some of the history. "Those women learned caring for people from their mothers."

"On-the-job training." Veronica picked up one french fry and nibbled it. "I guess some men were assigned to help."

"They were, but when the armies moved on, those men, soldiers, moved with them. Medical care was incredibly primitive. It's a wonder anyone survived," Adrianna added.

"But weren't the greater killers diseases?" Lynn asked.

"Yes," Veronica replied.

"Being so close to Cedar Mountain, seeing bloodstains still on the wood floors of Constance Hall, I've become maybe not as obsessed as my sister, but, fascinated by the aftermath. Ultimately, by the end of the war, twenty thousand men and women served as nurses. Some of the nurses were Black women. In its way, the war got women cooperating. Some nuns nursed, too, and to think it started here."

"Women thrown into the chaos. The sounds of war, seeing blasted bodies, hearing those men cry, having them beg for help, how did they do it?" Adrianna marveled.

"You do what you have to do," Lynn replied. "There wasn't time to worry about yourself, to dream of a better world. Those women had to be exhausted."

"I think there are all kinds of heroes. They were heroes," Adrianna said.

"Yes. You probably know the story of how Constance Hall got its name. The Duncans, four generations, owned it. At the time of the battle, their two pretty daughters took care of the wounded. After the war, they lost everything. One daughter married a Confederate soldier she had nursed. They moved to Richmond and scraped by. Times improved. The beauty who married a Union boy moved to Philadelphia. He made a fortune in stocks. When the estate fell into ruin, he bought it as a gift for her, restored it, and named it Constance Hall in honor of his wife. They would spend Christmas here. The neighbors considered him a carpetbagger but they knew her, of course. Little by little her husband, Dennis Knight, guided by her, helped her friends. He finally opened a bank in Orange, leaving Philadelphia. Funny how things worked out. He would visit home. He continued to invest in stocks, using his old firm in Philadelphia. People also began calling the farm Constance Hall as a form of thanks to her. No one used the name *Duncan Hall* anymore."

"Now, that's a pretty story." Lynn absorbed every word.

Baxter, noticing his mother's attention to Veronica, boldly reached out for another french fry.

Adrianna pretended not to notice. Lynn shrugged. She'd given up. Adrianna did notice, she also noticed some of the men at the bar leaving with young women. Adrianna diverted Lynn's and Veronica's attention to it.

"Some of those guys are getting lucky."

Lynn, looking up, nodded. "Luck comes in many disguises."

Veronica raised an eyebrow. "Good for business."

CHAPTER 8

November 9, 2023, Thursday

Nestled deep in her tidy den, Aunt Netty curled up on the old blankets, bits of clothing she had stolen from both the Lorillards and the Bancrofts.

Pattypan Forge, thriving for two centuries, finally shut down shortly after World War II. Some windows were broken but the stone building held up, as did the slate roof. If one had old straw or blankets, the forge was good shelter.

Her den rested under a northwest-facing window. Some wind blew over her lodging, not in it. Had she built her den in the middle of the floor, it would have been colder.

The Bancrofts, at After All Farm, and the Lorillards often put out cartons filled with clothing for the mailman to pick up. He knew who needed what, so the items found their way to the right people. They found their way to Aunt Netty's abode as well.

The aging fox, red with a tattered tail, shared the large room with a stone-laid floor with hibernating toads, birds who, upon finding the solid forge, decided why build a nest in a tree? Mostly she had the place to herself. She did not consider chipmunks equals, so there wasn't much conversation. She put her old stolen sweaters outside her den, should the chipmunks want them. The pickings were so good at the Bancrofts' and Lorillards', she often redecorated. She even had an old, torn thick cashmere sweater arranged on the blanket inside the den.

The den itself had three good-sized chambers, plus one small one. Three entrances gave her choices if the hounds or a coyote came in. She'd cuss the hounds. As to the coyote, she thought he was worse than the hounds. Her mate, Uncle Yancy, so messy, had moved to the Lorillard mudroom. He enjoyed the heat that escaped from the kitchen into the mudroom. A pile of folded towels on the floor covered his way in. He'd then jump from old trunks up to the shelf over the kitchen door. The shelf spanned the width of the mudroom. Torn down jackets, old beach towels, all folded, lined the shelf. Sam and Gray, who had restored the old place, forgot about the shelf. The coats neatly hung on pegs.

Uncle Yancy also had a den under the front porch, as well as one in the stone-walled graveyard. The other dens led hounds away from his true treasure, the mudroom. Aunt Netty didn't envy him. She liked Pattypan Forge, especially in summer. Those thick stone walls kept the place cool.

As for winter, she had plenty to eat, since the Bancrofts especially threw out delicious morsels. They always blamed the tipped-over garbage cans on the raccoons.

The old fox possessed a keen sense of weather. This allowed her to stay home on good scenting days. She had no desire to give hounds a run, whereas her husband adored making fools out of them.

Today she felt snow coming in late morning. She'd gathered everything she needed last night so she could stay put. An entire box of Nabisco crackers, lifted from the Bancrofts, part of a thick sausage, some old cheese she picked up from the Bancrofts' sat in the corner of the middle chamber, her favorite and warmest room. She luxuriated.

Hounds were speaking in the distance. They sounded as though they were heading west. No, they stopped. Coming back. They drew closer, staying on the farm road between the Bancrofts' and the Lorillards'.

Yancy must be giving them a go.

He wasn't. Hounds picked up the scent of a coyote, heavier than fox, down by the Bancrofts' house. Given the dry conditions, his scent provided a bit of sport on an iffy day.

All he did was tear straight down the farm road, fly past the turnoff to Pattypan Forge. As hounds gained on him, he cut left into the woods, much of it overgrown with vines, prickers, turning back toward Pattypan.

As the sound turned, Aunt Netty popped out of her den to listen.

Coming toward the forge.

The coyote, seeing the forge up ahead, ran toward it then swerved again to move through the brush, in the direction of Roughneck Farm, as the two farms abutted each other.

Following as best he could, Weevil knew there was no way to get through the woods. He turned around, running back toward the path to Pattypan Forge. Hearing hounds' cry, then hoofbeats, Aunt Netty slipped into her den.

Weevil stopped at the forge as the path stopped. The club needed to open a path between the forge and Sister's property, which would be rough going. Somehow the club members found excuses not to attack this mess.

Frustrated, Weevil turned and blew back. Sister wisely did not go toward the forge, thinking she could follow the narrow path if hounds kept speaking. They did not.

Within a few minutes, the pack ran out, Weevil flew behind

them now running down the farm road. Betty, who knew the territory better than anybody, had already galloped to the covered bridge. Given the path of the run, plus the dry day, she figured scent would soon give out. She also figured they were on coyote.

Tootie, on the other side, had nowhere to go so she, too, was now on the farm road, but behind everyone.

Hearing furious hoofbeats behind him, Bobby Franklin moved to the side of the road.

He called out, "Staff."

The back of First Flight, hearing this, also moved to the side of the road, as did Sister. So now Tootie had a clear shot.

Once the second whipper-in passed both fields, riders then squeezed their horses. The farm road, dry, hard, jolted everyone. Sister hated to run on a hard road, but given the speed at which everyone was moving she charged forward.

The thunder as everyone galloped through the covered bridge deafened both people and horses.

On the other side, Sister caught sight of Weevil's scarlet coat. She slipped down the road embankment, picked up the trail heading to her house, jumped the simple coop in the fence line.

Hounds did as their huntsman told them to do. When they lost the scent, Weevil had a good idea the quarry headed west. The few times they picked up coyote scent the animal tended to utilize more difficult territory once out of the bush. As one traveled west, the roll of the land became more prominent, until finally hitting the back of Hangman's Ridge, a climb up and a climb down.

Sister galloped along the tidy path, hugging the fence line, reached the hogs' back jump into her own property, and easily took it.

The hounds, already on the wildflower field, shorn of color now, worked to pick up the line. Sister fell back to a trot to watch.

Noses down, dust going into sensitive nostrils thanks to the dryness, they struggled to pick up anything. Weevil urged them on, praising them.

Jethro, next to his littermate Jinx, moaned, *"I can't pick up anything."*

"Me neither." Jinx sneezed.

The coyote, adopting some fox strategies, had circled back, heading east.

Weevil walked beside his hounds. They'd been out an hour and a half. He thought, what if he drew around the rear of Hangman's Ridge?

"Come along." He called to the pack, taking them by his place, to the farm road to the bottom of the ridge.

The path around there would eventually come out on the other side of the ridge, which faced Foxglove Farm in the distance.

Finally, Weevil realized he was defeated, so he drew back toward the Bancrofts'.

Foxhunting can be spotty; the field had one good run, so no one was disappointed. All were glad to just reach their trailers and then go to the breakfast, hosted by Tedi and Edward.

The large dining room, crammed with people, was noisy. The food, as always, mixed breakfast dishes with lunch.

Sister, tired, sat in a chair in the living room. Usually hungry after a hunt, today she simply wanted deviled eggs and a hot cup of tea.

Tedi, the hostess, now in her early eighties, sat with the Master.

"What do you think of these new riding boots with a zipper all the way down the back?" Tedi asked.

"Tedi, you know we are both sticklers for tradition, but I can understand why someone not so," she thought aloud, "married to the old ways would like them. Easier to get on and off."

"Yes." Seeing someone over Sister's shoulder, Tedi motioned for the woman to step forward. "Veronica, meet the Master."

An attractive woman walked around to the front of the chair. "Mrs. Arnold."

Sister put her cup down and held out her hand. "That introduction before the hunt was mercifully brief. Hounds wanted to go. I'm pleased to truly meet you."

The younger woman smiled. "They are keen."

"Thank you," Sister replied.

"Sit down," Tedi more or less ordered, then leaned forward. "Is it true you and your sister bought all that land across from Close Shave? Wolverhampton was once a beautiful estate."

"I have a lot of work to do," Veronica answered.

Sister realized where she had heard Veronica's name. "You own that beautiful home by Cedar Mountain. Constance Hall."

"I do. My sister and I own it. We restore properties. It's exciting, really."

"You're hunting with Bull Run?"

"We are. Adrianna told me to visit Jefferson Hunt's home territory. I'm glad that I did."

"So far it's been a dry Season. Tough scenting, but little by little I trust it will pick up. I'm delighted we have another foxhunter in the Chapel Cross area. It's spectacular."

"When we were looking for properties, I drove down here on a whim. The sign for the 1780 House drew me in. The proprietor, your road whip, gave me her card, wrote on the back the best hunting places. I looked up Chapel Cross on my phone, drove out, and lost my heart. Seeing the sunlight on the Corinthian columns at Old Paradise." She placed her hand over her heart. "Magic. History. Beauty."

Sister smiled. "It is magic. I assume you heard the history?"

"Oh yes. Sophie, who became wildly rich during the War of 1812 by raiding British supply trains. No Redcoat ever suspected a woman."

"It's a great story. If you want, we'll introduce you to the owners, the Howards, who have restored everything, even the graveyards."

"I would love that," Veronica enthused.

"Dare I ask what your plans are?" Tedi boldly asked.

"Fell in love with it despite huge potholes in the driveway, a tree growing up through the back hall, a huge front room. Love! I promise you I will restore it to its former glory. I have a team of women workers. That makes it even more fun." She did not reveal her plans for after the restoration.

"If we can help, we will. We all take great pride in Chapel Cross and the Crossroads." Tedi folded her hands.

"Honey," Edward called from the next room. Tedi looked as her husband waved at her. "I love him. I have loved him for sixty-five years but there are times when he is helpless. This is one of them. He has his 'What do I do?' face. Excuse me."

The women laughed as Tedi rose to rescue her husband, whose face registered relief as she stood up.

Sister chatted with Veronica longer, making a point of introducing her to those coming to talk to their Master.

Later that evening, after a hot shower, Sister and Gray lounged in the library. He had the TV on, watching college football, sound low.

"Without prompting, she offered Wolverhampton for hunting," Sister finally started.

"Babydoll, you could talk a dog off a meat wagon." He looked at the screen. "Idiot! The right tackle missed his blocker."

"Sounds gruesome."

"Given that the quarterback is left-handed, it is. Sorry. Couldn't help myself."

"What I worry about when you watch football is your blood pressure."

He put his arm around her shoulder. "Worry about it when I look at you. Okay." He groaned. "The offense is falling apart."

"Yes, dear." She laughed.

He started laughing, too.

"Playing safety in college hooked me for life. I could see the entire field from my position."

"Never thought of that."

He looked at her. "Wolverhampton, hope it all works out."

"She just offered, unprovoked, so to speak."

"Really? No wooing?"

"Really." She took the remote, turning down the sound. "I'm borrowing this for one minute, then I'll give it back so you can turn up the sound. If you're going to yell at the offense let them have it. Quick question. How much do you think it will cost to restore Wolverhampton?"

"I have no idea. Worker prices rise and fall. Windows, doors, plumbing. Things are so volatile. A rough guess for a good job, including the farm road, one million. That's watching the money, house only. Not including fencing."

She handed him back the remote. "I see. It might be less for the Sherwoods, as they work with women at risk. Teaching them construction. That will keep labor costs down."

"Jerk! You are such a jerk!"

"Jerk," she yelled at the television with him, then they fell into giggles like two kids.

Raleigh, stretched out next to Rooster, raised his head. *"I love them but . . ."*

CHAPTER 9

November 10, 2023, Friday

Sister opened the back door of her car, picked up two bags of groceries. At the mudroom, she sat them down, opened the door. A UPS carton sat in front. First she carried the groceries in, then walked back out and picked up the carton, which was somewhat heavy.

Before she shut the door, she made sure she hadn't left the back door of the car open. She'd done that once, and rain came up with wind and the backseat had been soaked. So she double-checked everything.

Sometimes an interruption will make one forgetful. The phone rings, you notice papers on the floor, those little things could divert her concentration from the task at hand.

However, she kept her mind focused in the hunt field. It was never an effort.

"All right, I can do this without doggy help."

"But I smell meat in this bag." Rooster's eyes were bright.

"Come on, now. Get your nose out of there," she chided him.

Raleigh and Golly, sound asleep on the sofa in the library, heard the bags rattle, roused themselves to wander into the kitchen. It's always good to know what new food is in the house. After Sister put the meat in the fridge, she picked up a shiny bag, pulled the top open, which took a minute, dipped her hand in, retrieving two long, skinny sausage chews.

"*My fav.*" Raleigh took one as offered.

"*Me too.*" Rooster, as polite as he could be, enthusiastically grabbed his.

"*I'm waiting.*"

As if knowing what her cat said, Sister fetched a little tin out of one of the shopping bags. "What a good kitty you are."

The reward was divine catnip.

With everyone happy, Sister proceeded to put away the groceries. Two fresh oranges sat in a bowl, she arranged two apples next to that. The lemons and limes she dropped in the refrigerator in a special tray for fruits. Nearing the end of this chore, she snapped a crisp bit off the Romaine lettuce. This she offered to J. Edgar, who was happy.

She folded the bags, opened the door to the mudroom, colder air rushing in, and placed the heavy bags on a pile of other saved bags. If it could be useful, she was loath to throw it out.

Finally, she sat down, exhaled, and picked up *The Wall Street Journal.* Gray read it cover to cover. She read anything to do with agriculture, letters to the editor, opinion pieces. She especially enjoyed the weekend edition, reading Peggy Noonan's column first.

The door opened, Gray walked in. "Getting colder."

"I didn't hear you drive up." She looked at the dogs. "What's the matter with you? You're supposed to announce visitors."

"*Gray's not a visitor,*" Rooster replied with his mouth full.

"Tired?"

"A little. Grocery shopping wears me out. I bought potatoes, carrots, peas, basic stuff. Meat. But I forget something. Every time."

"What was it this time?" He pulled the screen away from the fireplace in the kitchen. The fireplace had served since the early 1800s when this house was built. The original log cabin with an addition, occupied by Weevil and Tootie, was built earlier. Money rolled in during Monroe's administration, which was when the big house was built.

"Paper towels. How can I forget paper towels?"

"Honey, I don't know how you remember what you do."

"I make a list."

"Still." He crushed old newspapers, then placed a small fire-starter chunk in the middle of them. The actual logs he crisscrossed into a square finally placing a top log catty-corner over that. Then he pulled open the flue, dust from prior fires floating down. The kitchen matches rested on the mantelpiece. Sneezing, he picked up the large matches, struck two together, touched the papers, replaced the screen. Watched his handiwork.

"You build good fires."

"My mother taught me. It was the heat for the house. The coal-burning furnace did a good job, but there is so much wood at the farm, fallen limbs, why spend a lot of money if you don't have to spend it? I like to hear the crackle."

"Me too. Takes the chill right out of the room. Which reminds me, at some point in the next few years, we are going to need a new furnace."

He washed his hands in the sink, dried them, sat down. "Let's wait it out. Too much uncertainty, thanks to the federal government."

"How can Congress tell us how to heat our houses?" She pulled carrots out of the fridge and began cutting them into small pieces.

"People have been telling others how to live for thousands of years."

She realized she hadn't washed the carrots so she spoke above the running water. "Didn't work, did it?"

"Oh, it does for a while. Mostly what it does is create distrust, rebellion, disgust. My analysis."

"Your analysis is good enough for me."

The phone rang. They kept their landline; being out in the country, the ability to hear a caller or speak to same remained steady. The cellphones were not steady that way. Sister figured this had to do with satellites, plus they were so close to the mountains.

Gray got up and answered the phone. He listened, not speaking. Finally, he said, "I guess that's good news of a sort."

Sister looked at him. He put his hand over the mouthpiece. "Walter." Then he spoke into the phone. "Just told Sister it was you."

Walter replied, "Tell her I cleared the overgrown back trail to Birdie's. Just in case."

After a few more brief comments, Gray hung up and told his wife, "No drugs in Trevor's system."

She picked up a potato she just washed, began peeling it. "I don't know. Does that make it better or worse? I guess a little better. He did what most kids do. He tried stuff. Scared Birdie, but he wasn't a druggie."

"The other thing Walter said, apart from the fact that the medical examiner's office got to Trevor quickly, was that he had a small tumor in his lung."

"At twenty-four?"

"That's what they said. Cancer."

"Does cancer spare any family? But Trevor didn't smoke, at least I never saw him. I don't know, sweetheart, I've begun to think cancer is a true epidemic. We can't seem to face it."

"Maybe because it's natural. Even the pharaoh's doctors recognized cancer in ancient Egypt. But nobody knows how to stop it. Well, we can stop some kinds, but how it starts?" He shrugged.

"I hope this gives Birdie some comfort. At least he hadn't strayed into drugs."

Gray thought a moment. "Let's hope so, but what I think of is, if he wasn't strung out, was clearheaded, why was he shot in the head?"

She turned from the sink to reply. "What's worth a human life?"

"Maybe the question is, 'What is a human life worth?' "

"Right . . . I have no answer. As I age, I find there is more and more I don't know."

"I understand." He folded the paper into vertical quarters. "I see you've been reading."

"Citrus took a hit last year. No one knows what will happen this year, and I read about John Deere's profits."

The phone rang again.

"My turn." Sister shook her hands, then grabbed a dish towel. "Hello?"

"It's always good to hear your voice," Kathleen Sixt Dunbar greeted her. "Called you with a thought and news."

"I'm ready for both. Is that Abdul in the background?"

"He says hello, too." Kathleen motioned for her Welsh terrier to come over to her while she was sitting.

He did, leaning against her.

"Veronica Sherwood just rented the apartment behind the store. She said there is nothing to rent out at Chapel Crossroads. She needs to get stuff rolling. She doesn't want to drive back and forth from Culpeper every day. Said she wants to stay on top of it. Her sister can manage a smaller restoration in Orange County."

"Actually, she'd better rehab the farm manager's house first. Wolverhampton is a big project."

"I've never been in it."

"Lovely, not as big and grand as Old Paradise but has a fabulous curving stairway. Marble surrounds on the fireplaces. Big rooms. A small cubby here and there. When I was young, Ray and I spent a lot of time there with the Tates, shoe family, had owned it for generations. At any rate, you've hopefully gotten a good tenant."

"I think she'll be fine. As my business is chicken one day, feathers the next, I am happy. But here's what I want to talk to you about. She said she rides okay but she probably won't go out when it's bitter cold. Also, she doesn't want to keep a horse here. She has one at home. Rented, she said. I suggested, if you agree, that when she's here, she ride with Aunt Daniella and myself as a road whip. It's one way to learn the territory."

"Fine with me. Aunt Dan has the last word."

"Right, but she'll ask me if I talked to you first. Aunt Dan follows all the rules."

"When everyone is looking." Sister laughed.

"I suggested a few boarding stables when she's ready. She borrowed a horse when she rode at After All."

"We have some good ones. It's actually smart to rent a horse for a Season. Until you know what you're getting into. But I think it's a good idea and I'm glad you have that apartment rented."

"Me too."

After they hung up, Sister relayed the news to Gray.

"I don't blame her for not wanting to hunt on those icy cold days. I force myself to go out."

"If you're on a good run, you warm up."

He smiled at her, as hunting was her great passion. "Yes, dear."

As he read the paper, she put the ingredients for a stew on the stove; Sister checked the clock, making note that this would need to be stirred from time to time. Then she took expensive hamburger out of the fridge, taking half of the package and sprinkling all that into the mix. She was convinced good meat made good stew. She wrapped up the rest, put it back in the fridge, washed and dried her hands. The phone rang again.

"Freddie," Sister answered. "What can I do for you? Give you over to my husband?"

"No," Freddie replied. "Two things. Have you picked a day for us to hunt Bull Run?"

"No. I need to call Adrianna. I'll do that tomorrow morning. Any suggestions?"

"No. I'm curious about the fixture. Great fixtures."

"Yes, they are. And well maintained. What's the second question?"

"Not a question, just a report. When I came home today, someone had tried to get into my house. Fortunately, they were unsuccessful, but I had two packages on my front stoop. One from UPS and one from FedEx. Both were opened, but nothing was taken. The UPS was books and the FedEx was a box, too. Had caviar packed in ice with those plastic ice packets. So if you can double-check your security system."

"Yes. I guess we can assume the thief, or thieves, doesn't like caviar."

Freddie quipped, "That would be the first thing I would steal."

"And who sends you caviar?"

"My brother. He sent it early. Why wait until Thanksgiving is his attitude, plus by then delivery services are overwhelmed."

"I'd steal the caviar, too. But thanks for telling me."

"I guess the holidays inspire this kind of thing."

"Oh, people will take packages right off your porch. I suppose if they like something they keep it. If not, they sell it. Creeps."

She relayed this information to her husband while stirring her stew.

"Ben would know the statistics. I'm willing to bet theft shoots up over the holidays. Which reminds me, what do you want for Christmas?"

"Peace and quiet."

"Ah." He laid the folded paper on the table. "That's a tall order. I'll set the table."

The stew proved delicious. The wind came up as they finished eating, branches from a tree close to the back window scraped it, a horror-movie sound, then one of the logs popped in the fireplace, making both of them jump as well as the dogs and Golly.

"It was a dark and stormy night," Gray joked.

"Do you think someone really wrote that?" She smiled.

"Bet we can find out."

They cleaned off the table and then sat back down. He, for a light after-dinner drink. She drank some green tea. They talked about Ukraine, and the uproar in the Mideast, then switched to what their friends were doing, Saturday's upcoming hunt.

Full, Gray leaned back in his chair. "Thinking about no drugs in Trevor's system. You know whoever killed him wanted no mistakes. Truly wanted him dead. I wonder if Trevor had warnings and paid no attention. Quick and brutal."

"It is. I wonder what he did."

CHAPTER 10

November 11, 2023, Saturday

A low overcast sky, crisp temperature kept the scent down, although still somewhat dry, hounds had a chance with fresh scent. Hounds stuck to a line for the last thirty minutes. Heading south on Old Paradise's vast lands, the Jefferson Hunt was enjoying a day that felt like a late-fall hunt. Fall temperatures, blue skies, and falling leaves testified to winter's approach.

Sister on Rickyroo, a keen Thoroughbred bay, kept hounds in sight. The territory was beginning to steepen. She passed a big rock outcropping. She knew a young fox had a den in there, but hounds didn't swerve to it.

The fox, Sarge, had moved down to the stables at Old Paradise. There was the grand stable for former racehorses during the glory days, the stable for farm horses, and the elegant Carriage House, where Earl, an older red fox, lived in enviable comfort. The Carriage House was reasonably warm, with little traffic. Earl used to live in the grand stable, but too much commotion pushed him to the Carriage House. The farm horse stables also had blankets, folded, some human blankets in each stable tack room, plus many ways to get in and out of each stable. This way the two foxes could visit but not get on each other's nerves with one at the Carriage House, the other at the farm horse stables. Sitting outside the farm horse stables, they watched the pack disappear in the distance.

"Well?" Sarge asked his mentor.

"Bishop's Gate. Whoever this is is heading straight for it, and it's a couple of miles away. I don't know who they're chasing."

"The closer you get to the crossroads, the easier it is to find food. Especially at the chapel itself. That old fellow there is, well, old."

"He is." Earl had observed the sexton for most of his years, watching the fellow decline.

"Summer is the best. He sits in the graveyard, eats sandwiches, cookies, sweet stuff, forgets it." Sarge beamed, thinking of those easy pickings. *"He drinks. I can smell it."* Sarge wrinkled his nose. *"That stuff is awful, what he drinks."*

"He's supposed to keep the graveyard tidy. He does." Earl listened as the cry faded. *"That's going to be one tired pack of foxhounds. I rarely go beyond that back farm road full of potholes, that divides these pastures, wilder acres from the thick woods. No need. Everything I want is here."*

"You know, my old den is there if you ever get caught lolling about. Not that you would. You know this pack too well."

"They're fast. If anything slows them, it's the territory, but in an open field they stretch out. Cover a lot of ground. I don't know why they do it. Hunt, I mean."

Sarge agreed. *"They are fed every day. What's the point?"*

Earl pondered this. *"They were bred to hunt, and I guess even if they are fed and have fancy places to live, they still want to hunt. Same with the humans. Some want to chase something. Seems like a lot of unnecessary work."*

"They are a strange animal. Sometimes I hop up on a low windowsill to watch the nice lady at her desk. Sitting still. How does she do it?" Sarge

mentioned Marty, who had a second office at Old Paradise as well as at the estate she and her husband built before they bought Old Paradise.

Earl strained. *"Can hardly hear them."* He changed the subject. *"I'll be glad when deer season is over."*

"Why? No hunting here."

"Some of the other places allow it. Those fellows, always seems to be men, get up before dawn to sit in one of their platforms. They think we don't know because they wear camouflage. Some of those tree stands have fake foliage. Humans have no idea how good our sense of smell is. We know they are up there. But I don't go on those fixtures, just in case."

"You don't look like a deer." Sarge twitched his whiskers.

Earl nodded. *" Some people just want to kill things. They'd shoot me or you if they saw us moving. Not everyone, mind you, but there is a type of human that likes to kill things. Mostly they like to kill one another. Very odd."*

"Yes. They don't need to fight over territory. By the way, have you ever seen the amount of food the tall, thin fellow carries into Tattenhall Station? His lady friend helps, too. They get this stuff from buildings." Noting Sarge's raised eyebrows, Earl continued. *"Yes, buildings. Humans have buildings full of food. They go in and bring it out."*

"Have you seen this?"

"No. My mother told me about it. She said when she was young the Gulf station at the crossroads had a store. They sold gas. Had a place for people to eat and also to bring food out to their cars. All gone now, although the fellow that owns Old Paradise bought everything, since the Gulf station belonged to this place. I never saw it myself, but people still use the station to repair cars. Not many. I think it's private, like our dens are private."

Sarge considered this. *"So that orange sign means food?"*

"I don't know, but those pumps out front are, or were, for people to pull up and fill their cars. Even here if you go by a car or truck, you can smell the gas. Awful stink."

Sarge sighed. *"I will never understand humans."*

Earl laughed, a little puff sound like a dog's laugh. *"They don't understand themselves."*

Those humans riding today may not have understood themselves, but they understood they were on a rip-roaring run. Small clumps of earth flew up from hooves. A lone coop up ahead announced the end of this huge pasture.

Ricky never faltered at a jump. Sister barely knew she was momentarily airborne, he was so smooth. On the other side, the footing became trickier, as this was a cornfield used for silage. Instead of weaving through those irritating rows, she stayed on the outside, rode toward Chapel Road South, turned right following the fence path to the farm road, woods on the other side.

Hounds stopped. So did she, just as Kathleen, Aunt Daniella, and Veronica Sherwood turned onto the old road. Kathleen stopped. Sister waved her on, staying put.

Weevil, in the cornfield, stood still as hounds struggled to find lost scent. One usually doesn't lose scent in standing corn or even harvested corn, the fallen kernels bring in foxes and other animals. Corn is a high-calorie food. But there he sat, then slowly followed along as they ransacked the various rows.

Barrister, nose down, inhaled large amounts of scent. *"Dead something."*

Bachelor, his littermate, young, inhaled this odor as well. *"I don't know. Nothing we know. Not a deer, raccoon, even a bear."*

Diana, in her prime, came over. She lifted her head. Put it down again. *"Dasher."* She called her littermate. *"Come here."*

He did, studying the scent. *"Human."*

"I think so, too. Not recent."

"The line is somewhat protected by the rows. Not much. Let's follow it, but not open. We can't open on a scent that isn't our game," Diana reminded them.

The pack followed the two D's. They slowly walked through the row. The scent grew fainter as they emerged on the farm road. An abandoned rented delivery truck stood there. Beat up, the name of the rental company on the side, it looked forlorn.

Weevil came out of the corn rows behind his pack. Betty waited in front of the truck. Tootie came out closer to the road where it intersects with Chapel Cross South. She stopped. Both Tootie, Sister, and First Flight, Bobby leading Second Flight, waited.

Foxes vanish all the time. But conditions were good enough, they might pick up another. However, what they couldn't see was the pack sitting by the truck.

Weevil waited as Kathleen drove up and stopped. "Can I help?"

"No. I'll cast around this, maybe head across the road to Beveridge Hundred. They are sniffing this truck. Thought I'd wait a minute or two."

"It's the back of the beyond here." Aunt Daniella had run down her window.

Veronica, in the backseat, agreed. "Who would want to drive out here? Do you know where it goes?"

Aunt Daniella replied, "There's a better farm road, not so ripped up, maybe a half mile on the right. That goes back to Old Paradise. This road heads due west and stops at the mountains, where it turns into a foot trail."

"I see," Veronica answered.

Kathleen put the car in park, got out, and walked over to Weevil. "They are at the door. Your side."

"I'll pull them off. Could be our fox ran here. But I would think the scent would still be pretty fresh."

"I'll look in the truck." She opened the passenger door and then gasped. "Blood."

Weevil dismounted, throwing the reins over Kilowatt's neck.

Fortunately, he had four fabulous hunt horses at his disposal, so no one became overworked. Kilowatt stood like a champ. Betty didn't move, just in case the pack did. Her Huntsman was now on foot.

Weevil beheld the blood all over the passenger seat, some splashed on the door. It was black, having been there for days, at the least.

"That's a lot of blood." He tried to take it all in.

"I can't stand it. What are they doing?" Veronica put her hand on the doorknob.

"Don't. You'll get in the way, and that's not going to help you with Jefferson Hunt," Aunt Daniella ordered.

Veronica did as she was told.

Kathleen, not a panicky type, looked up at Weevil; he was six feet tall. "We'd better get Sister to call Ben Sidell. I think he's working this weekend."

"You have a cellphone, right?" Weevil kept staring at the blood; so much.

"I'll do it right now. What are you going to do?"

"Under the circumstances, I don't think I can keep hunting. You tell Sister. I'm going back to Old Paradise. I want to retrace my steps through the corn." He waved to Betty, mounted Kilowatt, and rode back into the row from which he came. This was easy, as the hoofprints proved clear.

Kathleen, now in the car, backed out slowly. Tootie followed Weevil from her position, which meant she had to pass both flights, all of whom turned their horse faces toward the whipper-in. You don't turn a horse's backside to another horse or human. Sister asked Tootie as she passed, "Drawing back?"

"I don't think so."

Sister rarely spoke to a whipper-in, best to allow them to concentrate on their duties, which could be perilous. Her job was to stay with hounds, but before she could turn, Kathleen had backed out to the good road. She stopped, quickly got out, hurried toward Sister, who asked Ricky to slowly walk toward Kathleen.

"Are you okay? You look a little peaked."

"Sister, there's a ditched delivery truck up ahead on the old farm road. The passenger side is full of blood."

"Good Lord."

"No other signs. If there was a body close by, you know hounds would have found it."

"Yes." Sister well knew the allure of decay to canines, as well as vultures. Nature's garbagemen.

"I'll stay here if you don't mind. I'll call Ben Sidell."

"Good idea, Kathleen. Plus Aunt Dan knows more about this territory and the history of it than anyone. If there's an old foundation, she'll know where it is. After Ben arrives, come back to the breakfast. I don't think we should say anything. People react in many different ways, some of them not at all helpful."

"Yes." Kathleen nodded then turned as Sister turned, riding past the two flights.

"Lost the line. We'll save heading to Bishop's Gate for another day."

As Kathleen called Ben, Veronica, listening in, turned to Aunt Daniella. "Good Lord. This is horrible."

"Way back here, it's tempting for people to pick up illegal substances, I think, but in the old days the homemade liquor boys used it a lot."

"Somebody dangerous is back," Veronica gasped.

Aunt Daniella opened her voluminous purse, pulling out a .38 special. "Carry a pistol. I have always liked shooting. Used to go to the firing range with my late son. I still go. It's good for me."

"That's a small barrel," Veronica noted.

"It's a snub nose. A longer barrel is more forgiving, but with practice you can be accurate to about fifty yards. Protect yourself."

"I'll think about it."

"You can't think about it when you're dead," the older woman stated.

Veronica studied the weapon. "Would fit into a purse."

"Or into a coat pocket," Kathleen, now off the phone, observed. "The key to stopping crime: Don't allow men to own guns. Only women."

Aunt Daniella dryly commented, "Kathleen, there will always be crime, gender be damned."

Veronica interjected, "True, but there would be less if only women owned guns."

Kathleen checked the indoor heat. "This is a subject for a long discussion."

Aunt Daniella plopped her expensive gun back in her bag. "For another day."

As the field, large, for it was Saturday, trotted over the pastures, people chatted, compared notes on the run. Back at the trailers, Sister quickly rode over to Weevil, Betty, and Tootie, loading hounds. They eagerly got in the party wagon, drank fresh water, and ate cookies. Once home, hounds would enjoy a warm mash, always a big treat after a hunt. They talked among themselves about the blood. Hounds knew enough about human behavior to know blood means trouble.

"Betty, Tootie, Weevil, come here a minute."

Weevil held Kilowatt's bridle, Betty walked over to the Thoroughbred's left side. "Come on down. I'll guide you."

"Not a bad idea. I know my voice can carry." Sister threw her right leg over the sleek animal's back as Betty reached up, holding her torso as she slid down.

Turning to her friend, Sister said softly, "Another sign of creeping age. Well, maybe it isn't creeping."

"Piffle." Betty smiled at her friend, for Sister could still ride.

But then again, even a terrific athlete must bow to the years.

Placing her arm around a friend she had loved for decades, Sister smiled. "Relentless Time collects his dividend."

Weevil and Tootie, by Kilowatt's head, leaned toward their Master, who was now right up with them, half whispering. "Say nothing. No point starting the gossip mill."

"Yes, Ma'am." Weevil always properly addressed his Master and was surprised when American staff did not. People might think he was an American, but he was not. He was a Canadian and there were certain manners of conduct he followed to the T.

"Did you see it?" she asked the blond young man.

"I did. The seat back, and seat itself, covered in dried blood. Was on the door. When hounds drew through the corn, they lost our fox, or our fox lost them. But after casting about they moved toward the road. No one spoke, as you know. I think they were on a blood-line, because they went straight to the passenger door once we reached that truck."

"Well," she paused in thought, "if there were a body anywhere within a half mile, I believe they would have found it. Or more blood. Any sense of how old that blood might be?"

Weevil shook his head. "It was dried. There was so much of it."

"Ben will have his forensic team on it. They're amazing. It's a science." Sister then took Ricky's reins. "I could never do it."

Ben reached the truck forty minutes after Kathleen had called. After answering his questions, he told her to drive back to Old Paradise with the same advice Sister gave her staff.

Jude and Jackie, his other young assistant, closely examined the truck. The forensic team came out, only two of them since there wasn't a corpse, only blood. He trusted their expertise.

After enough time, they began to feel the creeping cold. Ben turned to his team. "Let's get the truck back. Jude, call the tow crew. We'll meet here tomorrow at eight. Should be light enough by then. We'll scour this area, and Jackie, make sure we have drones."

"Yes, Sir."

"All right, then. See you tomorrow."

He and Jude climbed into the squad car. Shutting the door, Ben turned on the heat as he backed out. "Has that raw feel."

"Yes, Sir. Have you ever seen anything like that truck?"

"All the blood?"

"Yes, Sir."

"I have. It always amazes me how much blood is in the human body, between eight and twelve pints."

"It's possible whoever was hurt or killed was transferred to another vehicle."

"Then another vehicle would need to be cleaned." Ben paused. "There are services for that. Organized crime is very organized." A half smile crossed his face.

"The big crime families are organized and smart. Look how long they've been in business." Jude was grateful for the heat.

"It fascinates me how brilliant people can have crime as a career. I suppose if you're born into it, it's natural. Although this may not be organized crime."

"Whoever did whatever they did, probably murder, knows this area. Remember when we were back here once and caught the two guys who had been digging in the graveyards at Old Paradise? Boy, they were a long way from intelligent."

Jude recalled a case a few years ago when two fellows thought they would discover the hidden treasure supposedly buried by Sophie Marquet. They fulfilled the definition of *trespasser* more than *criminal*. One was illiterate, the other could read and write. Having grown up in the county, they knew the Chapel Cross area. As it turned out, there were buried coins in the old graveyard. Crawford found it, more by chance than design.

"I almost felt sorry for them. What kind of future do men like that have? All they really have is their bodies. Sooner or later the body breaks down. What kind of skill can they learn?" Ben drove through the crossroads, heading back toward town.

Jude thought about this. "Leather repair? Lots of horse people. You wouldn't need to read or write."

"Right. Detailing cars. Not a whole lot, but there is stuff."

"So you think whoever dumped that truck is from around here?" Jude liked law enforcement the longer he was in it.

"I do. Maybe not from around here, but someone who has learned back roads, dirt roads. That rutted mess isn't a road most people would know about and even if they lived in this area they might take a look at those ruts, the big potholes, and figure there was nothing scenic enough to risk their tires."

"Find the truck owner first?" Jude asked.

"It's a start."

When Kathleen left Aunt Daniella, she drove back to the 1780 House. Veronica knew Kathleen was shaken. Kathleen gave her a condensed version of walking up to the truck.

Veronica asked, "Is being a road whip always this dramatic?"

"Look at it this way, you weren't bored," came the reply.

CHAPTER 11

November 12, 2023, Sunday

The quiet of Sunday recharged Sister. Church in the morning, listening to Reverend Taliaferro's sermons, started the day off with ideas and calmness. Usually she and Gray would have dinner at the home place, Yvonne's, or Aunt Daniella's. This Sunday, Gray went to the Lorillard place to help his brother stack even more firewood for the coming winter. They'd spend time in the late summer, early fall splitting wood, a chore they'd accomplished since young men. The brothers would do the same for Aunt Dan, Yvonne, and Sister. Everyone had a shed near their houses filled with split logs, perfectly dried. Every fireplace had a small stack next to it. If the weather looked bad, wet, or snowy, then everyone's mudroom also had wood stacked so no one needed to trudge out in the wind, the wet, or push through snow.

Sister had the house all to herself. When the sun hovered close to the horizon, she bundled up to sit on the back porch, watching it glide behind the mountains. The cat and dogs stayed inside, as she didn't ask them out. She had her coat, gloves, scarf, and lumberjack hat. They had their coats, but when it got really cold, she put winter coats on the dogs. Golly stayed warm in the house.

Inhaling deeply the cold air, it was about forty-two degrees Fahrenheit and falling, assailed her nostrils, even reaching up into her sinuses. She pulled her scarf over her nose, wondering how people in Canada survived those minus degrees. She found the cold invigorating, but she had no desire to stay in it for a long time.

The sun dropped, half of it below the mountain topline. Then, poof, it was gone, a fierce red gold outlined the spot, the top of the Blue Ridge awash in gold. Sliding cirrus clouds moved toward her, more clouds pushing behind them. The colors fascinated her, as no sunset duplicated another. Gold turned to copper with scratches of magenta. The hot magenta slicing through the deepening gold and copper would impress anyone looking at it. Sometimes fingers of aquamarine would move along with the clouds, contrasting against the usual gold or pink of those clouds. The colors deepened, as did the chill. Scarlet turned to a faded red then a diffuse lavender. Finally, the sky shone a light gray with darkness creeping in behind like a curtain.

Some sunsets lasted for close to forty-five minutes. Others, the sun dropped like a stone; the color, pale, evaporating. Watching a sunset, she never knew how it would transform the sky, but she knew it would always transform her.

Mountains, valleys, streams, rivers, huge ancient oaks next to saplings, even underbrush captured her attention. So many creatures lived beyond her porch. They prepared for winter in their own ways. About all she could do was put on layers, wear thick gloves and a warm hat. A hunting helmet was not warm, but if the day was to be very cold, she'd pull on a thin lumberjack cap, then a larger helmet over it. Rarely did she do that, but some days that hunting helmet felt so cold. Keeping her hands and feet warm drove her crazy. Even if she put toe heaters in her boots, they finally stopped giving out heat and it felt like you had lumps of charcoal under your feet. A hand warmer on the inside of her gloves, at the back, helped, as did hand warmers in her pockets. Sometimes she had Gray put a square pad on the small of her back, which emanated heat. The one thing that could keep you warm was a good run. Watching the sunset, followed by twilight, she wiggled her toes. Those two pairs of socks, one silk and one cashmere, helped, but it was time to go in. The day birds, a twitter here and there, settled in for the night. In the distance, she could see the whites of deer tails as they came out to graze. Since she didn't allow deer hunting they flocked to her. If she kept still, they'd come quite close.

The hounds, silent, already asleep, curled up in their condos or in the main kennels. The kennels gave hounds a choice. Each indoor quarters had a dog door they could go through if they wanted to be outside in one of the big runs. The condos, insulated, each with a dog door; deep straw inside enticed some of the hounds, who liked listening to wildlife as they fell asleep: bat twitter here, the crunch of a larger animal passing the runs. The larger animal was often a bear. The deer trotted by also. They could curl up closer to their buddies in the condos. It was warm and cozy. Then they'd run inside in the morning to be fed plus all the water inside hadn't frozen. They had water buckets inside that often remained unfrozen except for the bitterest nights. It was a good life.

Finally, she rose, and walked back into the house. Gray had a fire built for her. All she had to do was light a match. She took off her down jacket, the fleece vest underneath, draping them over the end of the sofa.

Then she lit the fire as her dogs walked in to greet her. Golly, already asleep in her bed in the library, opened one eye then closed it again. Her bed was a whale with a big open mouth, the inside lined in fleece like Sister's vest. It was perfect.

As the fire roared, she picked up the phone, hearing a familiar voice. She started talking.

"Adrianna. Hi. How was your hunt yesterday? One long run and that was it here."

"Scent is getting better. We had a terrific day. Cubbing made me wonder." Adrianna liked giving hunting reports.

"Me too. I'm calling to ask if we can come over, November 25 or any day you like. Then you all can come to us on a Saturday. You pick in December or January. Actually, we can come earlier, say the eighteenth. It's a TBA on my fixture card, so this makes me look good." Sister laughed.

TBA meant *To Be Announced.*

"Let's fill up your TBA. November 18 sounds great, and we'll be at Tattenhall Station, one of my favorite fixtures. How about if I push the time back?"

"No. We can get there by ten. It's not a big problem. You get up one hour earlier. My weather app predicts the day will be maybe forty-seven degrees. Good." Sister agreed on the time and date.

"We're on."

"Yes." Sister hung up, happy to have filled the weekend, and with such a good hunt.

Joint meets, usually great fun, could give masters and staff fits. Everyone just knew deep in their bones if you were going to have a blank day, it would be when you had guests. Mostly that depended on the time of the Season, but it remained one of those quirks. Masters and staff always want to show good sport.

Sitting in front of the fire, boots off, socks off, her feet warmed up. They weren't miserably cold in the work boots, but no matter what she did, some cold seeped in her boots, two pairs of socks or not.

She picked up her cellphone again, dialing Betty.

"Sister. Hear anything about that truck?"

"No. If a body turned up, I think we would hear. You'd think we would be safe here in the country, and to a great extent we are. Nothing like the crime rate in the cities."

"More people." Betty took a breath, which made Sister interrupt.

"Are you smoking?"

"Just a puff."

"Do you have a pack of cigarettes there?"

"Well," a drawn-out silence then. "I have a pack in a ziplock bag in the refrigerator. Bobby never sees it because I have it stuffed down in the baby carrots. He isn't going to take out baby carrots and eat them unless I cook them. And don't lecture me."

"I'm not lecturing you."

"Every now and then I crave a smoke. I can go months without a cigarette and then I have to have one. I have no idea why. Am I stressed? No more than normal. Business has been good, so I'm not worried about money. Just wanted the taste of a cigarette, the smell of tobacco."

"I can't say anything. I never smoked. Made me queasy."

"You know, it never did me, not from the first puff." Betty paused. "I didn't see the blood in the truck. Weevil did. Said it shocked him. Preys on my mind. Over the years we have run up on odd things, people squatting in abandoned buildings, especially down at Bishop's Gate. Stuff like that."

"Any group of people has its miscreants. Over time you see a lot. In some ways, I can understand murder better than plotting to rip people off, make money."

"Me too. One is emotional, hot-blooded. The other is cold-blooded, but that doesn't mean it can't lead to murder."

"You're right. How did we get on this? I was talking about you smoking."

Betty giggled. "Yes, you were."

Sister laughed. "You do this to me every time. Get me off track."

As the two dear friends nattered on, Ben Sidell sat at his computer, he scribbled notes. He had found the registration for the truck and checked it out. The vehicle had been stolen from a small delivery service in Orange.

He called the owner, who verified the truck had been stolen, two weeks ago. He reported it, but no luck.

"What kind of deliveries?"

"Local stuff. We can deliver groceries or packages. Kind of like a local UPS. That truck was old, but I kept it for short runs. As long as something runs, I'm using it."

"Any idea who might have taken it?"

"No. I told our police here what I am telling you. I can understand someone stealing one of my new trucks, but not an old one. Like I said, it ran but would shake the fillings out of your teeth."

Ben then gave the fellow his number. If he had any thoughts, call.

Returning to his notes, Ben circled the length of time the truck had been missing.

An old truck wouldn't arouse much suspicion. The only identification on the side was a simple word painted in script: DELIVERIES. No business name, just *deliveries*. Less to paint, less to pay for. Being a small company, Ben figured most everyone in Orange knew who to call or who might leave a package. He'd work on that tomorrow.

He'd also find out who was delivering Amazon stuff, how was UPS faring and the other delivery company that rented new trucks from Hertz. Those trucks said HERTZ. Not much to go on. He had one murder on his hands. Did he now have two?

CHAPTER 12

November 13, 2023, Monday

"Here. Look." Kathleen pulled out the center drawer of a Louis XVI desk. "You can see how the wood fits together without nails."

Veronica bent down. "Such precise work. And this is really from the reign of Louis XVI?"

"The black and gold remains popular. You have to give it to the French, whether it's country furnishings or Paris interiors."

"Lot of fakes out there?"

"Some of them are well done. I have no problem representing a reproduction. After all, many of them are two hundred years old, or close, say, a hundred. The design is just about perfect to my eye."

"How did you get interested in antiques?"

"Probably the same way you got interested in corrugated cardboard and restoring old properties. Fell into it."

"Yes. I doubt anyone goes to college to manufacture cardboard. Can I say I was fascinated by the process? Cardboard is amazingly strong. I was fascinated by the profits."

Kathleen laughed. "Well, I am fascinated by materials, design. I learn about history. I wonder who opened this drawer? What was in here? They had to be literate. That was a mark of class back then."

"Still is." Veronica peered into the drawer again then slid it shut. "Easy."

"Couldn't resist showing you. We'll be hunting out Tuesday if you can make it. Wanted to give you this book about hunting."

"Thanks. There's a lot to learn. I've been talking to some of the girls about it. Good exercise."

"Ancient sport. We still do some of the things pharaohs did in Egypt. Mostly what foxhunters do, how they dress became set end of the eighteenth century, beginning of the nineteenth. It's not that people are rigid traditionalists, it's because it works. Horses and hounds don't change. What changes is our shift from familiarity with country life. Most people live in cities and suburbs now. They know little about wildlife, forests, cultivation. So many think we're out there killing foxes. Not so." She sighed. "I begin to think people believe what they want to believe. The facts have become irrelevant."

"I hope not." Veronica took the book. "Wonderful photographs." She flipped it open.

"It's a photogenic sport. Anyway, I'll leave at eight AM because I have to pick up Aunt Dan. The hunt starts at ten."

"That's okay. I'm an early riser."

"I thought a lot of corrugated cardboard was made in China, to change the subject."

"It is. I'm so small. I can create decorated boxes, special designs for special occasions. Mostly I make extra-sturdy boxes for books, shipping china. Stuff like that. I will say, when the price of cardboard rises, the economy is moving up. That is my experience. Helps me make purchasing decisions, like Wolverhampton."

Abdul trotted over as he had awakened, putting his head under Kathleen's hand.

"He's a nice dog."

"He has opinions." Kathleen stroked under his chin.

Veronica laughed. "Let me get back upstairs. I'll be at the car at eight AM. I have a lot to learn here but then again, I know Aunt Daniella will fill in the blanks."

Kathleen grinned. "She can tell you who had affairs with whom. Granted, the information may be sixty years old, but she relishes it. For her, it's scandal too good to be true."

Veronica lifted her eyebrows. "Speaking of scandals. Not Louis XVI, but his forebearers, the XIV, XV. They didn't miss much."

"When you have that much wealth and power, who is going to say no? And the estates they bought for their lovers! By comparison, we are dull." Kathleen laughed.

"Ah, but they are French."

As the two women chatted, Ben Sidell sat across from Birdie Goodall at her house as Jude took notes. Sitting on the coffee table was a brown paper bag, its contents sitting on the table. Those contents were forty-eight hundred dollars in cash.

"I heard the car, but by the time I reached the front door, it was gone. Noticed the red flag up on my mailbox and when I walked outside, this is what I found. I nearly passed out."

He picked up a note, reading it again. " 'Mrs. Goodall, Trevor was making good money. He wanted me to give you this if anything happened to him. I waited until I didn't think so many people would be around.' "

Jude peered over. "No signature."

"Any idea? Did you know your grandson's friends?"

"I'd see them from time to time when Trevor would stop by. He used to have so many friends, especially in high school. Then he,"

she paused, "he sort of drifted off. He never spoke of fights or anything like that."

"I've looked into the jobs he held. Mostly bartending."

"No direction. He wasn't lazy, but he didn't go to college.
Didn't like book learning. And COVID ended so many jobs. All
those little stores. He'd tend bar, quick money. In time another,
more expensive bar, would hire him away for more money. Better
tippers I guess."

"Did you know he was doing okay?"

"He bought me a new kitchen table this summer. My birthday is
in June. But I didn't think about it. It's not extravagant, but it's very
nice."

"Mrs. Goodall, let me write you a receipt for this. I'd like to fin-
gerprint the bills as well as the paper bag. Worth a try."

Jude began writing out a receipt.

"Of course."

"I'll bring it back tomorrow. There's no reason to believe this is
stolen, contraband, etc. This money is yours."

Her eyes, teary, made her reach for a handkerchief in her apron
pocket. "He wasn't dealing drugs. I know that. He wouldn't. When
anything is wrong with people, especially young people, they think
drugs."

"I understand. Do you have any thoughts about what kind of
business might have attracted him?"

"Not sitting behind a desk."

"Liked people?"

"Yes. He did. Could talk to anybody."

Ben stood up. "Mrs. Goodall, you were right to call. I hope this
helps us. This has been a difficult time for you."

Jude pulled on his thin rubber gloves, put the money back in
the bag.

Driving back to town, Ben said, "Check with every pawnshop. Take a photo of Trevor. The one in his file will do it."

"His file. Not much of a criminal record, so much as a guy with shaky friends."

"Let's bring those in, too. We'll find some. Birdie wouldn't really know who his friends are now. He loved her. He would most likely hide anything suspect. All we have recently is one speeding ticket, plus he was at the scene of fistfights at Jolly Roger. Then again, he was tending bar."

"Okay."

"I'll get this fingerprinted." He slowed for a red light. "You never know."

CHAPTER 13

November 14, 2023, Tuesday

Mother Nature does as she wishes. Sister, on Aztec, waited at a loss. Hounds needed to again pick up scent. The fixture, Skidby, ran up to the base of the Blue Ridge Mountains. She watched as a blanket of fog, as if pulled down the east side of the mountains, was aimed right for her. It was eleven in the morning; fog should be lifting, not spreading.

Hounds in front of her, noses down, searched for scent. The run, a bracing twenty minutes, ended at sparse woods. One would think it would intensify, but no, it disappeared.

Within minutes all she could see were the sterns of those wonderful foxhounds. Weevil's voice was clear. She turned to look behind her. The field, slowly enveloped in mist, began to fade.

"Get 'em up. Get 'em up," Weevil encouraged.

Zorro, determined, pushed a bit into the woods.

Weevil couldn't see him anymore.

"Found it," Zorro called to the others.

The pack ran to him. He was a proven hound, so they honored his call. The whole pack opened.

Weevil, as baffled as Sister, could hear his hounds. As he closed, he could see them somewhat, but the woods, low branches, the odd log here and there slowed him.

Hounds roared.

Aztec, not one to be idle when hounds were speaking, fussed. *"Let's go."*

Sister asked him to trot, which irritated him. This kind of music called for galloping. There was no way anyone could trust moving that fast in this blindness.

She heard Weevil up ahead, cursing. Betty and Tootie remained silent. A low-hanging branch caused her to duck, her face on Aztec's neck. This was a last-minute sighting. Sister pulled up. She couldn't in good faith ask the field to follow. The last thing she wanted to do was lose her hounds, but better to lose the pack than for someone to hit their head.

Listening, she heard a good run. Weevil, now far behind, wisely chose to walk. The fog thickened. Hope of it dissipating soon faded.

"This is what it is to pray for patience," she whispered to Aztec, still fussy. "Just hold."

Hounds moved farther and farther away, and then silence.

Aces lifted his nose. *"Where are we?"*

Dreamboat replied, *"I don't know."*

Nor did Weevil, but he realized he didn't want his hounds to find the line again, especially if it went up the mountainside.

"Come along. Come along. Betty, Tootie, where are you? Can anyone see?"

Betty, close by the sound of her voice, called back. "I'm here by the steep creek. Tootie, where are you?"

"I'm on your left," Tootie replied. "There's no farm path that I can see. Just woods, and I can't see them either. Where are you, Weevil?"

"I'm heading toward Betty. I have the pack. Follow the horn and maybe we can get out of here." He tooted one sharp note.

Carefully picking her way through, Tootie, like a good hound, followed the horn call. Betty waited at the creek, wide, running hard.

She whistled so Weevil could keep his bearings.

Alert, Weevil and the pack veered toward the whistle. The hounds had a better sense of the direction than he did.

"Dammit." Weevil came up on a fallen tree.

"I'm close," Betty encouraged him.

"I'll find a way around this damn tree." He called, "Tootie, can you hear me? This is a whistling bitch." He used the old Southern expression.

"I can."

"If you come up on this tree, you have to go around the back. The roots are huge, and so is the hole. That's about all I can see, and I can only see it because I damn near fell into it. Be careful."

Betty advised, "Wait for her, Weevil. It will be easier."

Realizing the prudence of her words, Weevil gently said, "Hold up. Hold up. Good hounds."

The pack did that. They couldn't see either. Gunpowder snorted. Iota, Tootie's horse, snorted back.

Weevil patted Gunpowder on the neck. "Good boy."

Within minutes Tootie came alongside. The two picked their way toward Betty, who whistled again, as she could hear them.

Hounds patiently walked.

Sister turned. She could neither see them nor hear them. She was maybe a football field's length in the woods, on the remains of a deer path. She couldn't see it, but Aztec easily found his way out. In the mist, the riders looked like apparitions.

Joining them, she said, "We'd better wait for staff and the pack. That sounded like a long run."

The field, six this Tuesday, agreed. Those side by side could see one another, although the mists floated by in a strange manner. You'd see someone's features clearly for a moment, then you wouldn't. The fog enveloped everyone.

Betty, happy to see hounds, Huntsman, and Tootie, said, "This is an old fixture. If we follow the creek, we should come up on the big hay shed in maybe fifteen minutes. We've covered a lot of ground."

Weevil and Tootie agreed, for no one knew territory better than Betty, who had been whipping-in for close to thirty years. Staff members like Betty are dipped in gold.

"Come along, good hounds."

"*Smell that?*" Aero mentioned to Cora, out today although she neared retirement.

"*Ignore it,*" the older girl ordered.

"*What is it?*" the young hound asked.

"*Bear,*" Pickens called up to him. "*She's right, leave it.*"

"*But we can hunt bear,*" the keen youngster said.

"*We can,*" Cora informed him. "*But we can't see in this. We can use our noses, but we can't leave the humans. And they can see better than we can. It's no noses. They won't be able to smell their way back.*"

"*So what?*" Aero sassed.

"*Do you want warm gruel tonight and your bed? You could be out for a day, even with your tracking collar. And don't sass your betters, you little creep,*" Zorro, not the most tolerant fellow, ordered.

Back with the group, Gray now up with Sister, she called to the others so those in the rear could hear. "Let's wait, and if we hear hounds, we'll start back. If we don't hear them or staff in fifteen minutes, we should be able to pick our way back."

Gray put the collar of his coat up. "Getting raw. I don't remember a fog coming down in the morning like this."

"Well, I guess if the ground is just right and wind comes down the mountain or a front moves in, it can happen. Pretty much I've come to the conclusion anything can happen."

The rawness affected toes as well as necks. As horses weren't moving, people sat still. It seeps in.

Weevil tooted.

Sister called out, "Over here."

Betty called back, "Sister, come to the horn. We're at the stream. Will take us back. Otherwise, God knows where we'll wind up."

"Okay. Weevil, toot again."

Walking slowly, the field moved toward the toot. Another one told them they were closer, and within minutes hounds' sterns appeared in mist, disappeared, some reappeared. The fog was moving quickly, not just sitting or lifting.

"Everyone here?" Sister called out.

"Yes," Bobby Franklin called from the rear, with Second Flight.

"Lead on," Sister told Betty.

Betty, taking the lead, walked along the north side of the creek, bubbling, so at least one could hear the sound. After a slow twenty-minute walk, Betty hollered, "We're going to turn right. We should be at the trailers in, oh, five minutes. Don't run into one."

True to her word they reached the trailers, which seemed to appear out of nowhere, a fragmented vision. One rider almost collided into the back of a trailer. Others found the spaces between, dismounted, and walked to find their own trailer.

Weevil, Betty, and Tootie reached the party wagon, opened the door. Hounds bounded in quickly, snuffling down in the heavy straw.

Sister reached her trailer along with Gray. Betty would be over with Magellan, her second horse, as soon as hounds were all inside the special hound trailer.

Betty picked up her cellphone. "Where are you?"

Kathleen answered. "At the crossroads. Had to get out of the car to read the road sign."

"Come on back. We can't do a thing. Go slow."

"Will do."

Ben Sidell was driving back with Jude from the pawnbroker's.

He'd intended to send Jude to the pawnbroker's alone but decided to accompany his young assistant. The pawnbroker recognized Trevor from the photo. He went to his office, brought out a file, and pulled out the papers for a Panerai watch, as well as a diamond necklace. He produced the purchase receipts. He acknowledged how valuable the items were.

"Good work. Those receipts." Ben kept his eye on the road, as it was foggy.

Not as foggy as Skidby, but nothing to fool with.

"Fakes?" Jude asked.

"I don't know but where would Trevor Goodall get the money to buy that kind of watch or necklace? Plus, he wasn't married."

"Professionals? Professionals can make good copies. Then again, Trevor may have taken some very good stuff. He crossed somebody important."

"Without a doubt."

"A smart pawnbroker would know that," Jude responded. "Don't you think?"

"Yes, he would, but if he has the paperwork, why turn away an expensive item? He can put it out for sale in thirty days if it's not claimed. Those two pieces were brought in for quick cash, so they were instantly released."

"How would Trevor know good jewelry?"

"He would be taught. A little bit like Fagin." Ben mentioned the Dickens character.

"Virginia is a rich state." Jude was thinking. "And this is a rich town. Someone would have to know where the money is."

"That's not too hard. Think about it. Theft is a business like any other business. I'm not talking about someone who pinches a wallet, but a company, an organization, who goes after the big stuff, silver, diamonds, gold, and watches. Any organization has its own outlets. I expect this group does and I also expect Trevor perhaps did some work on the side. Cost him his life."

Jude leaned forward to peer ahead. "I guess you don't fool around with those people?"

"No. Your loyalty has to be absolute for organized crime, even smaller organizations."

"Yeah, but what's the draw apart from money?"

"We can only see money. Maybe you will get used to it. You learn 14 carat gold from, say, 24 carat. You learn silver from silver plate. Stealing is pretty easy." Ben thought for a moment. "You get used to the money."

CHAPTER 14

Later

"I still can't see out there." Sister looked out the window in the library, the pane cold to her touch.

"It's dark." Gray came up next to her, putting his arm around her waist, still small.

"Look."

He squinted. "I can't tell if that's still fog or heavy mist. If you think about it, late autumn and early winter are often foggy in Virginia."

"True. Seeing that heavy white fog roll down the side of the mountain mid-morning was a surprise."

"Next it will be snow. I don't mind looking at it. The mountains turn baby blue. The crunch underfoot is a unique sound." He thought a moment. "Who was it that wrote, 'Fog comes in on little cat feet.'?"

"Carl Sandburg."

"Such a great image, although today those were big feet. Is that how one continues the image?"

"Oh, honey, I don't know. But it was raw and it's still raw."

"It will freeze tonight."

"Yes." She walked to the big sofa, sat down. "Aha, speaking of feet." She reached up as Golly's hind paws dangled over the sofa back.

"Watch it. I was here first." The calico blinked.

Sister reached up, grabbing the luxurious tail, holding it under her nose. "How do I look?"

"Uh, better without the moustache."

"Gray, your moustache covers wrinkles. We all get them on our upper lip. If I had a moustache, I'd look younger."

He laughed. "You look wonderful the way you are. You know who you look like? Gladys Cooper, Dame Gladys Cooper, the English actress."

"Didn't she play against Bette Davis in *Now, Voyager?*"

"She did. Older then. But she was a ravishing beauty, and if you think of it, her career lasted from silents to the stage, to talkies, to color, and even television. There are other beautiful actresses, but I can't think of anyone with her career span."

"You flatter me."

"You're radiant. Really radiant. You always have been. You and Aunt Daniella have something. You walk into a room and people know you're there."

"People love Aunt Daniella. Now, there was a wild woman. I was never wild; determined, but not a manslayer."

He laughed. "Well, I can argue that, but, oh, it feels good to sit." He grabbed a pillow. "Back to whatever I was going to say. Which I forget."

The two dogs snored in their plush library beds, placed close to the fireplace.

"Listen to those dogs."

"Why? Lower life-forms. I never snore," complained Golly, who did.

Sister reached up again to stroke Golly's lower hind paw, then put her hand under the throw, which Gray had pulled on her legs. The fire, perhaps twenty minutes old, had not yet warmed the entire room. Taking the chill off isn't instant.

"We had some shocking events. Do you think the changing seasons affect people? Maybe they take chances they wouldn't otherwise?"

"Those who suffer from lack of light start to slide during the fall. Everyone tries to prepare their house, car, stable, whatever, for winter, and every year it's more expensive. More stress. The seasons affect people."

"They do. But let's think about what has happened. First, and horrible, Trevor Goodall is shot in the head and kicked out on I-64. Then hounds run up on an abandoned delivery truck, an old one. The passenger seat is full of dried blood. We didn't see it, but Weevil is not given to overstatement."

"Could a woman have plotted Trevor's murder?" Gray said.

"I doubt a woman would have committed it. She could have paid for it."

"Why couldn't it have been a lover's spat? She loses it and shoots him," Gray said.

"What if it was a male lover?" Sister posited.

Gray shook his head. "I doubt it. If Trevor were gay, Walter would have picked up on it. Trevor would stop by the office. Or Birdie might have known. She would have told Walter."

"Maybe that's why his father was so cruel to him."

"Possibly, but his father was an awful person. Anyway, honey, we'd probably know if Trevor were gay. Mercer gave me gaydar." Gray mentioned his late cousin.

"I sure don't have it. But while we are groping in the dark, we have to admit these events are completely out of the ordinary."

"Yes, but not related."

She leaned over on him. "Maybe. We have no idea of what's going on. If Ben has come up with something, I'd think we'd know."

"I hope so," Gray said.

"The watch. We forgot the watch."

He looked up at the ceiling. "We did."

"According to Betty, this is all related somehow to murder," Sister simply stated. "She can hop from a found watch to mayhem."

"Well, I sure hope not but I'll wear it to the Thanksgiving hunt. Lots of people."

"You'll have your sleeves down."

"Right. But I can push them up when we come back in. Then again, everyone will run home for dinner. I need to wear it at a breakfast." He was decisive. "I can't imagine that anyone will recognize the watch or, if they do, admit it."

CHAPTER 15

November 15, 2023, Wednesday

Yvonne sat at the kitchen table at Beveridge Hundred, which she owned, although she lived in the dependency. To the older couple who had owned the wonderful large farm, Cecil and Violet Van Dorn, she gave them life estate. As Cecil was failing, she thought perhaps another year before he would be placed in assisted living. One of their daughters would take Violet. As it was, Yvonne loved the dependency, a simple farmhouse with a center hall, rooms off each side, and three bedrooms upstairs, one being very large. Every room had a fireplace, as the clapboard home was built before coal heating. Then later, electricity.

Tootie sat opposite her mother; both had papers in front of them.

"Oyster dressing." Tootie scribbled the ingredients. "Mom, that's hard to make."

"Make it anyway. Your kitchen is good and Weevil can help."

"He's a good cook."

"As men like to eat, they often make good cooks."

Yvonne smiled then looked down. "He loves his Godzilla toy."

Ribbon, her Norfolk terrier, had fallen asleep on the kitchen rug, Godzilla toy in his paws.

"He hasn't torn the stuffing out."

"Yet." Yvonne tapped the pencil on the table. "Okay, if you've got the oyster dressing then I've got the vegetables, the deviled eggs. Doesn't seem like enough."

"Betty and Bobby are making the turkey. Sister, Gray are doing the pound cake with vanilla icing, plus a devil's food cake. Let's see, Aunt Daniella is making the biscuits; Kathleen, the salad and carrot sticks. Freddie is cooking the ham. Everything goes to Aunt Dan's, and when we're finished hunting she'll warm it up. Kathleen will probably get there first after hunting. We've got to shower."

"Still seems like something is missing."

"I'll double-check with Sister. But this is what she said Aunt Daniella gave Gray. Well, the bourbon is missing."

"Should Weevil and I buy a bottle?"

"Bobby will bring Blanton's. Sister and Gray will bring Woodford Reserve. Kathleen says we should, too, so maybe she'll rearrange the bourbon. Something unique: I'll bring a few bottles of soda water, Schweppes. Some people like a mixer or water. All I want is champagne."

"Well, who will bring champagne?"

"Tootie, that's a good question. I guess I'd better get some. That will fill out my puny list."

"What's Sam bringing?" Tootie asked.

"I don't know. He said he and Gray had it figured out. They took a truckload of firewood over last week. Sam likes to do physical things for his aunt, but he'll bring some kind of food. Maybe I should ask him."

Tootie replied, "If he has to get Crawford's horse ready, he won't have much time to do anything. Crawford and Marty often come to the big hunts."

"They do. Well, he has enough on his mind. I'll wait and see. Okay, what else?"

"That's it."

"Hungry?"

"Whatcha got?" Tootie smiled as Ribbon stirred then fell back asleep.

Godzilla had sapped a lot of energy from the dog. Subduing a monster is a big job.

"I have avocado to start, and then how about I warm up chicken soup? I made my mother's famous chicken soup."

Tootie sliced the avocado, placing it on the lettuce, setting out oil and vinegar while her mother stirred the soup.

Then the two sat down to eat, catch up, and give Ribbon some soup. The aroma wakened the terrier.

"I took a peek at Wolverhampton yesterday after hunting." Yvonne chewed her slice of avocado. "The chimneys are huge, and to my surprise Midnight Sun, the same guy who cleans my chimney, was there with his crew. He said houses built in the early eighteenth century like this one duplicate what people had known in England. That's why the chimneys are often paired together, at the ends of the houses. And Wolverhampton also has huge chimneys in the center of the roof. He said they were surprisingly in good shape."

"You had enough servants, those fires could keep burning. Can you imagine the payroll of a Renaissance king or duke? Every chore was done by hand. All the cleaning, the cooking, you name it. Must have cost a fortune."

"Well, you could offer housing, clothing. Stable boys, house servants wore livery, didn't they? Plus the status of working for the king. But you're right, what an expense, plus you had to feed everyone, house them. I don't know, but Wolverhampton no doubt had a large crew. I'm dying to go inside."

"Sooner or later I bet you can. Sister told me the new owners said we could hunt it." Tootie wanted to see it, too.

"There were trucks at Wolverhampton, young women working. Carpenters, people with tape measures. Bet they'll be glad they can use the fireplaces." Yvonne added, "Helps with light, too."

"I thought construction people used propane heaters," Tootie said. "It's noisy."

"Well, I didn't go inside, but I would guess electric lines still go to the buildings. The Sherwoods will need to open an account, check wires, etc. They may have already done so. Takes time to make sure wires are safe, I guess. But I was surprised to see so many women workers."

"Good for them. I think they're being trained by Women at Risk. Sister said something like that. Guess we'll find out."

"I have never had the slightest desire to do construction work. I don't even like to change a lightbulb." Yvonne sighed.

Tootie laughed. "I know."

Yvonne laughed, too. Then changed the subject. "Yes. All those years I lived in Chicago, my view was what happened in Chicago. Moving here brought history home in a new way. You know the graveyard in the back of Beveridge Hundred? There's the white section and the Black section, like at Old Paradise. The white monuments are bigger, but the graveyard for our people is tidy, carved monuments for some and inscriptions. They were remembered. Like every generation, you remember your grandparents. You might have a slender memory of your great-grandparents if they were alive when you were a child, but then it fades. All that's left are the stones. 'Beloved Mother.' Every now and then there will be something a bit different. Like 'An Angel on Earth, She's Gone Home.'"

"Let's walk off our lunch, Mom. Let's go to the graveyard."

Once in the graveyard, carefully tended, they pulled their scarves tighter, walking between the rows. Over two hundred years of people who worked and lived on this land now rested beneath it. A large estate, it bustled with activity. Some years the harvests were good. Some not. The white male owners had investments, as did many wealthy men, but they had to work. Everyone had to work. Both mother and daughter tried to imagine the hive of activity as they walked among those sleeping.

"We really don't know history, do we?" Tootie walked apace with her mother.

"Not really. If these people could rise and speak to us about what they lived through, we'd be surprised. It probably won't be as clean as what the history books make it. We all bump into the future." They reached the end of one row.

"Wish I could talk to Maggie Walker. Imagine starting a penny bank in 1903, and she made millions."

"That's a story I'd like to hear." Yvonne stopped for a moment, looked toward the last row of graves, the thick timber pushing the edge. "Tootie. Look."

"Huh?" She followed her mother's brisk pace to the last row.

"This is disturbed." Yvonne pointed to a grave that had leaves pulled over it. She brushed her boot over the leaves. "No grass."

"Wouldn't be much now, Mom, it's the middle of November."

"I know that, but there's no dormant grass. This, it can't be," she took a deep breath. "Might be a fresh grave."

CHAPTER 16

November 16, 2023, Thursday

Jefferson Hunt rode at Wrexham today. It's the most northeastern fixture. The wind was light but cool, feeling degrees below what the mercury registered.

Sister watched the pack search, eyes cast over this territory. She knew, like so many other masters, that Jefferson Hunt's days were numbered here. Development encroached, big expensive houses on two-acre lots. The two fixtures abutting this would resist, she hoped, but how many country people really want to live by a development where the residents, tidy, demanded more county services, which she understood, but how long before a subgroup of those new people began petitions against foxhunting? Some didn't bother with petitions, they directly created problems at the state house.

The glory days of her youth and early middle age retreated, now facing an onslaught of people who knew nothing about the country ways, wildlife, or how one acts as a neighbor. Political beliefs, important to them, determined their friendships and who they might help or hinder. Sister knew she couldn't afford to pick her friends due to political affiliation. She needed her neighbors. Looking over the field, she had a good idea what each person's politics were, as she did with her neighbors. None of which matters a whit if your bridge collapsed or your barn caught on fire. To view people in such a manner meant one was insulated. You didn't truly need people, but when Mother Nature flattened you or some other large event then you *did* need them. By then it was too late.

She told herself many did learn, they also brought new ideas.

Allowing herself a wave of nostalgia, she watched her beloved hounds do what they were born to do, as she felt she was doing what she was born to do: follow hounds.

Weevil blew "Lieu in," better understood as *Find your fox*, although the Norman French meant *Go in*. She mused on how much music had developed from hunting with horns and hounds. Thousands of years. There were some museums who had some of those old horns going back centuries. Some were tiny, the falconer's horns, and some were large. A man wore the horn over his shoulder, a precursor to the French horn, essentially. As sound travels miles, depending on the weather, humans could communicate with one another and their hounds. Then again, in battle, there was a trumpeter, who wore reverse colors, who sounded orders. A shudder ran down her. For how many millions of men over the centuries was that the last sound they heard?

The sound she now heard was a yip. Then a yap. Then a few more hounds agreeing to the scent, and then full-throated hounds all together. If that was the last sound she heard in her life, it would have been a good life. Anything would have to be better than a nurse asking, "And how are we today?"

The small field trotted over the generous territory. The farther east one traveled, the land became gentle until it grew rather flat by the ocean. By some rivers there were deep banks, even on flat lands.

The soft roll of the land gave hounds and horses the opportunity to reach out once cry increased.

Any thought Sister had in her silvered head flew away. The second she was living in, the smells, sounds, and sights were all that mattered. It was divine happiness.

As Jefferson Hunt settled into a fine day, Ben Sidell, Jude, Jackie, and a crew with shovels worked and watched at the grave at Beveridge Hundred. Yvonne had given up her hunt day to be there. For one thing, she felt she owed it to Violet and Cecil. She was also curious. Not that she had a desire to see an old skeleton or worse, a moldering corpse, but she should be there. After all, she was the one who called the sheriff.

After an hour of preparation and then digging, Jude, who put his weight on the shovel, said, "Boss, it's hard as a rock once we cleared off the leaves. The rains haven't sunk in this deep, plus there hasn't been enough rain."

Ben knelt down. "Right. The drought burned this to brick."

"Do you want us to keep digging?"

"No." He stood up.

"We can get a Ditch Witch," Jackie offered. "That would still be difficult, but it would eventually get down to a casket or old bones."

"No. It's a good idea, Jackie, but we aren't looking for old bones." He slapped his thigh. "Damn."

"I'm sorry, Ben. I've wasted your time and the department's time."

He looked at the sensational-looking woman, whom he had grown to admire for her willingness to learn, open up, be part of the group. "Yvonne, you did the right thing. And if whoever was in that delivery truck was brought here, pretty easy to do in darkness, this would be a good place to put the body. There had to be a body. After our team crawled over that truck, there was even more blood. Some had run under the seat, on the console, all over. Could someone survive? Maybe, but they would have had to be rushed to the hospital, which I doubt happened." He looked again at the paltry progress. "Thanks, guys. We've hit a dead end, forgive the pun."

Yvonne offered everyone lunch, and something to drink. Instead, they left for headquarters. She walked with Ben back to her house, as he had left his squad car there. The team had driven around the property to come in the far back to the graveyard.

"You have good people."

He smiled. "Thank you. It's a line of work that will never disappear. And I like the young ones coming into law enforcement. A different breed of cat, for the most part. Very technologically savvy."

"I can see that. Won't you step in for a moment? It's a lot warmer inside."

He agreed, walked into the back porch area, and wiped his shoes. As he reached the kitchen, he breathed deeply.

"Cold air tickles your lungs." She smiled as she put on the coffee. "I know you can't drink on duty, but I'm willing to bet a hot cup of coffee will warm you up from the inside. I'm also willing to bet your team will stop and get cups at the first gas station. Imagine when you could do that out here at the Gulf station."

"Thank you, Yvonne. Thank you again for your vigilance. So many times in my line of work, it's the small detail, an errant observation that turns out not to be errant, that puts me on the right track."

"Good. I don't want to go on record as a nosy neighbor."

He smiled. "No danger. What good coffee."

"Jamaican. I'm spoiled." She sat opposite him, her own coffee steaming. "So we do have a second murder on our hands?"

"I believe we do, but I'm not making that a public statement. All I've said is, a truck was found and it raised suspicion of theft and possible wrongdoing. The press can actually help us, but it also gets people stirred up. Creates more demand on the department. I need to focus on the crime, not smoothing ruffled feathers."

She laughed. "That's the county commissioners' job."

"They don't like doing it any more than anybody else, but I agree, that is part of their job. Mine is to find the criminal, and then the legal system takes over. It's often depressing. If one has enough money, well, you know."

"I do. I've seen a lot of it in my business, which is an old boys' club. It's under pressure right now from Me Too, and even gay men fighting back, but in the main you dangle money in front of someone and they shut up. I guess it's what we are and always have been."

"Yes. You know, this really is good."

"I'll give you a bag. My freezer is filled with it. I can't run out of coffee so I buy vats of the stuff." Her laughter, light, was warm.

"Yvonne, I hunt, but I'm not in the middle of the social circle. I don't have the time, really, but if you hear anything, a stray comment, tell me. I've got two murders on my hands. Trevor's and this as-yet-undeclared murder. I have ideas, but I'm a long way from home base."

"Willing to share some ideas?"

"In any university town, there are young women and young men who will sell their bodies for cash. It's been going on since whenever. It's an easy way to pick up cash. What I know has been happening here to a small degree, and in places like New York to a larger degree, is young women going into bars, men get loaded. The women have figured out who has money and who doesn't. Who has an expensive watch, a big ring, stuff like that. They strike up a conversation, go outside or to a room. He gets blindsided by a couple of young men. Or he sleeps with her and then goes to sleep himself. She lifts his wallet, and his watch, and rings. Maybe she leaves the credit cards. Maybe not."

"Why is that?"

"Using a credit card can be easy to trace. Lifting jewelry, cash, not easy. It's another reason cars aren't usually stolen. Too easy to be traced, cars. Cleaning a man out is easier. Then there are sex gangs. The john is photographed, videoed. He has to pay up."

"Gangs?"

"In some cases, yes. Sometimes a few kids working together. But I wonder if there aren't better organized gangs. The stuff has to be sold."

"On eBay?"

"That's one outlet. Another is, and this does take organization, it's sold in other countries. That's beyond your average college student or the pretty girl willing to sleep with a man who seems rich to them. As to simple theft, they are handed cash and sent on their way. It's a good deal for both sides. The fence, not really the right term, gets high-end goods. The kids get quick cash, far less than what the item is worth but it's clean."

"I had no idea."

"No one does, really. Oh, the sex stuff has been going on since Abelard and Heloise. Okay, they were in love, but there's nothing new about the young using their bodies for gain. Or being used."

"Birdie Goodall's grandson?"

"He was tall, strong enough. It's possible he worked with a few girls or an organized group. I'm trying to cast a large net. That's what Sister says when Weevil casts the pack. The larger the net, the quicker you get on terms with your quarry."

"And who could be your quarry?"

"Anyone desiring large profits, no taxes, and easy cover. After all, if you're in on the fence, you aren't in too much danger unless an employee, and I use that word loosely, turns on you."

"I would have never thought of this. Well, prostitution maybe, but lifting wallets, rings. Wouldn't the lures have to know the value?

A diamond ring or heavy gold one has to be worth more than a simple thin ring."

"They do. Either they're taught or they read magazines like *GQ*. But most kids can tell an expensive item from a cheaper one. We're assaulted with ads, stuff to buy, every day."

"We are." She was factoring in what he had told her.

Looking at the cat clock, eyes moving, tail ticking, he finished his coffee. "Thank you for this. I didn't realize how cold I was."

"You're welcome. I will keep my eyes and ears open. If this is a prostitution ring, say, setting a man up with a college girl who will be his mistress, better than prostitution, would there be good money in that?"

Ben nodded. "One takes a percent. College towns have all sorts of educations."

After two and a half hours of mostly trotting and some hard gallops, the hunt ended at Wrexham. Back at the trailers, the small number broke out their Yeti mugs filled with hot coffee or tea.

Sister, observing this, asked Betty, "How does something become so popular?"

"Like fashionable?"

"Right. Who would think a mug would be fashionable?"

"I don't know, but they do keep things warmer or colder longer. Being in the cold, people want something warm."

"Makes sense. Anyone catch your attention today?"

"The B's are coming along. It's all sinking in."

"Good. Good bloodline, my B's." She looked around. "Betty, we're going to lose all this. The land, easier to build on here it's not so rugged. Wrexham is right on the edge. The owners rarely use it."

"I know," Betty plaintively agreed. "It is a long way from New

York. Used to be easier, but so many flights were cut back over the last decade. You could commute."

"Right." Sister sat on the bumper cover for the trailer wheel for a minute. "My legs got tired. Doesn't happen very often, but today I feel it."

"I generally feel it when we start cubbing. Even though you and I ride during the summer, it's not the same."

Exhaling a long puff of condensation, Sister agreed.

"Well foxed here." Betty admired the setting. "And the house, small, is perfect for a weekend getaway. You couldn't ask for more if you're a city person who wants to be a country gentleman."

"Right. Farming is a lot of work. Fewer and fewer people want to do it anymore. I love it. I just love it."

"I'll bring you seed catalogs. Makes you happy. I don't believe the big companies can really modify seeds that much. I think it's like selling cars."

"Well, we need both. And yes, I do think seeds can be developed to be, say, cold resistant."

"I'll believe you when Bermuda grass makes it through the winter here. I see all this beauty and it makes me sick to think we'll lose it."

"Our grandchildren will never see what we have seen. Not that I will ever be a grandmother."

Betty knew Sister rarely spoke of her lost son. "You would have made a great grandmother. You would have done short rides with the baby on your saddle."

"I would." Sister smiled. "Well, sugar, let's load up."

As the two women drove the horses back to Roughneck Farm, Betty's phone rang.

"Yvonne. How was it?"

"Pretty good. We missed you."

"Let me tell you what happened." And Yvonne did just that.

"That is odd. Let me make a suggestion. Someone had to have driven back there. It's at the far end of the property. No one heard or saw a truck or whatever. Put up some cameras. They aren't cheap, and if someone sees them they can shoot them out, but do put them up. Might really help one of these days. You feel safe?"

"I do. Pretty much I do, plus Sam is here a lot."

"Those Lorillard boys can handle anything. Do you mind if I relay this to Sister?"

"No. I am hoping you do."

"You'll hunt on Saturday?"

"Wouldn't miss it for the world."

"Thanks, Yvonne." Betty then informed Sister of all that tran-spired.

"Lord." Sister exhaled. "I just hope this doesn't have anything to do with us."

"I do, too, but whatever is going on, it's too close for comfort. In a strange way, it would be easier if this were about drugs. We'd all know more. Drugs are inescapable now."

"Yes." Sister turned off the paved two-lane highway onto the farm road. "Maybe money really is the root of all evil."

CHAPTER 17

November 18, 2023, Saturday

Three spoiled dogs rode with Kathleen Sixt Dunbar and Aunt Daniella. Abdul; Baxter, Lynn Pirozzoli's Jack Russell, ever chatty; and Magnum, Adrianna's retired foxhound.

"Look at all this territory!" Baxter, nose pressed against the windowpane, remarked.

"Thousands of acres back here at Chapel Cross," Abdul bragged.

"You should see our territory. Beautiful houses, fencing everywhere, and all painted, too. Lots and lots of jumps." Baxter felt a tug of competitiveness.

"They're off!" Abdul watched as Weevil and the Jefferson Hunt pack climbed the hill behind Tattenhall Station.

Magnum noticed everything, feeling he should be out there even if it wasn't his pack.

"Frost. Won't start to melt for another hour," Aunt Daniella predicted.

"Scent will lift?" Kathleen loved learning all the ins and outs.

"Yes, but that doesn't mean they can't catch some of it now.

Also, the open pastures will warm up first, so they should begin to get a little something. The woods will stay cold. All of this works to the fox's advantage."

Adrianna and Lynn, in the field, rode up front with Sister. Visiting masters and guests usually were invited to ride up front in the two flights. Sometimes an old member would grumble because he or she felt they were entitled to ride in the master's pocket. Not much of that at Jefferson Hunt, as Sister drilled protocol into everyone, and fortunately for many of her members, she need not have bothered. But the new people need reminding.

The Bull Run ladies were going to leave their dogs at Tattenhall Station. Aunt Daniella told them to put Magnum and Baxter in Kathleen's car.

Hounds walked at a good pace, noses down. To their left, a long terrace rolled down to the old Norfolk and Southern railroad tracks. Given the shimmering frost, it would be slippery.

The three women in front already felt their faces tingle. Their cheeks were red.

Twist stopped, stern slowly feathering then whipping faster. *"Faint."*

Giorgio, the pack's most beautiful hound, walked over, nose down. *"Let's just walk it. It should heat up."*

The other hounds, noticing the concentration, came over, until the entire pack moved deliberately toward Beveridge Hundred.

"Let's go," Dreamboat urged, as the scent was now strong.

Hounds opened at once, charging across the pasture. Where the frost had melted, bits of turf flew from their paws. Larger chunks flew from the horse's hooves.

Bobby, keeping a respectful distance behind First Flight, looked around at his field, twenty-one eager souls. Numbers were picking up as the Season moved toward winter.

He noticed Veronica Sherwood riding in the middle of his

flight. She looked secure in the saddle, as did the other visitors from Bull Run. He pressed his horse's flanks, surging forward.

The first jump between Tattenhall Station and Beveridge Hundred was maybe three feet, two inches. Originally, it stood at three six but time gave the obstacle a welcoming sag.

Sister soared over, followed by Adrianna and Lynn. The field made it. No problems. Hounds raced for the main house, then stopped. Large deciduous oaks, a few maples, not as large, the Leland cypress that had been artfully placed around the old mansion over the decades, centuries, gave shade in the summers. Their expansive breadth also kept the frost secure underneath. Hounds struggled.

"Scent will pick up. Keep moving," Diana ordered everyone.

Weevil trusted his hounds. If they trotted behind the house, he knew they'd come when he blew the horn. Another group moved over to Yvonne's dependency. Ribbon barked from inside. The main body continued in a straight line, fanned out but moving south.

Yvonne created a special area to feed foxes. She knew who visited her. She had one red and two grays. They had a large doghouse, but the opening was small so a hound couldn't get in other than to stick his head in. She had self-warming beds, plus she put out kibble and treats. Sister said it was one thing to get foxes through a harsh winter, it was another thing to give them steak bones plus berries season round.

Yvonne couldn't help it. If she passed good-looking raspberries at the market, some fresh French bread, she had to buy it.

A line of scent led to this doghouse.

"He's here." Barrister excitedly yelped.

"Even if he's there, we have to find another fox," Giorgio sternly said. *"She feeds them."*

"So he's not in there?" Poor Barrister felt cheated.

Giorgio called, *"Are you in there, Gris?"*

"No. Go away," called the gray from Tollbooth Farm.

"See, he's not there." Giorgio had a sense of humor, as did the gray.

From behind the main house a roar alerted everyone. The section of the pack back there shot out, heading for the woods.

Weevil rode to get behind them, urging the rest of his hounds to get with it. This they did. Scent would be hot then fade, but they kept moving, whether at a trot or a gallop. They hung on the same line.

Old timber jumps appeared in old fence lines. This part of Beveridge Hundred remained in timber, but the old owners had fenced their entire property. Far less expensive to do then than now. Most of the jumps were lashed-together logs. Everyone took them at pace.

Finally hounds emerged into Prior's Woods, much thicker than the timber at Beveridge Hundred. Prior's Woods needed a select cut. The owner, from the Midwest, paid little attention to this land. He inherited it from his family. No one was left in Virginia. Pushing through slowed everyone. Sister knew an old path lay up ahead. She was going to get on it and head to the Chapel Cross Road South. There wasn't much you could do in the woods. No need for her guests to bushhog was how she looked at it.

Finally out on the road after a few impromptu jumps over fallen trunks, Sister moved parallel to the pack.

Betty, up ahead of her, strained to hear. Sound would come close then move away. Finally sound grew louder. The whole pack shot out in front of her, Tattoo in the lead. Dreamboat and Aces right behind. They ran tightly together, crossed the road; the woods on that side wasn't great either, slowed them down, but they turned left, heading right for Bishop's Gate.

Within forty-five minutes the whole group had covered four miles and were now hitting the fifth. Betty galloped ahead. She knew if she got to Bishop's Gate, she had more room to maneuver. If hounds went up the mountain, there wasn't much she could do, but she figured maybe this fox would head straight. If not, she'd do the best she could in untended woods.

The pack did head for Bishop's Gate. The old church, the few outbuildings—particularly the firewood shed—offered dry space; some warmth; and for the stacked wood, mice.

The fox zoomed to the side of the church, ducked into his den under the church but he had some openings into the church itself, mostly the side room. Unless that door was opened, one would never know.

Hounds dug furiously.

Weevil, having caught up, for they were flying, blew "Gone to Ground."

He dismounted, praised his hounds, patting them on their heads. Betty remained behind the church. Tootie stayed on the road turning off Chapel Cross Road South into the Catholic church. Better safe than sorry.

"Let's go," Audrey said once Weevil was back up on Hojo. *"Old scent back there somewhere."*

"It's not fox," Dasher admonished her.

Audrey disobeyed, ran behind the church to the old graveyard. She ran back again. *"Dead body. Torn apart."*

The younger hounds, fascinated, followed her. The older ones stuck with Weevil, who was frustrated.

As it was her side, Betty rode back, cracked her whip, which brought everyone's heads up. "Leave it."

Betty did not look closely at what she knew was a human body left out in the elements for two weeks, maybe three. The arms were torn off. She didn't want to look at what else was shredded.

She didn't look because she knew if she did she would never forget the horror of it.

"Leave it!" She cracked the whip again.

"She means business," Angle announced. *"We'd better go."*

Reluctantly the youngsters obeyed Betty.

"All right." Weevil stared down at the hounds, all now with him, turned his horse to hunt back.

"Weevil, wait a minute. Come to me." Betty rarely asked such a thing, so Weevil knew it was important.

"Yes?" he asked, ready to get on with it.

"I didn't want the field to hear. There's a dead body in the graveyard. Decomposing. I didn't look closely. If you head back toward Tattenhall Station, I'll tell Kathleen to call Ben Sidell. It's another working weekend for him."

Weevil's first thought was, *Is this whose blood was in that delivery truck?* "Oh, Betty. Well, yes, sure. You alert Kathleen and Aunt Dan. Are you all right?"

"As best as I can be. Weevil, something awful is going on. We can worry about that later. Let's not lose the pack, and I wouldn't put it past the young ones to return to that gruesome sight behind our backs. Decay holds a wicked fascination for their noses."

He grimaced. "Right." Then he blew his horn, hounds obeyed.

Betty watched them ride out; she kept a bit behind, waving Tootie on. She made the "Time Out" signal for Kathleen. Rode up as Kathleen was turning around.

"Kathleen, call Ben. We have a corpse back there. No one has seen it but me. I didn't look closely."

"Dear God," Kathleen exclaimed.

Aunt Daniella said nothing as Betty kicked on, needing to get to hounds, and Kathleen was already dialing Ben's number. Once she transmitted the gruesome news, Kathleen clicked off her phone.

"Let's stay here. I don't want to go back there," Aunt Daniella advised.

"Right." Kathleen kept the motor running, the heat helped in this cold. "I can't grasp what is happening, but we found a truck full of blood and now a body."

"Yes. They may not be connected."

"And then again, they may. People don't just kill for the thrill of it. Wait, I take that back. Some do, but most don't."

"I agree."

They waited for Ben. He made it in a half hour, then they drove back to Tattenhall Station, figuring the breakfast was on. It had taken the field an hour to get back to the station. They'd covered a lot of territory.

Once inside the restored station, neither said anything, although they went up to Betty.

"Let's not tell Sister," Betty, a bit shaken, suggested. "She has all these guests. Let her do her entertaining. I'll tell her once we're back at the barn."

The breakfast put everyone in a great mood. The hunt lifted spirits. Magnum and Baxter strolled around, making friends, begging for tidbits.

"Lynn, how did those dogs get in here?" Adrianna asked.

"I don't know. Kathleen must have brought them in."

The two friends walked over to Kathleen. "We're sorry. We should have waited outside for you and taken our dogs."

"They were good passengers."

Aunt Daniella added, "That little one is a pistol."

Lynn agreed. "Yes, he is. Thank you for tolerating them."

"Oh, it was fine, plus they made friends with Abdul."

The Welsh terrier hung with them. They had their "we need food" act down perfectly.

After forty-five minutes, Veronica and Sheila thanked Sister. They told the Master they were taking Adrianna and Lynn to see Wolverhampton. Would Sister like to come?

"I would, but I'll take a raincheck. Best I stay with the group. How did you do today?" Sister didn't want anything to spoil the day for Bull Run. This was a help.

"I didn't fall off." Veronica smiled.

Yvonne, standing next to Sam, looked out the front windows to see Ben go by in his squad car, plus two other sheriff's cars behind him. She put her hand on Sam's arm.

"Ben and his team are out there." She walked to the windows in time to see him turn left, now heading on Chapel Cross Road South.

"Poor guy doesn't get a break. He would have had a great time hunting today. We don't have enough law enforcement officers."

"No, we don't. Sam, I have a terrible feeling this has something to do with the disturbance at the graveyard at Beveridge Hundred."

He put his arm around her waist. "I hope not."

CHAPTER 18

November 20, 2023, Monday

Finding a body makes news. Sunday the local TV news covered the event. As nobody yet had any information such as DNA, all the reporter could do was question how the body was found.

Ben shielded Betty from being questioned. He said a foxhunter spotted it and immediately reported it to him. He also emphasized she did not get close, so nothing was disturbed.

Hearing the news, Veronica called Adrianna. "This happened at the hunt? At the church?"

Adrianna replied, "It did. Sister didn't find the body, a whipper-in did, but she and her staff kept it quiet so as not to frighten people. She called this morning to explain, which was good of her."

"Sheila and I have an investment property out there." Veronica's voice wobbled a bit. "It's not safe!"

"No one knows what's going on."

"I have people working there."

"Veronica, if you or your girls were in danger, I'm sure you would be notified. I can understand your concern." Adrianna again repeated herself.

"Apart from how awful it is, something like this could ruin our investment."

"Probably not. Give it some time." Adrianna's voice was soothing. "Best not to act in haste."

After the conversation ended, Adrianna didn't know if she'd calmed Veronica. There wasn't much she could do.

Naturally, people called Sister, who said it was not she who discovered the corpse. She gave credit to her hounds. They found the remains, a woman, before any rider did.

People were sure Sister was withholding something.

She wasn't. She truly knew nothing except that Betty found the body. She kept that to herself, except when she spoke to Adrianna.

After breakfast, driving home, Betty did tell Sister. They wondered what kind of evil was brewing out there.

Monday, enough time to think, talk to her husband and Yvonne, who called and told her about the disturbance at the graveyard at Beveridge Hundred, Sister was bedeviled with questions.

As the hard-core hound crew walked the pack, they kept their scarves over their mouths. Once hounds had their morning exercise, happy to be inside again because the food awaited them, as did the warmth, the two old friends went to the kennel office. Sister built a fire as Betty pulled out the list of able-bodied hounds. Twenty minutes later, Weevil and Tootie joined them. The feeding room had been hosed down. Hounds were back in their kennels. All was peaceful.

Raleigh and Rooster, who often accompanied the hounds on hound walks, rested on an old rug on the floor. The wood floors bore testimony to the years of use so Sister threw used but still thick rugs over them. With the fire popping, that and a rug underfoot her feet kept warm as well as the rest of her.

They pulled their chairs up to the fire.

"You know my legs are still sore from Saturday," Betty confessed.

"Cold. Makes the kinks last longer." Sister felt it, too.

Weevil, now that they could relax, informed them, "That TV fellow called me."

"He did?" Betty and Sister spoke in unison.

"I said it wasn't me. I was down Chapel Cross Road South before I knew of the, uh, problem. Okay, I fudged a little, but I didn't see the body."

"I can tell you I didn't study the scene but she wasn't in one piece. I expect the coyotes got at her. What in the hell is going on?"

"I think we won't know until Ben has the ability to make a DNA comparison between those remains and the blood in the truck," Weevil answered.

"Won't be long," Betty projected. "Ben will push. Don't know when he'll get a full report from the medical examiner, but DNA can't be that hard."

"I don't think it is." Sister got up and grabbed an old pillow, held it up; no takers.

She put the pillow behind her back as she sat down.

"Back stiff?"

"Don't gloat, Betty."

"I'm not." Betty then looked at Weevil and Tootie. "Do you ever get stiff backs?"

"Sure. Those days when it's bitter, raw, and windy, and we have a good, long run, I feel it. And we know the horses can feel it if we don't have enough padding on them. You taught me to keep the saddle on after a hunt. It does keep them warm. You throw the rug over them and by the time we're here, we can wipe them down. A little Absorbine. Rug back on. I'm learning a lot." He smiled.

"Thank you. You never know what people remember from you." She thought a moment. "It has occurred to me, a far stretch but still it has crossed my mind, what if Trevor's murder and this, shall we say potential murder, are connected?"

A silence followed this.

Tootie punctuated it. "A girlfriend? A relationship gone sour?"

"I'd say that's really sour." Weevil reached over to poke her upper arm. "Maybe another possibility is they were killed because of the same activity, business."

"Okay." Betty, ever ready to put her mystery-watching to use, declared, "Start with the girlfriend. What if she was his girlfriend? Was she killed before him, after him, or at the same time?"

"We won't know that until Ben has some answers from Rich-mond," Sister said.

"We know exactly when Trevor was killed. It may be slightly in-exact for the woman." Tootie had watched a few shows herself, plus she read every Karin Slaughter book as it came out.

"Do you think this has occurred to Ben?" Betty then answered her own question. "I'm sure it has. He'll have to ask Birdie questions again. You know, like did Trevor have a girlfriend?"

"Maybe she doesn't know. He might not have brought her to meet his grandmother. And I don't recall him being the going-steady type," Sister informed them.

"But what if they were connected in some way? Maybe they worked together." Betty wasn't giving up.

"Yeah, but what kind of work? What is going to get you killed? If in fact the corpse was killed."

"I don't think there is any doubt. She isn't a hiker who dropped dead of a heart attack. I'm not saying she knew the Chapel Cross area, but Trevor did."

"Her killer did." Tootie felt certain of that.

"Go back to business. More likely than a lovers' fallout." Weevil pulled closer to the fire. "What kind of business can get you shot in the head?"

"Espionage, spying," Betty forcefully answered.

"Does Trevor strike you as the kind of person who would be a spy?" Sister looked at Betty.

"No. I think to be a good spy you need to be educated, seem trustworthy. He was too young as well." Betty inhaled. "We should consider everything, no matter how crazy. So we can set aside spying. He could have had valuable information, though, about criminal activity. Maybe he wanted money?"

"Blackmail?" Weevil's eyebrows raised.

"It's an old standby. It's amazing how many people think they can get away with it." Sister nodded. "People will think drugs, but Trevor evidently steered clear of that."

"You mean he didn't take them himself?" Tootie wondered.

"As far as we know. I doubt he was mixed up in that," Betty replied. "If he was, I think Birdie would have asked Walter for help. She worked in his office for decades. Birdie ran a tight ship."

"So she probably saw a lot." Tootie stared at the fire, then looked at Betty. "Sometimes, though, when you're close to someone, you don't see it."

"True, but after a while it's hard to hide. Addictions make people unreliable." Weevil didn't know Birdie as well as Sister and Betty did.

He had only seen her when hounds made it to her house or in passing at an event at Walter's house.

"Walter will know how long DNA lasts in dried blood." Betty was back to the blood in the truck.

"Given that DNA can be taken from corpses hundreds of years after they are gone, just bone, I guess as long as the dried blood is not wiped out by moisture, what, at least a month or two? You can get DNA from anything," Weevil told her.

"So we'll know if the body was in that truck?"

"Or not," Weevil answered Betty.

"I keep coming back to what is so important that people are being killed? Even if only Trevor was killed, the Bishop's Gate body is something else, but what could drive someone to this?"

"Rage," Tootie said.

"Money."

"The thrill of it." Weevil held up his hands. "Some people are that twisted."

"And the fact that you think you're invulnerable. You won't get caught," Sister remarked.

They sat there, warming, disturbed. No one wants to believe they are in the middle of something dangerous, criminal.

Sister broke the silence. "Do you all think people are born killers? Or criminals?"

"The two aren't necessarily related." Weevil wasn't being difficult, just precise. "But do I think people are born with the criminal mind? I do."

"No help for it?" Betty then added, "But murder is different, in that you are taking another human life."

"I think murder is the easiest crime to understand if it's not premeditated. You kill to defend yourself or those you love. You kill out of rage, like Tootie said, or you kill out of fear. It's the premeditated crimes that puzzle me. A person spends how much time and work to steal?"

"Wouldn't it be easier to spend that time learning an honest trade?"

"Maybe, but it probably wouldn't be as exciting." Weevil moved closer to the fire, stretching his feet out. "If you, say, rob a bank, the old days of bank robbers as celebrities, you get attention, right? You've fooled how many people plus the police? And you think you're smarter."

"They are. Armed robbery takes brains and guts." Sister threw this out. "But why not do it once, make off with the loot. Except that's not what happens. It's a high. I really think it is."

"The money sure is. No taxes." Betty found that a happy thought. "Can you imagine? The dollar you make or stole is yours. A hundred percent."

"Society would crumble," Weevil added. "How would roads be built? The poor fed? Schools?"

"Ah, but study ancient Greece and Rome. They had different systems for those needs. Well, take Rome, it's closer to us. The people with extraordinary wealth could build roads. The Flavian Way, Pompey the Great building all those fabulous buildings. The public was served and you were famous, powerful. Perhaps beloved by some. Your name was everywhere," Sister generalized. "But make everyone pay, oh, that never makes anyone happy, no matter how necessary. Human nature."

"It's also human nature to kill." Tootie half smiled at her Master.

"Well." A long pause. "Yes. We can't stop ourselves. We kill in war. We kill to steal or, as you said, rage. And some kill because it makes them feel powerful. A huge adrenaline rush."

"Can it be identified early? Like in childhood?" Weevil wondered.

"Some perversities can." Betty felt recent events were perverse.

"Not enough, and even if you do realize that ten-year-old is dangerous, no conscience, you can't do anything about it until he does kill at some point." Weevil, quiet for the most part, was a thinking man.

"Okay, let's assume the body in the graveyard was murdered. I think we all do." Sister looked around. "I come back to, for what?"

"A sex killer," Tootie said.

"That could be so," Sister agreed. "We seem fascinated by serial killer stuff, but I keep thinking this is about money or status," she paused, "or power."

"What an awful thought." Betty shuddered.

"Killing is awful. That's what started this discussion. We are each disturbed, angry perhaps. Not only are we upset at Trevor's bullet to the brain, blood in a truck seat, a partially dismantled body, we are horrified it's on our turf," Sister quietly said.

CHAPTER 19

November 21, 2023, Tuesday

A crack of thunder made the horses flinch in their stalls. Sister, in the heated tack room, stepped outside into the center aisle. Everyone settled down. It was so unexpected. Thunderstorms in November, uncommon, sneak up on you. The low rolling clouds, dark, added to the sense of peril.

Everyone wore their blanket and had good food. They were warm enough. The hunt horses had trace clips. Thoroughbreds usually don't grow heavy coats, so apart from suitable blankets, a rider rarely clipped them down to that sleek fabulous look one sees on the racetrack. Given their thin coats, they looked sleek enough. But a trace clip, depending on how fancy the clip, allowed them more of their coat. The crossbreds are often heavier coated; they also had trace clips. Worked for the winters, which could bounce from a fifty-one-degree day to a plunge into the mid-twenties. This could take place in a few hours, or it might be a slide that allowed one to prepare.

Life by the mountains presented weather drama; but then, one could endure weather drama almost anywhere. What seemed apparent to those who were older was that the weather had changed.

Shutting the door, grateful for the heated tack room, Sister sat down in a comfortable chair as she inspected torn stirrup leathers.

Raleigh and Rooster, her shadows, stretched out on an old upturned blanket; the fuzzy interior felt good. As both the Doberman and the Harrier lacked heavy winter coats, they also had real coats. Once inside, Sister took them off, and when they walked back up to the house, she put them on.

"I hate to throw these leathers out. They can't be used for stirrups anymore. No point sewing them back together. Rip apart in a heartbeat."

Raleigh lifted his head and then put it down again. He tried to appear interested, but the storm's low pressure system made him sleepy.

Sister rubbed her fingers on the English leather, real English leather. "I can't throw this out. I just can't."

The phone rang.

"Walter, how are you? How about this storm?"

"I'm glad we aren't in the middle of a hunt. I called you because I just talked to Ben. They haven't identified the corpse, but they have identified the DNA. Same as the blood in the truck."

"Oh dear." She had no idea what to say.

"He's gone over missing person information for Virginia. Nothing close. Caucasian, perhaps twenty-three or twenty-four. No one fits that. Once he sends out the dental information, that might help. Richmond does a good job on that, according to Ben. He wants as accurate information as he can get. He said he's looking at missing persons reports from other states."

"Dreadful. And in our territory. People will be afraid to hunt with us. You know how people get."

"I do. Given the stirring the pot, endless conjecture and gossip, I expect we'll have more people hunting with us."

Sister half laughed. "Hadn't thought of that. But you're right. People love gruesome stuff. I don't think any of this should go in our newsletter."

"Alida is too smart for that. She'll do the usual report of the hunts as she does with flair, list upcoming events. Since we don't know anything, there's nothing to say."

"Yes."

"Ben also said he visited Birdie. He didn't tell her all the details, like blood in the truck, but he did ask her if Trevor had a girlfriend. She said he had girlfriends, friends . . . not romantic interests. She didn't think there was anyone special in his life."

"What was his last job?"

"Bartending. He liked the cash he made tending bar. He moved up the line of bars to ones with rich clientele."

"When one is young, you don't really know what you're getting into. I think he should have stayed put. Not jumped around. He worked the longest at the Jolly Roger."

"True, Sister. It doesn't take long for someone to get a reputation as a flake. It's bad enough for a young woman. Worse for a young man."

"Sexism is alive and well." She drew a long breath, then said, "But I tell young women to use it. If men underestimate you, you can often get ahead of them and they don't know it until it's too late."

"Worked for Angela Merkel," he agreed. "But Trevor wasn't going anywhere. Or so it appeared."

"Did Ben say if he mentioned anything to Birdie about two killings being connected? Again, it's only a thought."

"He didn't. I doubt that he would. It would only add to her woes."

"Right, and the holiday season around the corner. Poor Birdie."

"Let me get back to work here. I'll see you at Thursday's hunt."

"Thanks for calling me, Walter. I'll phone Betty, since she's the person who found the body."

"Good idea."

Sister dialed Betty, who picked up the phone. "I know."

"Oh," Sister simply replied.

"Ben kindly called me since I was the one who found her. Well, hounds found her. He's a thoughtful man. Gross. It's just so gross."

"Is." Sister rubbed the leather between her fingers of her right hand. "Walter told me Ben did ask Birdie if Trevor had a girlfriend."

"Right. It's a blank wall, isn't it? Oh, there's another boom." Betty felt her room rumble a little.

As she said that, thunder rattled over the stable.

"I could feel that one," Sister remarked. "Crazy weather. Crazy times. I have no ideas. Do you?"

"No. It gives me the creeps. Murder in our backyard, so to speak."

"Me too, but that doesn't mean the murderer is someone we know."

Betty rejoined, "I hope we don't, but whoever this is, they know our territory."

"Maybe not, Betty. Anyone can go down a dirt road like where the truck was dumped . . . and then again, Bishop's Gate isn't that far away. I don't know."

"Too coincidental. He or they know the territory."

"I hope you're wrong, but I can't argue the point. Since Craw-ford has restored Old Paradise and opened it up for research, special days for the public, more people do come here than before. Let's change the subject. I don't feel like talking about death during a thunderstorm."

"Too much like the old *Frankenstein* movie."

"Betty."

"Well, it is."

Sister shook her head. "I have my old stirrup leathers, that good English leather. I've saved them. Can't throw away English leather. Maybe I could make a belt out of the longest one."

"Sure. Your waist is still small. But you have enough belts. What would you wear it with, that old leather?"

"My jeans."

"Make a sissy strap, that's more useful."

"I don't need a sissy strap."

"We all need one. I have one."

"You're whipping-in. You have to do more than I do."

"I'm getting older. Our territory can be rough. If I'm heading up a steep hill or it's slippery down, I want to reach up and grab that strap."

"Is this your way of telling me I'm old?"

"No. But even the late, incredible Jill Summers had that strap around her horse's neck. Why take chances if you don't have to do so? It's not like we're riding for the Three-Day Olympics. We're fox-hunting. An undetermined course, as it were, and anything can happen. Sometimes the ground gets churned up in front of a jump or worse, it's mud on top and ice underneath. The absolute worst." Betty mentioned the late Master of Farmington Hunt.

"Well," she paused. "Who could make it? Shouldn't I have short leathers connecting it to my saddle?"

"Some people don't, but I do. Why take the chance of the strap sliding over your horse's head if he puts his head down for balance."

"Or to buck." Sister laughed.

"We don't have much of that," Betty bragged. "My boys are angels. Go to Sam."

"That's not a bad idea. Doubt if he gets much time, though. Crawford keeps him busy."

"He'll find time for you. Do it. You'll be surprised how useful it is."

"Okay. Betty, are you worried?"

"For myself? My own safety?"

"Yes."

"No. Are you?"

"No. But I'm uneasy. We have no idea what any of this is about. Including that damned watch."

"I think we're safe. The only thing that could change that is if we get in the way somehow."

CHAPTER 20

November 22, 2023, Wednesday

"It seems a bit extreme, but then again," Sister said.

Alida, sitting across from the Master in the kennel office, fire roaring making it pleasant, said, "Money seems to be no object with the Sherwoods."

"Could all be majestic again. Someone with vision will come along."

"Veronica seems to be freaked out. Finding the truck and then the body was too much for her. The sisters haven't made up their minds about the property. Few properties sell in winter. It's a bad time," Alida said.

Sister sighed. "Right. I expect having young women doing construction work has factored into the decision. It's understandable."

"Whatever work they've started is still going on. It will be a tough sell unfinished." Alida thought this was a real mess.

"Recent events have been gruesome." Sister also thought it was a real mess.

"Yes, but blood and a body aren't going to happen every day. So why am I here? I have talked to my husband, of course. Do you think it would be possible, or advisable, to form a syndicate and have the Hunt Club buy Wolverhampton?"

"Alida, what would we do with it?"

"We can revitalize it, put it back on the market. Make a healthy profit. This area is so unique."

"Our money would be tied up for about two years. It will be one year just to restore the house, and then consider fencing. Hundreds of thousands of dollars in fencing, Alida."

"Yes. The one thing about being an accountant is I have a pretty good sense of value. This area has phenomenal value. We would make a reasonable profit. Fifty percent would be average. If the economy shoots back up, maybe more."

"Whoever buys Wolverhampton wouldn't be taking out a mortgage," Sister wisely remarked.

"Here is another possibility. Kasmir and I would be part of this. I'm sure you have already figured that out. But we could rent it as an extravagant, high-end, hunting box, retreat. Possibility one. We could also use it as a clubhouse. Possibility two. Visitors would see it, stay in it like a hotel, if it weren't rented. Possibility three. And anyone who lives out there loves it. *Loves it*," Alida emphasized.

"Be a hell of a clubhouse and hotel." Sister laughed.

"Green Spring Valley, Radnor. They have made it work. Talk about perfection."

Sister folded her hands and stared into the fire. "You've intrigued me." She smiled at a stalwart on and off the hunt field. "Remember, both Radnor and Green Spring Valley have had consistent, brilliant leadership for decades. Decades."

"We have you."

"Is that flattery?"

"You're a strong Master. Fair, respected by non-hunting people, and Walter has come into his own as your joint master."

She tilted her head. "Thank you for the compliment."

"It's the truth. Think of clubs with consistent leadership. Apart from the two we've mentioned, what about Orange, Deep Run, Rockbridge? I mentioned them because those are the three with whom I have capped over the years more than the others because of my friends there. And Bull Run, a transformed club with visionary leadership. Other clubs are thriving thanks to a change in leadership, but consistency always pays off."

"The late Sally Lamb was a big help for Bull Run during upheavals." Sister mentioned a woman she had known and adored for over fifty years who had recently passed away. "She'd put so much energy into Bull Run, a club growing quite a bit. If you had Sally in your corner you were going to succeed. Didn't mean there couldn't be long, even heated discussions, but they lead to solutions, solutions that brought people in, didn't drive them away." Sister paused. "We'll never see anyone that generous again. The number of people she threw up on a horse. It's not like she was making bundles of money but she got people hunting. She gave horses to other clubs to compete at Warrenton and hunter trials."

"Don't you think that in every successful club whether it's foxhunting, beagling, bassett hunting, even a bridge club, there are one or two people who, thanks to personality and, for some, resources, give, make others welcome, help them along? You always have an extra horse or two. Kasmir goes over the top, as you know." Alida smiled. "Freddie, Ronnie, and Gray will have a good idea of what is possible when it comes to a syndicate." Alida went back to that idea.

"You may be retired but as an accountant, you haven't forgotten how to add and subtract," Sister teased her.

Alida grinned. "Let's say we sold shares at five thousand dollars apiece. That's not a big hit, but not negligible either. If you, my husband, and I, Yvonne, and Gray bought shares, that's a start. And I've even thought of Crawford, although he, well, I don't know, he might buy a few shares for goodwill."

"You know few of us have the kind of money you do or Yvonne does. But Yvonne, given the demands of building her media empire, can see things we cannot. Will she do it? I don't know. Here's my idea. I need to talk to Gray. If he says it's a good idea, then let's you, me, and Ronnie, our trusty treasurer, talk to people. Quietly. Face-to-face with a clear plan in writing."

"Nothing will happen until January. Even if the Sherwoods immediately put it on the market, we have a bit of time. After the New Year, we might be facing higher interest rates. But what I do know is, if Veronica is truly scared, we might be able to get this at a bargain. Even less than what she and her sister paid for it."

"Alida, I'm glad you're on our side."

"I'm not saying we take advantage of her but the situation favors cash."

"Any situation favors cash." Sister nodded. The phone rang. "Excuse me a minute."

"Hello." She listened intently. "Walter. Just calling to tell me there are no updates. No ID on the corpse."

Alida grimaced. "If Forensics creates a mask, you know how they do that, of what the victim looks like maybe someone will recognize her. Those people are magicians."

"Yes. No missing persons report. A facial reconstruction might provide identity, some background ideas. Again, Ben says he has checked, as has his staff, missing persons reports all over, not just Virginia. Nothing comes close," Sister said.

Alida sighed. "How many lost souls are there? A kid runs away and gets a false ID. Maybe gets some kind of job, waiting tables, stuff like that. New name. Who would know? No abduction. No sex work.

A woman was unhappy at home. Or even someone sleeping on the streets who was lured into criminal activity or sex work. Or someone who has mental problems. There really are a lot of lost souls."

"I don't know. I mean, I know what you're saying is right, it's that I have no ideas. Not one."

They heard the door open to the kennel side.

"Are you feeding twice a day?" Alida asked.

"We do for a few hounds that have trouble putting on weight. Like people, there are bloodlines prone to putting on weight and then the reverse. Weevil and Tootie come in for that and he wants to check everyone's pads. He's now using that Musher's stuff. Musher's pad protection wax, I think it's called. He tried it and thought it was better than everything else."

"Good team."

"Makes a hunt club flourish." She leaned closer to Alida. "I'll get back to you right after Thanksgiving. Actually before. We'll hunt that morning. Gives me enough time to talk to Gray tonight. Thank you for thinking of the club, of the future. I'm lucky to have you and Kasmir."

"We're lucky to be able to do what we love. To be outside and be close to other creatures, the smells, everything. Even gardening is a relationship with nature."

Sister smiled. "It is. Should you have any thoughts about these disturbing events, well, tell Ben first, but then tell me. It preys on my mind."

"My husband says this is about money or revenge."

" 'Revenge is mine, saith the Lord.' Think I am close to the quote."

"Sister, there are some people so arrogant, they think *they* are God."

CHAPTER 21

November 23, 2023, Thursday

Hounds were close enough to the old gristmill to hear the whap, whap, whap of the waterwheel.

Overcast, raw, good for scent, they moved, sterns up, ears forward. Faint scents curled up their nostrils, but not of quarry.

"How many turkeys live here?" Aero complained.

"Too many," Andy answered.

Jerry, a young hound, eager to learn, asked, *"Why can't we chase them?"*

Dasher stepped in as this was too much talk. *"They fly away. Now, noses back down. Do you want our huntsman to think we're babblers?"*

As it was a gentle chastisement, all did as directed without a quibble. This should have been a day to get on quick terms with your quarry. It wasn't.

This crossed Sister's mind as she slowly followed her hounds. They walked on the pastures behind the impressive eighteenth-century mill still in good working order. If there was one thing she had learned over the years, it was that she knew less and less about

the weather and scent, not more. Why was this day proving so difficult?

She caught herself. Nobody really knows. Why should *she* know?
Shut up and take what comes.

The farm road, gravel in the potholes, proved a bit slick, but not
bad footing. Bad footing was when one could barely stay upright.
Although if she jumped in and out of the fenced pastures, she'd keep
a tight leg.

Giorgio, picking up a snootful of turkey, sneezed.

Barrister came over and inhaled. He sneezed.

The field, forty strong on this holiday morning, silently observed. The old hunting hands asked themselves the same questions
Sister was asking.

"*Bear,*" Dreamboat, next to his sister, said.

She took a whiff. "*We can hunt bear. Let's go.*"

Dreamboat and Diana opened. The pack followed, noses down.
Soon all were speaking, moving at a lope.

Keepsake picked up a trot as Sister focused on her hounds.
They moved straight ahead, steady.

A fox can, and sometimes will, run straight. Often, once a fox
feels hounds are getting closer, he'll be evasive, or just jump in the
first den, whether it's theirs or not.

Sister wondered, did they pick up coyote scent? If so, they would
probably be moving faster.

Weevil, on the right pasture, rode behind the working hounds.
Were they a clockface, he would be in the place where the two hands
come together. Hounds would be at twelve o'clock. This was the ideal
placement but anything could change it quickly. The point was to
keep moving.

The pace picked up. Weevil glided over a coop at the back of
the pasture.

Sister, still on the farm road, started down the hill, fairly steep.

Kathleen and Aunt Daniella were far enough behind the field not to be a nuisance. They drove more slowly.

Hounds kept speaking and reached the bottom of the steep hill. They were in the woods.

"Damn," Dreamboat cursed.

Bear scent, heavier than a fox, should stick. It disappeared. Hounds diligently searched. Weevil, a bit above them in the woods, watched. He didn't know for certain if they had switched scents. Did they lose what they were originally on, and what was it? The scent could so easily fool humans, but there were times when it fooled hounds. They always knew what they were on, but they could become confused when it vanished quickly.

"Come along," Weevil called, as no point wasting more time.

He rode down to the old hayfields at the part of Mill Ruins called Shootrough. Hounds trotted down. A bit of scent lifted, enticing them. It was fox.

Fanning out, they reached the closed large toolshed. The fox was in there and had no reason to come out.

"Come out," Audrey yelled into the den opening at the side of the building.

Grenville, the fox, had one on the other side as well.

"Get lost," he called back.

"He's enjoying hearing us out here. He's full and warm. He'll stay right where he is. Come on. We'll find something else." Giorgio encouraged the youngster smarting from the fox being rude.

It never occurred to the hounds that they might be rude.

As hounds moved toward the creek, the dirt farm road deteriorated badly. Hounds worked the creek beds. A few already had swum over, their double coats offering protection from the cold even though they were wet.

Trooper, head down on that side, hollered, *"Got him."*

The other hounds hurried across the creek. Weevil waited a moment to be sure. Then he and Showboat crossed the swift-moving creek, which wasn't deep at that point. The remnant of the old wooden bridge, on his left, gave hope that someday it might be rebuilt.

Betty was already across the creek. She knew of an old deer path farther down, got over, and was now behind the hounds. Weevil began to catch up, so Betty moved into the woods on that side, which had been timbered twenty years ago. The underbrush could still be a problem, but she shot up the hill, keeping her eye on Weevil's red jacket, as well as the hounds.

Tootie rode behind Weevil, looking for a place to veer left. She couldn't find a decent clearing until they reached the top of the old farm road.

Sister crossed the creek, and listened to the splashing behind her. Bobby followed, telling his field the water wasn't deep but it was fast running. If anyone wanted to stay back they could, but listen for the horn.

Now in full cry, hounds ran through Birdie Goodall's farm, out to the mostly forgotten state tertiary road, then headed parallel to the creek down below, obscured by the woods. They were above the Mill Ruins land.

Down they plunged. Weevil followed. Once out of the creek, the situation changed. The banks, deep, forbade crossing. Hounds managed to wind up on Mill Ruins' back pastures, as they could scramble up the banks.

Weevil turned, struggled up to the road, flew past the field, Birdie's farm, back down the road to the crossing to Shootrough at Mill Ruins. He could still hear his pack but feared losing them.

Aunt Daniella, once hounds crossed to go to Birdie's, told Kathleen to turn around, go back up the rutted farm road, turn left up the steep hill, then stop at Mill Ruins' high meadow. They could hear better.

"They'll probably circle back," Aunt Daniella mentioned. "Given enough time, lead time, a fox circles back to his den."

Kathleen rolled down her window. Hounds sounded ahead of her, but she could clearly hear them. Not four minutes later, a flying Weevil passed them.

Betty, on the other side of the creek, found an old crossing she recalled from years back. She slid down the bank and put her feet on Outlaw's hindquarters while she hugged his neck. The water, deeper here, forced the good horse to swim. As he reached the other bank, lower, she sat up, swinging her feet into the stirrups. He clambered up. She paused as he shook. She knew where the hounds were. They blasted off.

Tootie sped past them. Behind her, the field would soon be coming.

"Stay put," Aunt Daniella advised.

Sister moved as fast as she could. She could hear rifle fire far away, not on Mill Ruins. No foxhunter wants to hear guns, but she silently gave thanks to those deer hunters, because some of the field lagged behind. This would goose them up to the others.

Finally, up the hill, she saw Kathleen and Aunt Daniella sitting in the car. She and the field rode past them, dirt flying from their hooves.

Weevil passed Walter's house, he was that far ahead. He galloped to the front field. Nothing. He couldn't hear a thing.

Betty, ahead of him on the decent bridge, a quarter mile to his right, threw up her whip hand. He rode toward her.

She pointed ahead of herself and made the motion of putting the horn to her lips.

He understood hounds were far away. He blew "Come to Me."

Kathleen, with Aunt Daniella's instructions, pulled near the front fields but stayed well out of everyone's way.

The field arrived. Everyone held up. They and their mounts needed their breath. They waited, waited. Weevil kept blowing.

Finally, Diana could be seen trotting across the far field, the T's behind her. Within ten minutes the entire pack assembled at Weevil's horse. Weevil praised them.

Betty and Tootie now stood by the pack. No cut pads or barbed-wire cuts on their backs, the winded pack awaited orders.

Sister rode up to Weevil. "That was a surprise."

"It's the devil when we get over on the other side of the creek. I can't stay with them and there aren't enough crossings."

"True. Everyone has Thanksgiving dinner ahead of them. Let's call it a day. We had a good run."

"Yes, Ma'am." He looked down at the hounds. "Come. Come along."

Gray wore the Rolex but no one noticed. The fast hunt captured everyone's attention.

Aunt Daniella's George III china made for a beautiful table. No one threw a party like Aunt Daniella. Her silver glistened. In her day she threw parties and large dinners often. Now not so much. She was determined to remember her glory days with the table setting, the food, the flowers.

At one end of the table, Sister sat on Aunt Daniella's left, Sam on her right. Gray anchored the other end. Yvonne was to his right, Betty to his left. Between these two ends, it was the traditional man, woman, man, etc. When the numbers ran out, Tootie volunteered to be an honorary man, to everyone's laughter.

To Gray fell the honor of carving the turkey while Weevil, his first time, sliced the ham.

Who could not eat themselves into a coma at a Virginia Thanksgiving? They talked about the day's hunt and then moved on to what people were reading and watching.

Aunt Daniella announced she was reviewing every year of *Downton Abbey*.

"What is it about the Brits?" Yvonne asked. "Generation after generation of fabulous actors."

Everyone weighed in on the talent of the British Isles, evidenced whether with horses, theater, or ceremony. Then again, how about their navy? Everyone had an opinion.

"That fox, whom we have run before, is too smart. He needs a Stanford sweatshirt," Bobby teased them.

"Northwestern." Yvonne stuck up for her alma mater.

"My alma mater is in trouble." Sam had attended Harvard, which they all knew.

"Seems to be tempestuous times at many of our better universities." Sister thought it depressing.

Kathleen agreed. "Crazy times. You know, I think if people gathered for other cultures' celebrations, we'd find ways to get along. Who doesn't want to party?"

"Oliver Cromwell." Sam speared a brussels sprout.

"He's been dead since September 3, 1658," Gray shot back at his brother.

Freddie, also an accountant, remarked, "Wasn't it Cromwell who said, 'No one rises so high as he who knows not whither he is going'?"

"Why are we talking about Oliver Cromwell? Look how long he's been dead." Betty shrugged.

"Because his ideas aren't dead," Gray answered. "God forbid anyone have a good time, especially Roman Catholics."

"I guess your choice was a king or an autocrat. I'd choose a king. Better clothes. Divine jewelry." Aunt Daniella smiled devilishly.

As they considered jewelry and then laughed, Sister said, "You do deserve jewelry, as do Tootie and Weevil. You three did so well today in difficult territory and a difficult situation."

"Thank you," each replied.

"Thinking of today's hunt and the ground we covered," Freddie asked Walter, "how is Birdie?"

"Doing as well as can be expected." He added, "You know she just retired, but I'm thinking work would help her. I'll wait a bit then see if she'll come back."

Kathleen agreed. "Mental activity helps during hard times."

They chatted about that then Yvonne veered off the subject slightly. "Do you think Wolverhampton will again fall on hard times?"

"It could happen. Ideally, another foxhunter will buy it if they sell."

"I thought that was the point. To restore then charge big bucks." Ronnie finally spoke, as all he had been doing was stuffing his mouth.

"I don't think we know, and maybe the sisters haven't made up their minds. They saw a good deal and jumped at it, plus it's a business where they've made money." Betty had found updating her kitchen awful; rehabilitating an entire house would drive her mad.

Gray, no fan of restoration work, said, "Well, Wolverhampton will be stunning. It really should be part of foxhunting. A hunt box."

"That's a hell of a hunt box." Ronnie laughed.

Freddie warmed to the subject. "True. People with means are always looking for beautiful escapes. Think of the rents in Manhattan or London, the desirable parts. Monthly rents in the five figures. Some even six. I guess one could rent it. I'm not sure we're in that category."

"Praise the Lord," Aunt Daniella jumped in. "Whether Wolverhampton winds up being a family home or a hunt box or even something more, all it needs is a good sex scandal. Oh, that will make it so desirable."

"Aunt Dan." Sam shook his head in merriment.

"What sells better than sex?" she retorted.

"True. True. True." Gray supported his aunt.

"What about a perverse sex scandal?" Ronnie was enjoying this.

"The idea for perversity is like a pendulum. Swings back and forth." Yvonne threw up her hands. "Thanks to Puritanism. Cromwell again. We are shocked by stuff that other times, other cultures, would find quite ordinary."

That got everyone talking at once. What was perverse now? Of course, thanks to the wonderful dinner, drinks with it, people proved more imaginative than others might have expected.

Aunt Daniella, in her glory, laughing, finally caught her breath. "Is everyone ready for dessert?"

They were, and out came crème brûlée, pound cake, and a devil's food cake. Sam and Gray cleared the table.

"I have them so well trained." Aunt Daniella dug into the crème brûlée when her nephews rejoined the table.

After dessert, they repaired to the living room, Gray and Bobby taking drink orders while Sam set out the glasses. Ronnie attended to the fire. Aunt Daniella sat close to the fire. As she aged, she minded the cold more.

Once everyone had their drinks, Bobby ducked into the hall, returning with a shopping bag with a bow on it. He placed it in front of their hostess. Now Gray was on one side of her and Sam on the other.

"Aunt Dan, it's heavy," Gray informed her.

"Tissue paper." She pulled up the tissue paper and started to lift the bag.

Her nephews put their hands under the bag, placing it in her lap, then helped her to lift out the bottle.

"What have you done?" Her eyes widened.

Everyone said individually then in unison, as Freddie directed them like a choirmaster, "We love you. Happy Thanksgiving."

"Pappy Van Winkle!" she exclaimed "But you all brought me bourbons. Blanton's, Woodford Reserve, Glenfiddich, Yamazaki. I mean, you each brought me a good bottle, and now this. I can't believe it. I just can't believe it."

The bottle the group had pitched in to present to her was an aged Pappy Van Winkle that cost $1,529.00. There were bottles aged more than this one, but they could break the bank. The one aged twenty-three years cost $44,999.99. This bottle was perfect. Also, everyone could afford to pitch in.

"Would you like a glass?" Sam bent over her.

"Of course. But give everyone a shot, will you? We all should taste it together."

Sam and Gray did as instructed. The group put their regular drinks on side tables, the coffee table, and stood to salute the grand lady. Then they knocked back their small shots. There was enough for people to get a good taste.

A warm glow spread through everyone.

Freddie smiled. "I always thought bourbon was wasted on me. I was so wrong."

Others agreed, as bourbon is an acquired taste. Most hard liquor is.

They reveled, laughed, and luxuriated in one another's company.

Aunt Daniella, who was not prompted but was highly intelligent, sipped her drink. "This Wolverhampton thing. Why couldn't it be bought by a syndicate? Saved."

Gray and Sister were surprised that she came up with it but a lively discussion followed, and to their continued surprise, most of the group thought it a good idea if possible. Maybe Alida had talked to some of them. It all hinged on the Sherwoods, but a quick sale can be very convincing. The longer you hold on to a property, the more money you are spending keeping it up. They all agreed on that.

On the way home, Sister and Gray talked about how this was one of the best Thanksgivings they could remember.

"Sometimes I forget how smart she is," Gray murmured.

"Think of you and your brother." Sister had always been dazzled with the Lorillard and Laprade people. "You've hit on something, honey. If Aunt Daniella finds the syndicate idea a consideration, it truly is worth our time."

"Well, I hope so. I say let the idea percolate. And it is possible the Sherwoods could change their mind."

"It is, but Veronica seems superstitious along with being frightened."

He turned onto the farm road. "Either that or they want an excuse to get out of it."

"They have a construction team. They had to know what this would cost, even with their advantage," Sister responded. "I think it's emotional."

"Could be. Chapel Cross is under a dark cloud right now."

As they walked into the kitchen to a rapturous greeting, the sheriff's department had released a reconstruction of the dead woman's face. How they could do these things with a mangled, exposed corpse from Bishop's Gate was amazing. The victim was young and reasonably attractive. The sheriff's department hoped someone would recognize her.

Two someones did. They were not happy.

CHAPTER 22

November 24, 2023, Friday

Holidays filled up the ER at hospitals. Walter hurried to the ER, as one of his patients had suffered a heart attack. The fifty-five-year-old woman was lucky to get a room.

After seeing to her needs, he sat down for a minute at the nurse's station.

"It's mobbed." He leaned back in the chair.

"I don't know what's worse, Thanksgiving, Christmas, or New Year's." The nurse in charge of the station scrutinized the computer screen.

"It's either too much celebration, too much exertion, or a car wreck," the other nurse chimed in.

"Well, thank you for your assistance. Mrs. Tartaglia fortunately had a mild attack, but do keep monitoring her. I'll check in. You have my number. Scared her. For which I am grateful. She didn't blow it off as indigestion or whatever. As you know, often heart attacks present differently in women than in men."

"Yes, Dr. Lungrun."

"She's sleeping." He stood up and glanced down the hall. "Where are you going to put all the ER patients?"

"In the hall," the head nurse simply replied. "There is no room. It's pretty intense."

"Yes, it is. You know where to find me." He patted the desk with his hand as he left.

In his car, Walter cut on the motor, sat there as the seat warmed up. He liked Thanksgiving. Pulling out, he thought he'd stop at the Jolly Roger. He wanted a quick beer, plus he was curious as to who else would be there as it was usually filled with people from the hospital, but it was a holiday.

Parking in the lot, half-full, he hurried inside.

Waving to the bartender, he then sat down at the bar. "The usual."

"Hard day?" Glenn asked.

"No. I'm glad I'm not an ER doctor. The place is full."

Next to him, a middle-aged man turned. "Dr. Lorenzo, Pulmonary. I got called in, too."

They chatted as Walter looked down the line of mostly men at the bar, interspersed with young women. "Full here, too, despite or maybe because it's a holiday weekend."

Dr. Lorenzo nodded. "Guys without families. Guys like me, needing a drink. Respiratory overload at the hospital. I've got patients on oxygen. Not COVID. These things come in waves. The press picks it up, scares the hell out of people."

"Yes, it does. I have to hold my temper when a patient or their advocate cites whatever they've read on their computer or phone. Everyone's an expert and everyone's frightened."

"Yep." Dr. Lorenzo knocked back his straight shot. "One cough and it's pneumonia. Or it's pneumonia and the patient doesn't believe it. I reckon doctors have always dealt with difficult patients, hysterical families, but now it's worse. I swear it's worse. If you were young would you go into med school?"

Walter thought about this. "Yes. I'm fascinated by the heart. But in my undergraduate years I faced strict classes. I had to master material that on the surface had nothing to do with my future career. Taught me how to think. Gave me a background, a sense of who we are."

"Me too."

"I think that's gone for most people in college."

"If I were young, I'd forget medicine. Too much interference. I want to practice medicine, not answer to the latest law checking us from the state house or have a lawyer looking over my shoulder, praying for a malpractice suit. I'm too old to get out. If I can hang on for ten more years, I can retire. The kids will be through college. My wife and I can travel a little. She's been a trouper."

"You're a lucky man."

"I am. Are you married?"

"No. I don't know how two people with high-powered careers negotiate it. In my case, if I get a call at three AM, I have to go. If I get an emergency call as I'm packing to go to Vienna, I have to go." Walter again looked down the bar. "I bet half the guys at the bar are doctors or work at the hospital."

"Or are lost," Dr. Lorenzo mentioned. "Holidays are hard for people without families."

"I think so." Walter noticed one fellow rise, and the young woman left with him.

Dr. Lorenzo followed them with his eyes. He raised his eyebrows as the man texted on his cellphone.

"Honey, I have to work late at the office." Dr. Lorenzo grinned, imagining the text.

Walter watched. "Maybe."

"It's a good bar. Good bartender. Good for pickups. Then again, maybe any bar near a university or hospital is. Sometimes you need a drink after a hard day. A pretty conversationalist gives you a lift."

"We're more vulnerable than we realize."

"We are." Dr. Lorenzo nodded. "If I feel a flutter of temptation, I think of my wife, who has stood by me, and I think how humiliated I would be if my kids found out. Meredith would forgive me, but the kids wouldn't, because I hurt their mother. Sobers me right up."

Walter listened, thinking that the second shot loosed Dr. Lorenzo's tongue but then, they were under pressure. Viruses sweeping into the area. Accidents. COVID mutating into more contagious forms. Drug problems.

"You're a wise man." Walter smiled at him. "When I was young, I picked up girls. Dated some. But maybe that's how you learn what you really want and need. I slowed down once I got into med school. No time, really. Now I wonder, am I capable of a marriage?"

"Maybe there is an optimum time to marry. I was thirty-one. Just worked, despite my career. But I don't know. I found the right woman."

Walter grinned. "There is that."

Another couple walked out. Both men observed. Walter then added, "I've never sat here long enough to see this."

Dr. Lorenzo checked his watch. "Time to go. Leftovers." He laughed.

"Better the second day."

"Right."

As Dr. Lorenzo left, Walter considered a second shot then decided he didn't need it. Tomorrow was a hunting day. He had to set out his gear. He kept watch on his drinking. The stuff tasted too good. He'd seen many a physician give in to alcohol or drugs. The profession; dealing with constant crises; people, some in the extremes of behavior, could drive one to escape. And often a doctor was exhausted. He took a deep breath, left a nice tip, as another middle-aged fellow walked out with a young woman.

Sliding into his Mercedes E Wagon, he watched the man open the door to a flashy Porsche SUV. He wondered which one of them thought she or he had hit the jackpot. Then he felt his steering wheel warm up; his seat, too. Made the drive home pleasant.

As Walter negotiated the deepening gloom as the sun set earlier and earlier, Kathleen picked up the phone.

"Hi. It's Veronica."

"Having a good Thanksgiving?"

"Yes. What about you?"

"Wonderful Thanksgiving."

"The events out in Chapel Cross really scare me. I'm not sure what to do."

"I can understand. One doesn't expect to find a corpse while hunting. All I can say is, this is upsetting to all of us," Kathleen assured her.

"I'm sure it is. And not a clue?"

"No, not really. As you know, the sheriff hunts with us. He has to be circumspect with information, but I don't think much is known."

"A mystery. Well, I will be out by you on November 30 and I thought I'd bring you some of my special cardboard boxes. You might like them."

"I am curious as to what you are doing with cardboard."

"Not exactly making it fashionable, but you'll be able to use the boxes for giving gifts, or the larger ones for your papers. The exterior will help you remember what is where." Veronica paused. "I'd like to talk to you then about Wolverhampton."

"Of course."

After hanging up the phone, Kathleen sighed. Abdul, sensing

her mood, padded over, put his paw on her knee. She put both her hands behind his ears, leaned down, and gave him a kiss.

"Abdul, that rent helps. It's either feast or famine in this business. I hope Veronica isn't going to leave. Sweetheart, we have to be careful."

"I love you."

Hearing his little murmur, she kissed him again. "You truly are my best friend."

CHAPTER 23

November 25, 2023, Saturday

A small group hunted that Saturday since so many members traveled for Thanksgiving. Despite the uptick in COVID's new variety and other respiratory bugs, people had restrictions lifted on travel, so off they went. For some people, they visited their families, which they hadn't seen in three years.

Sister never knew what to expect over holidays in the best of circumstances. A cold wind made her nose even colder; but if she ducked behind conifers or an old outbuilding, that helped.

The hunt started at Mud Fence, across the road from Tattenhall Station. The foxes at Mud Fence and Tollbooth had no desire to venture out in the dropping temperature.

Sitting behind Mud Fence's stout hay barn, Sister wondered why she was out in this. Hounds pushed north, finally leaving the old farm, so Sister and her small field abandoned what little shelter they had found.

Hounds trailed a line, but no one opened. Weevil pushed. Finally, Taz opened, crossed Chapel Road North heading west. Hounds and the field rode around the edges of the graveyard at the chapel itself. As they swooped past the old Gulf station, a blast of wind sent the old orange sign rattling, which frightened some horses.

Hounds trotted behind the station then turned toward the south crossing, over onto Old Paradise. This proved even colder than the other side of the road, as the pastures around the historic estate were wide open. No hiding from the wind.

Hounds worked the line, finally losing it a half mile from the Carriage House.

"Gris," Aero called and the pack turned, now heading back toward where they started, as Gris lived at Tollbooth Farm. The wind smacked everyone right in the face.

Another forty-five minutes of a trailing line was miserable. The sky darkened. Sister's teeth chattered. Usually she could keep warm, but today her many layers couldn't block the frigid air. Again on Mud Fence, Sister jumped one of the mud fences for which the place was named. The original owners, right after the Revolutionary War, had little money. They couldn't afford much, no stone fences, no wood fences, not even those pretty zigzag fences, so they built mud fences. Those fences held up over the centuries. As grass was sown on them, even a hard rain didn't wash them away.

Landing on frozen ground, Sister felt every bone in her body. Aztec cantered away from the fence. They wound up where they had started, behind the stout hay barn.

Shivering, Sister looked behind her. People pulled their collars up, tucked their faces into their ties. A few wise ones had used white scarves for a stock tie, warmer than cotton.

She motioned to Weevil. He nodded at her circling right hand, lifted hounds, and they crossed the road to Tattenhall Station, where the trailers were parked.

Once horses and hounds were attended to, the eleven riders knew they would live once they felt the warmth of the station. The fireplaces gave off good heat and Kasmir had put in a big furnace when he bought the property. This proved much easier than keeping the old fireplaces going nonstop. The station had been abandoned for so many years that new plumbing and a big heat pump were installed, plus a huge generator could keep the place warm if the electric went out.

The warm food helped. People sat at the long table.

Freddie poured coffee. Gray took drink orders. He only had two, himself and Walter. Kasmir stuck to hot chocolate, as did Bobby, who usually enjoyed a stiff drink after a hunt.

As they sat there chatting, Kathleen and Aunt Daniella came after wheel-whipping. Fortunately, they didn't need to warm up.

"Why does today seem cold? We've been out in lower temperatures than today." Betty grabbed a ham biscuit.

"Snow's coming in. The moisture makes it raw," Kathleen, sitting next to Walter, offered.

"When's the snow to start?" Alida asked. "My phone apps keep changing the time."

"Mine said six PM. Otherwise, I wouldn't have hunted. I don't want to trailer in the snow. Too many accidents, even if it's a light snow." Freddie was prudent.

"I don't care what the apps say. It's going to come in before that." Alida glanced out the window. "Look at how dark it's getting."

"It's not to be bad. Maybe four inches." Bobby ate his mac and cheese.

At every hunt breakfast, someone made mac and cheese. Everyone loved it. It stuck to your insides. Since most people didn't eat breakfast—or much breakfast—before hunting, they felt starved.

"Depends on who is driving," Walter, feeling the warmth from his straight scotch followed by a coffee chaser, remarked. "I was at the ER last night and people were lined up along the walls on gurneys. Holidays equal more accidents, heart attacks, name it, but accidents especially. People party, the rest you know."

"You think we'd get some sense," Betty said.

"Those of us who live do." Yvonne half laughed. "Partying loses much of its appeal. At least it did for me."

"You aren't spending time with the right people," Aunt Daniella teased her.

Sam teased right back. "Aunt Dan, I resent that."

This brought a laugh from the group.

Walter then told them, "I was wiped out, so I stopped for a pickup. Every now and then I'll stop at the Jolly Roger. It's near the hospital. Anyway, I never paid much attention to it before, but I was at the bar with another doctor and we started noticing the men at the bar and the few women there, too. The women might have been college students. Some of them left with the men."

"Walter." Sister laughed. "What's so strange about that? Men have been picking up women in bars or coffeehouses since the eighteenth century, forever."

"Well, that's just it. I think it was the women picking up the men."

This caused a brief silence.

Kasmir broke it. "Maybe the fellow offered dinner. Young people usually don't have much by way of funds."

"True," Kathleen simply agreed, then added, "But my late husband, who attended UVA in the sixties, told me there were a few houses of ill repute and the boys attended them. Not everyone, of course. But then, when he would come back for his reunions he noticed that was no longer the case." She paused. "He admitted going to Pearl's, his favorite. What can I say? But he said once women were admitted to the university, the fellows would date women their own age, and I expect in some circumstances more than that."

"Isn't that true in every coed university or college?" Tootie asked.

"To an extent," Freddie chimed in. "But dating, sleeping with someone, isn't the same as looking for maybe not cash, but an easier way. Not everyone can afford college. Scholarships only do so much."

"Freddie, what are you saying?" Sister was surprised.

"Maybe some girls are looking for a keeper," Freddie answered. "You meet him at a bar or a gathering. He's older and established and you get along with him and, well, you become his mistress. Your bills are paid. You study, but when he calls you come running."

"Really?" Sister couldn't quite believe it.

"Honey, these aren't the things, wait, let me rephrase that." Her husband continued, "These aren't things you would think about and I doubt there was much of it when you were in college. I can't speak for the men here, but let's just say the male body is hitting its stride. Lots of energy. You can only play so much football or whatever."

"You guys." Betty shook her head.

"Betty, they're made differently than we are," Freddie said.

Aunt Daniella knew of which she spoke. "A smart woman can write her own ticket. When it comes to beauty or availability, my experience is men can't think."

Gray, Sam, Bobby, Walter, and Kasmir looked at one another, then finally Bobby grinned. "Gentlemen, best we refrain from this discussion."

"Walter," Sister looked at her joint master, who was regretting bringing up his observation, "do you think those girls, women, were on the make?"

"How would I know? I'm sure some were. There are a lot of lonesome men in Charlottesville, and then there are some husbands looking for a jolt."

Weevil, who had stayed out of the conversation, finally spoke. "And they can justify cheating on their wife. Men feel entitled to sex."

"Weevil." Bobby stared at him.

"I believe that. Men feel entitled. I don't, but I come from a different generation than you all. I'm not saying men in my generation don't feel that way, but not to the numbers of older generations. It was a different time. Getting pregnant without the benefit of marriage could be a disaster."

This shut up everyone.

"That's true," Aunt Daniella gently said. "In my ninety-six years, I have seen countless women ruined and abandoned. In my time, if a woman got pregnant, the man could always say, 'How do I know it's mine?' Fortunately, no man can use that excuse anymore. Has behavior changed? Up to a point but, Walter, I am willing to bet some of those women you watched were looking for a sugar daddy."

"Good God." Sister threw up her hands. "I am completely out of it."

"Honey, don't worry. Any man would wish to be your sugar daddy. But you aren't that kind of woman." Gray came over, putting his hand on her shoulder. "Don't fret."

She patted his hand. "I can't believe I'm that naive."

Alida smiled at the Master. "It's not something I guess many of us have had to consider. But maybe a couple of those women didn't want a keeper, but they might steal his watch or the cash out of his wallet if he fell asleep. If he's married, he can't do a thing. And a young man can do it, too. Sex can be bought, sold, used against someone. Our media is full of this stuff."

"Would you want to be a kid today?" Betty grabbed another sandwich. "You can't stay one very long. I feel badly for them. Who needs to know this stuff?"

"True," some people said, as others nodded.

Gray, thinking, pushed up the sleeve of his coat.

Sam, noticing the Rolex, came over, really looked at it.

"When did you get this?"

"Actually, he didn't. I found it." Sister knew her husband was about to get grilled, as he was not a spendthrift.

"She did find it." Gray took it off, handed it to Sam.

"I was there when she found it," Tootie backed up her Master.

"A Rolex?" Alida examined it as it was passed around.

Sister and Tootie then told the story of how they found it on the grown-over trail leading down from Hangman's Ridge.

"I told her not to advertise this, because who knows who would claim it? A free Rolex." Gray took the Submariner back as it came to him.

"I've been looking for ads in the lost and found as well as on the computer. Nothing. You would think whoever owned this expensive thing would want to find it," Sister told them. "None of us lost it."

"We'll probably never know." Sam thought it strange.

Yvonne said, "Back to you, Walter. If a fellow leaving the bar slept with one of those girls, she takes his watch, his cash, whatever, would you try to find your watch?"

"No," Bobby said with conviction. "You'd leave yourself wide open."

"But what if this was stolen? How did it wind up where it did?" Kasmir offered.

"When I told my wife not to advertise, I told her I'd wear it. Maybe someone would recognize it. I wore it hunting. No one noticed. So much has happened around here. This watch is one more oddity."

"And none of us recognize it." Freddie shrugged. "You'll need to wear it to bigger events."

"What if whoever owned it is dead?" Tootie had thought that for some time.

"I said that in the beginning." Betty raised her voice.

"I know. I've had time to think about it. Maybe it's true," Tootie replied.

"Oh great. Another dead body out there." Freddie moaned.

"Well . . ." Betty reached into her pocket to feel her cigarette. She was dying for a cigarette but didn't want anyone to know.

"Let's hope not." Alida exhaled.

"To change the subject, I'm trying to set up a joint meet with Bull Run in their territory. Everyone okay with that, once Adrianna and I set up a day?"

"Great." Yvonne and Tootie echoed each other.

"Such wonderful territory. And we'll be at a normal hunt." Freddie looked at Betty. "No bodies."

CHAPTER 24

November 26, 2023, Sunday

"There. Many hands make light work." Sister closed the back door to the 1780 House.

"You've been so helpful but I don't think a master should be carrying boxes." Veronica's knees stung a bit. "Thank you."

"What did it take? Ten minutes?" Kathleen led the two women to the living room. "I need wine. I have a weakness, but I watch it. Love a glass at sunset. Who can I talk into joining me?"

"I'd like a greenie," Abdul said.

"I'll join you." Veronica pulled out a kitchen chair as Kathleen indicated she should sit. "I've noticed you rubbing your knees."

"Stiff. Every now and then I get a twinge."

"If you all have time, I can recite my aches and pains." Sister laughed.

"You don't look as though you have aches and pains." Veronica envied Sister for her posture, way of walking.

"Greenies." Abdul barked louder.

"Beggar." Kathleen gave him his greenies. "Who trains whom?"

"You must have thrilled your English teachers." Veronica laughed at her saying *whom*.

"Red or white?" Kathleen opened the kitchen cabinet where she kept a small supply of spirits, the larger being out in the shop.

"It's so cold. Red. Yes, red," Veronica answered.

"Sister?"

"Nothing, thanks. Let me help you carry the glasses and what looks like those thin Italian biscuits on the counter. Well, maybe I do need a drink. Those biscuits are too good."

"How about Perrier?" Kathleen asked.

"Okay," Sister agreed.

Once the drink order was set, the drinks on a tray with napkins and the biscuits, the ladies repaired to the living room.

"Oh, this chair feels wonderful." Veronica sank into it. "Don't your legs ever hurt?"

"No, I'm not riding," Kathleen said.

"After a long hunt, I feel it. Mostly in my thighs. Knees are okay. Sometimes the small part of my back talks to me but I don't think you can live long without aches and pains. That's why you have to keep moving."

"I'll remember that." Veronica looked at Sister. "I have so enjoyed being here. Sheila and I train women for jobs, especially in construction. Most of them are young, and come from hardships, disadvantaged backgrounds. We try to encourage good health habits as well as skills. We're worried about them working out in the Chapel Cross area."

"We'll all be glad when this is resolved." Kathleen took a grateful sip. "Everyone has theories, but no one has facts."

"True for any crime." Sister bit into a biscuit. "Once the crime is resolved, it all makes sense."

"One hopes," Veronica replied. "While I'm sitting here, let me ask you all, what are your theories?"

"I don't know. The two murders may be connected and may not. Who knows?" Kathleen answered.

"I didn't know cause of death had been found." Sister's eyebrows raised.

"Ben called me since Aunt Dan and I were there. Fortunately, we didn't see the body. Will be in the media tomorrow. Torn apart. The medical examiner found a .38 bullet in her. Her torso was somewhat undisturbed."

"Two young people shot." Sister sighed.

"See what I mean? It's too creepy."

"A woman was dumped at Bishop's Gate, Trevor was left on I-64. The two deaths may not be connected, but it is creepy."

Veronica said, "Trevor's grandmother lives out here. People have told me that. If I lived now in Wolverhampton every footfall I would hear, every leaf crunching, would scare me. I'm a big chicken."

"Given events, that sounds sensible to me." Kathleen, while she didn't feel quite that way, agreed with Veronica. "But the women working at Wolverhampton won't be alone."

"What's your theory?" Veronica asked Sister.

"I don't really have one. People kill for money, for love, to protect themselves, status, I guess. I can't imagine what this is about. To change the subject, these biscuits are wonderful. Kathleen, where did you get them?"

"Basic Necessities in Nellysford. Happened to stop by for French bread on my ride home from Lynchburg, the back way, and thought I'd try the biscuits."

"Ladies, let me get a couple of those boxes in the living room. I'll be right back."

Kathleen and Sister chatted. Veronica returned with two cartons, which she set at one end of the table.

Kathleen wondered, "What are you doing?"

"You'll see," Veronica answered.

"All right now." Veronica opened one of the large cartons, pulling out some smaller cartons. "Wanted to show you what I make. These are book-carton sizes. They're decorated, color printed, tiny books on the outside." She lifted out a few dividers from inside. "These are if you want to divide the books or put layers between them." She set them on the table.

"This is so pretty, one can forgo wrapping."

Kathleen picked up one of the dividers. "You even have quotes on them."

"Okay, now here's a bigger box. This is for clothing. Folded. And the sides are double thickness. Keeps out mold. Again, dividers if needed."

"How clever." Sister thought the boxes were.

"I can make anything in different colors. I can imprint people's logos on a carton. I can print special designs. It saves wrapping paper, especially book boxes. The double thickness makes them more expensive but much more sturdy. Good for china and glasses, too."

Sister picked up one of the book boxes. "They are heavy."

"Given how boxes are tossed around, whether by mail delivery or even UPS, best they be extra sturdy. Does my cardboard cost more? Yes, but it saves a lot of steps. Got the idea years ago when I was moving after my divorce. I swore I was not going to pack my books ever again only to have the box break."

"I can understand that." Kathleen finished her wine.

"It's both useful and clever," Sister praised her.

"Thanks. I'm the practical sort. That was one of the things that impressed me when I started hunting. The tack, the clothing. It's all practical."

"You can be out there for hours. The last thing you need is clothing that doesn't fit or boots that are too tight. Layers are the key." Sister picked up another biscuit. "Yesterday it was so cold, creeping-up cold. I had layers but not enough. Cashmere or merino wool are the best."

Kathleen smiled. "Aunt Dan and I are happy to be in the car."

"Sister, what I have noticed the few times I have hunted with you is the chain across your vest. Is that attached to a pocket watch?"

"My grandfather's. The face is so big. Easy to see, and I don't have to push back my sleeve, which I hate to do when it's bitter cold."

"Are you a watch person?"

Sister responded to Veronica. "I like them. My first husband was a fanatic. I'm not obsessed. He loved collecting watches. There are people who just love them."

"Yes, they do, and they'll pay a lot for them. If it's a rare brand or an especially beautiful one, out comes the checkbook. Women's watches don't seem as desirable as men's, especially the old ones."

"Too small." Kathleen thought. "I wear my late husband's because I can see it, like Sister with her grandfather's pocket watch. The face is big."

"It's a good thing to be able to tell the time." Sister smiled. "Goes so fast. The time."

"That's the truth," Kathleen echoed.

"Sister, do you mind if I ask what you did with your late husband's collection?" Veronica inquired.

"Not at all. I gave each of his closest men friends a watch. I saved one for myself. I was surprised at how touched his friends were. Ray was one of those men who had the gift of friendship. That and, unfortunately for a time, alcohol got him through our son's death."

As Veronica didn't know about RayRay's tractor accident, Sister briefly told her.

"I am so sorry."

"Thank you. He was a joy. But you go on. You must go on. For me, it's one of the ways I love him. To live life as fully as I can. And I guess that's why Trevor being shot at twenty-four, and the woman, what did they say, early twenties, why it seems so wasteful."

"People take chances. As you age, you grow more careful." Veronica then inhaled. "Doesn't mean we don't now take chances. Maybe we are better at weighing the facts."

"Such a hopeful thought." Sister laughed.

"I took a chance moving here. Taking over the store. Best thing I ever did." Kathleen picked up a box. "This is pretty. I like the books on the outside as decoration."

"That didn't take much imagination," Veronica confessed.

Abdul came in to sit next to Kathleen. Finally, Veronica looked at the mantel clock. "I'd better be going. Stuff to do at home."

As the other two women walked her to the back door, Veronica said to Kathleen, "I'll keep you abreast of what Sheila and I are thinking. I should bring her down to spend the night. We should go out to the old house together. She's working on a rancher we bought. Will be a quick turnaround." Veronica put her hand on the doorknob. "Sister, out of curiosity, did you give all of your late husband's watches away?"

"No. He had so many. I saved three: a Jaeger-LeCoultre, the old gold polo watch for Gray, and a steel one for me. Maybe in the back of my mind, I knew I would marry again. I gave the LeCoultre to Gray, as he knew Ray. Gray loves that watch. You flip it over so the crystal doesn't break when you ride. The others I took up to New York. I made quite a bit of money. Some of them were worth thousands. I had no idea. I had all kinds of ideas about what to do with the windfall, but then I thought about Ray. He would have wanted me to invest, so I did."

"He sounds very intelligent." Veronica had taken her coat from Kathleen, hanging by the back door.

"Yes. I am a fortunate woman. I married two industrious, intelligent men. I never thought I would find love again, I was in my early sixties, but I did. And Gray is a godsend. He is funny, warm, and sensible."

"Well, he's handsome." Veronica grinned.

"Yes." Sister grinned back. "A girl does have weaknesses."

"In the second big box is a smaller box for sending or storing china. Thought you might be able to use it," Veronica said as she opened the door, cold air rushing in. "Oh, Sister, can't help myself. What is the third watch?"

Sister smiled. "A gold Tank watch from maybe 1967. His initials are on the back, *RRA*. Again, because it's a man's watch, I can see the dial."

"I've never noticed you wearing a Tank watch." Veronica was so curious.

"I do. In cooler weather. A sweater sleeve covers it up. I like the clean design. I rarely wear watches in the heat. Uncomfortable. I like classic design."

The two women returned to the living room after Veronica left.

"I hope she stays. No one is alone in Wolverhampton. I don't think so, anyways."

Sister began rooting around in the cardboard boxes. "This really is so clever. I wouldn't think she would be that spooked by Chapel Cross."

"It is unnerving."

"Maybe Veronica could make heavy cardboard boxes for coffins," Sister stated.

"You're awful."

CHAPTER 25

November 27, 2023, Monday

Sister, Yvonne, and Alida stood in front of Wolverhampton. A calm but cold day made their cheeks tingle.

"Do you think she'll change her mind?" Yvonne wondered. "About restoring this place?"

"I don't know. None of us know her that well. Adrianna says Veronica has a sharp eye for property." Sister liked the windows in the upper stories of Wolverhampton. The lower windows all had an arch plus the fan window over the front door.

"Let's go in." Alida walked to the imposing door and opened it. "Aha."

The other two followed.

Pulling her coat tighter, Sister looked up at the curving stairway. "It's not much warmer in here."

Workers in down coats carried lumber and pipes.

"It's like the difference between a cold rain and snow. I feel warmer when it snows. Sort of." Alida noticed the light streaming through the windows. "Whoever designed this took advantage of the light."

"I think many of those early architects paid attention to light. Candles were expensive, especially beeswax. You know, I think keeping warm or having light has always been expensive. We're lucky until the power goes off. Then you'd better hope you're in an old house with fireplaces." Alida appreciated the big old house at Tattenhall Station.

"True." Sister walked into the library off the big hall. "Oak."

No one was working in the library, which had a fire going. There were books on the bookshelves.

"This must have been built before the mahogany craze." Yvonne, who liked architecture, thought out loud. "Or the owner figured they had so much walnut, why not use it?"

"I vote for the latter." Alida smiled. "Given the proportions of the rooms, the windows and glass were expensive, too. Are there any Tates left?"

Sister answered. "No. It's one of those stories where the male line died out. I think there are some female-line Tates in Fort Worth and in Wyoming. I don't really know, but if there are any left, they don't want Wolverhampton."

"Happens a lot, I think. Who can afford these grand estates that have been left to fall into ruin?" Alida posited. "This isn't that bad off, all things considered."

"Right."

"As you know, when I drove down here out of curiosity, the fireplaces were being cleaned and the fellow said they were in good shape," Yvonne remarked.

"It was built to last centuries and it will. The work is interior stuff, wiring, plumbing, sanding floors. The windows look pretty good. How long has it been empty?" Alida asked.

"This isn't exact, but I'd say maybe eight years. The last Tate died. He'd been going down, so the place was getting raggedy," Sister recalled. "That's the problem with farms and ranches, you know. If you don't have children to help keep them up, they unravel when old age hits. You can't do what you always did."

"Sister, one can hire people," Alida said. "Look at all these young women in here."

"To a point. Fewer and fewer people have farm skills or want to have them." Yvonne crossed her arms over her chest. "I'm not surprised that Tootie loves the outdoors. She always did, but she's rare. Most of her classmates at Custis Hall, now graduating college, they all go into law or medicine or business. City work. Even if you have the funds, I don't think it's easy."

"The Tates had money for generations. The usual number of fools filled out the sibling lists, but mostly the eldest kept it together." Sister remembered some of the Tates. "Let's check the kitchen."

They walked toward the back. The kitchen was empty. Most of the windows were in the large rooms and the hall.

"The old summer kitchen is outside," Alida remarked.

"A very sensible solution. Still is, really." Sister liked the idea of heat not being in the house during the sticky summer months.

"Amazing that the old wood-burning cooking stove is still here." Alida admired the huge stove, the opening for wood on the right side. "Boy is this big."

"Wonder if the Sherwoods intend to keep it? Rehab it. Wouldn't be that difficult." Sister knelt down to peer at it. "Our foremothers knew what they were doing. Even with servants, a woman had a lot of physical work to do. Just walking throughout the house and checking took some energy." She stood up and smiled. "They were tougher than we are. One just got on with it."

"What's the phrase? 'A man works from sun to sun. But a woman's work is never done,'" Alida recited the old phrase.

The three women walked throughout the house, saying a few

words to the women working but staying out of the way. They didn't go up the winding staircase. They went outside. Walked around to the back door, which they had just stood at when in the kitchen.

All around the back, truck and car tracks churned up mud.

"How many workers are here?" Yvonne wondered.

"A lot. Seems like a lot to me. Fifteen?" Sister then added, "Gray said they should renovate the farm manager's house first. Easier done. Then, say, Veronica could move in and supervise the rest of the work if she was so inclined."

"You know, it really would be the best idea to have someone here." Yvonne thought a moment. "If the Sherwoods want to sell now, we can buy it; even the manager's house would be perfect. Just kind of thinking."

Sister kept looking down at all the tracks. "I expect the Sherwoods have bills to pay."

Once home and happy in her warm kitchen, Sister filled in Gray, who had driven back from Richmond early, as to what she had seen.

"If we're talking about a syndicate, I guess I should go over there and look."

"Go with Bobby and Sam. They both have sense. When Bobby and Betty bought Cocked Hat, it was decent, but they've turned it into something special without being flashy."

"He's also in a business that reflects what's going on. Births, marriages, deaths, graduation announcements. The two of them know more than the rest of us."

"They are sensitive to technology, too. But I had a thought. A little weird, but I kept noticing the tire marks in the mud. What do you think if I ask Ben to come take prints? I bet they still have that bloody truck impounded."

"If they don't, Ben would have had prints taken, also photographed. He is a very thorough man. Thinks of stuff the rest of us don't. Then again he has to. That's a good idea, honey."

Sister called Ben, explained herself. He thanked her and said he'd check Wolverhampton's roads, parking spots.

"Probably a wild goose chase." Sister put the phone down.

CHAPTER 26

November 28, 2023, Tuesday

Ben peered at his computer. Impression evidence could be helpful in establishing time. However, it also suffered from so many variables that it often does law enforcement little good in the courtroom.

Ben wasn't interested in the courtroom, but in location. Fortunately, the truck was still impounded. He sent Jude to get photos of those tires. As for Wolverhampton, he listened to Sister. Her idea had some merit, so he sent Jackie there to take close-up photographs of all the tracks.

He focused on tread design. While that is consistent for different brands, all-wheel tires, snow tires, etc., there can be distinguishing marks. A vehicle whose tires are out of line might have more tread wear on the outside of, say, the right rear tire. A nick or a cut in the tire could be distinguishing. Unfortunately, nothing that clear showed up but the one tire tread that was somewhat clear looked like the tread on the old truck.

It was highly possible that the truck with blood all over the front seats had been at Wolverhampton. This would do little good in a courtroom, but he wasn't in a courtroom. He was in the midst of seemingly unconnected violence and death.

He thanked his assistants for their speedy work.

Walking back and forth in his office, he rubbed his eyes. Staring at the computer made his eyes itch and water. Was it possible that whoever drove that truck was working in Wolverhampton? Or more than one person?

Possibilities flashed through his mind. And those possibilities returned to *why?*

Had the truck carried contraband? What could be that profitable narrowed the possibilities. Cigarettes, and alcohol made from clear mountain water, made a lot of money when driven north. The counties along the mountains did a big business in those country waters, which wound up in expensive bars in Manhattan and elsewhere. Interstates 81 and 64, as well as Route 29, were heavily traveled corridors for drugs. Drugs were a lot easier to transport than a truck full of moonshine.

The two murdered young people did not have drugs in their systems. Finding traces of those powerful substances was a priority for medical examiners and the tools advanced greatly. Then again, a good drug dealer rarely used the stuff.

He walked to the end of his office, turned, walked back again. Pacing loosened his back. He'd been sitting too long, but the pacing wasn't doing much for his mind.

What else? What could be that valuable?

He leaned over his desk and buzzed Jude.

"Come on in my office. Bring Jackie."

Once the two sat before him, he dropped into his chair and rolled it in front of them. He reviewed all of his thoughts.

"What, apart from drugs, is easy to transport, will bring money anywhere?"

"Cash. Stolen cash." Jude spoke.

"Like from a bank?" Jackie questioned.

"Yes, but if it were from a legitimate bank, we'd know. Why couldn't one drug cartel or big dealer steal from another?"

"They could, but I think we'd have more dead people." Ben leaned back.

"What never loses value?" Jackie thought out loud.

"Apart from drugs and cash?" Jude rubbed his chin. "Women's bodies."

"True, but humans are hard to transport, and now there are better ways to identify human trafficking. Even the general public has seen posters about this."

"And you'd have to put women somewhere," Jackie stated the obvious. "Where could you secure women without notice? Even out in the country, sooner or later someone would notice people in houses and not coming outside."

Ben rolled closer. "What stands the test of time?"

Jude quickly answered, "Gold."

Both Ben and Jackie absorbed this.

"And?" Ben asked. "Diamonds, precious stones. Right?"

"Silver. Usually, it's melted down." Jackie picked up the ball. "Same with jewelry. Remove the stones, melt down the platinum or the gold. A stunning piece of jewelry could be recognized, say, if worn at a big fundraiser like the Met Gala. Easier to break it up. And it could be sold anywhere in the world."

"You'd need a team. Someone to break down the stuff," Jude said.

"Actually, Jude, you wouldn't. All you'd need to do was sell it to your contact in Washington or Richmond or wherever. You need good equipment to melt gold, remove diamonds. And I'm sure there are those who can do it."

"What about people who have a job at a jeweler's? They could do it on the side." Jackie's mind was racing.

"Yes. Not very smart, though," Ben opined. "I would think sooner or later you'd tip your hand or a contact would show up at the store. No, I think whoever would be dismantling the jewelry would be a business unto themselves, or part of the large business. It would leave their hands and go directly to the market. Right?"

"We've thought of value. What else?"

"Shares. People keep Apple shares in safes or at the bank."

"You mean quick money?" Jackie questioned.

Ben then pushed them a little. "Go back to the first crime. Trevor Goodall. He lived in Charlottesville, had a small apartment in Woolen Mills but he knew Chapel Cross intimately. He left cash for his grandmother. Had his fingerprints on it. Nobody else's, so whoever dropped the cash in Birdie's mailbox wore gloves. Given that it was cold, that may have no significance."

"How much does a bartender make?" Jackie asked.

"In Washington? I would guess a good bartender at a busy bar could make maybe a hundred fifty thousand or even more. Some of that would be declared, but you could hide the rest. It's enticing work." Ben always saw the pull of avoiding taxes. "Here? I don't know. Seventy thousand? Maybe if you slipped some contraband to a customer, some fabulous booze made right here in the mountains, you could make more."

"And you could also slip drugs." Jude had seen this when in college. "You have a flat packet, slide it under your hand to the customer, under a napkin for his drink. Or you take a quick break and go to the parking lot for a larger package. Pretty easy."

"So then, too, would it be easy to do business with women?" Jackie asked.

"Trafficked women?" Jude shook his head. "A girl for the night? Yeah, I think that's pretty easy. She gives you a cut."

"Is it worth dying over?" Ben pushed again.

"That depends on the profit. Depends on whether someone is

getting shaky and any of those young women can turn on you and say they were abused if the fire comes too close. You'd be cooked."

"True." Jackie nodded. "Maybe some of those women have nothing to lose, but others would. Be a fool to go public and initiate a lawsuit."

"So it seems." Ben tapped his foot on the clean floor. "I don't know that Trevor was that successful as a bartender. He moved between a few bars. No one accused him of stealing as a bartender. His mistake was stealing cars once. He seems to have been a drifter. Perhaps weak, easily led."

"But what if the bars he moved to had a connection?" Jude provided a new thought. "If you have a crime ring, they could be working more than one bar. Behind the scenes. It would be possible to do that without the owner knowing. Think about it. If your bartender is in on it, a few of the girls, who would know? You weren't stealing from the bar owner, which is what any owner would be vigilant about."

"That's very possible." Ben stopped tapping.

"Now what?" Jackie asked the obvious.

"You and Jude go to every bar where Trevor worked. To be safe, I suggest you go together."

"No woman will try to pick me up, then," Jude said, in complete earnest.

"You think?" Jackie couldn't help it, she laughed.

Jude's face reddened.

"Sorry. Jude, you can sit at the bar and I'll sit at a table, but my feeling is, I wasn't being mean, you are too young. If this is some kind of prostitution ring, none of those women are going to look at a young man. You don't have enough money."

A sigh of relief escaped Jude, which even made Ben laugh. "Well?"

"We can start tomorrow, but then can we come in late?" Jude liked his sleep.

"Well, don't close the joints down. You'll get an idea. I doubt some lonely fellow will sit there until two AM. My hunch is the girls are checking the clock. Maybe a woman can service two johns in a night. More money." Ben had known streetwalkers who on the weekends could pick up eight johns in one night. It was all cash.

"That's a thought," Jackie replied. "But how do we determine it has the potential to be more stable? Like a woman gets kept?"

"Doubt you'll be able to tell, but maybe some of the girls will talk about other girls?" Ben quickly added, "You have to be careful. No leading questions. If this is about sex and an organization getting a percentage of the cut, a woman who talked would be endangered. Best to watch. Maybe a light conversation here and there."

"Okay," the two agreed.

As they left his office, Ben rolled back to his computer. He didn't know if selling sex was behind this, or if it was something like stealing jewelry. He didn't think he was sending them into obvious danger.

With Christmas around the corner, there would be more accidents, more shoplifting, and more pressure. If nothing else, it would push the two murders into the background.

CHAPTER 27

November 30, 2023, Thursday

"Take your flashlight, even though it's broad daylight," Betty ordered Sister. "The brush is thick."

"Okay." Sister popped back into the mudroom, returning with a 9-volt flashlight.

The two women got into the mule, which they had driven up from the stable. Raleigh and Rooster hopped in, too. Sister fired it up, they drove past the stables, turned left, roared up the incline to the Hanging Field, drove down the other side.

"Today's hunt was better than I thought it would be," Sister spoke over the motor. "I put three rocks on the spot. We aren't far."

Betty held on to the bar on the right. Sister cut the motor, pulled on the brake in case it rolled a bit, as it wasn't exactly flat. "Okay."

"Glad it's warmed up a little." Betty looked down at the path.

"For now." Sister slowly walked. "It's here somewhere."

Betty, behind her, thought even with winter around the corner, or at least the winter solstice, the undergrowth looked thick with prickers and dried leaves.

"Okay. Here." Sister stopped as Betty walked up to the three mid-sized rocks.

"What in the hell was a Rolex doing here?"

"I don't know."

As the humans took in the surroundings, which they knew well on horseback but not so much on foot, the dogs sniffed.

"Rabbits," Rooster announced.

"It's a faint scent but you always know what it is," the Doberman agreed.

"Did you see a glitter?" Betty asked.

"No. I would have stepped right over it, but I stumbled and that's how I saw it. Those damn cows are worthless, but I wouldn't have found the watch if it weren't for them."

"I'll remember that the next time we're at Cindy's." Betty knelt down to look at the spot. "We aren't far from the road."

"No, we aren't. Someone with a decent pitching arm could have given it a chuck. And don't tell me there's a body. If there were, I would think the watch would have been on it."

"You don't know. Two people have a fight. The watch goes first. And you don't know if the car was stopped or not. The driver could have pulled to the side of the road as they fought."

"If they were fighting." Sister knelt down with Betty. "Although, why else would someone pitch a valuable watch?"

"If they had killed their passenger, it's possible they wanted to remove any trace of him."

"Maybe. Or whoever threw this did it to make a point. 'Keep pissing me off and I'll kill you.' When people fly into a rage, there is no logic."

"If one didn't know that, being a mother sure proves it." Betty knew of which she spoke. "I rarely get to see Jennifer since she stayed in Maine after graduating from Colby, but as a child she could blow. Scream. Vile thoughts crossed my mind."

"Old vulture tracks." Raleigh ducked under an overgrown bush, following the marks, a long-faded scent.

Rooster noted a feather caught in a low branch.

"Vultures are smart. Usually, they nest where they can see for a distance," Raleigh pointed out.

"If anything was dead, a deer, say, something big, there'd be bones left behind, no matter how long ago. That's the confusing thing about deer season. Too many carcasses left about. If we bring a leg home, Mom has a fit."

"She's not squeamish. Give her that." Raleigh noted, *"I think the smell gets them. It is such a wonderful scent."*

"Their noses are different."

The two canine friends slowly walked, inhaling everything. Not much scent other than rabbits, a gopher here and there.

Sister and Betty looked around then walked to the road. Given that this was an old road, few cars drove on it, and those were usually whoever lived on Soldier Road, not many people.

"Here." Sister handed Betty a rock about half the size of a baseball. "Give it a pitch."

Betty, good arm, did just that. "A bit past where you found the watch."

"If a driver was heading west, threw this, it would fall not quite so far."

"But what if a driver was heading east? Stopped the car and threw the watch? Close, I would think. There's no way to tell the direction of the vehicle. Then again, what if it wasn't thrown from a vehicle?" Betty looked again at the distance.

"No one walks this road," Sister said. "The only time I would think anyone would walk Soldier Road is if their car broke down."

"Well, that's true," Betty agreed. "So we don't know any more than when we started."

"No." Sister felt disappointed.

"Clouds are coming in." Sister put her hand over her eyes as a shield. "Skidding down the mountain."

"All right. Let's head back." Betty knew the temperature would drop.

The mercury hovered at about fifty, unusual for this time of year but not impossible. Once the cloud cover took over, the temperature would dip into the mid-forties.

"Raleigh, Rooster," Sister called.

"What have you two got there?" Sister reached for a single turkey feather.

Back in the kitchen, Sister and Betty admitted defeat. They knew no more than when they started.

Jude and Jackie, driving from Yancy Downs, were also frustrated. They had visited two bars, this being the second in two nights. Not much was going on.

"I wonder if weekends will be better than weeknights?" Jackie asked. "And how long do we have to do this?"

Jude spoke. "I say weekends. Everyone is looser. As to how long, go to the boss."

"One of the things I like about our work is you have to think, unless the perp is standing there with a smoking gun. Happens more than people know."

"Crimes of passion or of the moment." He turned up the heater. "Getting cold again."

"Well, it is almost December."

"Haven't gotten anything for Mom and Dad. Better think of something."

"Is their house warm?"

"Some rooms are, but they're trying to save money by turning down the thermostat."

"Boy, do I understand that. There are some really nice small one-room heaters on sale on Amazon. I'll text them to you."

"You cold, too?"

She smiled at him. "The landlord turns the heat down at night. I hate waking up to a cold room. Anyway, I'm going to get one of those heaters."

"A lot of cheapskates out there. Then again, a bad tenant can cause so much damage." Jude was sympathizing.

"That's something we haven't thought of. If a woman was picking up tricks to take to her apartment or house, it would have to be pretty decent.

"Damn." Jackie wrapped her arms around herself. "These last few weeks have been strange. But you know, we'll figure it out eventually."

Jude smiled at her, then his eyes returned to the road. "It's the eventually that worries me."

CHAPTER 28

December 1, 2023, Friday

"Can you believe it's December?" Adrianna marveled, speaking into her phone.

"This year has been a blur," Sister confessed. "Before I forget, have you seen Veronica? She's questioning restoring Wolverhampton."

"Yes, she was out hunting the other day. She said all she could think of was going out by the back pasture and finding a body. I replied that she lives near close to a thousand bodies that have never been found." Adrianna paused. "She said while it was a little creepy, that was so long ago it didn't frighten her. I can't say that all those Union and Confederate missing unfound dead frighten me, but I'm aware of them."

"Yes," Sister simply replied. "The dead are always with us in one way or the other. Things zip through my mind. This morning I was thinking about Pompey the Great. Is there anyone in our country today with his mind, courage, and wealth? People recognize Caesar, but they don't think of Pompey. Oh well. How did I get off on that? I don't know, Adrianna, but there's so much going on here. Back to Wolverhampton. People don't readily buy properties where there have been murders, not that there's been a murder at Wolverhampton, but right now Chapel Cross is under a dark cloud."

"Speaking of dark clouds. The weather is going to be good on Saturday the ninth. Want to bring your people up here for a joint meet? The fixture is Quiet Shade. All I have to do is tell our people it's a joint meet. No fuss, really. The more people, the more fun."

"Mine will be fine. It's a TBA. So now I can announce it. Lynn will be riding, right?"

"She'll be in my pocket. Actually, you'll be in my pocket. Lynn will be behind you."

"Adrianna, you can put me wherever you please. I don't have to be up front."

"Better to see hound work."

"That's the truth. Bad as this year has been, with the drought finally ending, my hounds have done well. I feel so guilty when I go out and there's no reward. Very little scent. They try so hard."

"It's getting better and it's getting darker. I never really get used to it. I think it may intensify the scent."

"It could be. Can we bring anything?"

"Of course not." Adrianna smiled, hearing Sister's offer. "Maybe before Season's end we could put your pack, Deep Run's pack, and ours together. A real old-fashioned triple meet. Remember how we used to do that? A triple meet."

"It was the leishmaniasis scare that ruined joint meets with joint packs. Slowly, slowly, we're getting back to it, but you know, the new housing developments, the new roads, they all impact what we can do. Where can you take, say, seventy hounds for a meet? In the old days, I knew hunts that took out fifty couple on weekends. What a thrill that was. The music alone lifted you right out of the saddle." Sister paused. "You're too young to remember that."

"I remember big packs. Hunts that had fifty couple. But really, who can afford the costs? Everything has skyrocketed. Doesn't matter if it's food or bedding or vet costs. It's not just hunting, obviously, but I don't see how Americans can afford themselves."

"That would be funny if it weren't so true." Sister found Adrianna's insights, so clearly stated, refreshing.

"Veronica said she brought you and Kathleen some of her cartons. Aren't they something?"

"Yes. Clever, and can hold a lot of weight. I don't know how people come up with these ideas. I'm not creative. I can improve things, but I can't invent them. I don't know if I said that correctly. I marvel at Yvonne, whom you met. She came up with something new, exciting. Who would have thought of a Black media network? Now it seems obvious. Her riding is getting strong, by the way."

"Oh, I'm sure the men in my club will notice." Adrianna laughed.

"There is that. All right, Madam, Saturday the ninth. What time? We can come at any time."

"It's getting colder. Come at eleven. The fixture is at the large stable. Won't be too late. I am betting there will be plenty of scent."

"Sounds good." Sister hung up her kitchen phone, happy to have something to look forward to with a club she much admired.

It was easy to take shortcuts, and Bull Run was not taking them. She fed J. Edgar, who chirped. Then she gave Golly special crunchies. The long-haired calico was beside herself. The dogs received regular crunchies topped with a short but thick beef bone. Life was good.

Life was neither good nor bad at the Jolly Roger, where Jackie and Jude were sitting. People getting off work from the hospital stopped by. No one wore scrubs, but you could tell who was a doctor and who wasn't. There were three or four at the bar for an after-work shot.

"Maybe we should have started here first," Jackie remarked. "This was where Trevor tended bar for some time."

Jude flipped over the brief menu. "I don't know that it would have made much difference. Do you want anything to eat?"

She reached for a menu. "I am kind of hungry. What about you?"

"It's the start of the weekend, so we might be here a bit longer than we were our last two nights. Yeah, I'm hungry."

They ordered hamburgers. No alcohol, as they were working. He ordered a Coca-Cola and she ordered iced tea. As they sat there watching the place fill up the bar was packed by the time their food came.

"I swear I know that woman." Jackie reached for her tea.

Jude turned to look at the woman about Jackie's age. She wore big earrings, a tight sweater with a plaid shawl draped over it. She was nice-looking, talking to the man beside her and also to a woman on the other side of her.

"It will drive you crazy. Does me when I can't place a person."

"How much longer do you think we'll be on bar patrol?" Jackie asked.

"Maybe another week. Nothing has happened very slowly." He cut his hamburger in half.

"You are so tidy." Jackie followed suit. "I'll do it, too." Then she lowered her voice. "She's looking at me."

"Well, don't look back." He giggled. "Maybe she wants to pick you up and not the guy she's sitting next to."

"Thanks." Jackie lifted one eyebrow.

Being devilish, Jude said, "Hey, you're attractive to everybody."

She blushed. "Well, well," she repeated herself. "Jude, I am so tired when I get off duty, I can't imagine being attractive to anybody. All I want to do is go to sleep. I'm not complaining. I'm learning a lot, but I hope we get better hours when we come up for review."

"I think we will." He finished off half his sandwich, being hungrier than he realized.

Jackie's face changed as the woman walked over.

"Excuse me, are you Jackie Anstine?"

"Yes, I am."

"Gerri Kendall." She held out her hand, which Jackie shook.

"I can't believe it. Forgive me for not recognizing you."

"It's been ten years since we graduated high school. And I've had a little work done," Gerri confessed.

"Uh, well, you look great."

"I wanted to look better. I went on a diet. Best thing I ever did."

"Excuse me. This is Jude Anderson."

He stood up, shook Gerri's hand. "Would you care to sit with us?"

"No, thank you. I'm with the fellow at the bar. Jackie, I don't know where I heard it, but did you go into law enforcement like your father?" She smiled.

"Yes. What about you?"

"Interior design." She smiled reflexively. "Do you have to do dangerous work?"

"Sometimes. A lot of what I do is routine," she answered.

"No car chases or murders?"

Jude watched silently.

Gerri said, "Both would be pretty exciting. The guy who used to tend bar here was murdered."

"Yes. I know." Jackie nodded.

"Do you think there might be a killer here?" Gerri wondered.

"Well, I guess there might be information wherever he spent time but we were hungry, close by, so we came in. We weren't thinking about the bartender. Now that you've reminded me, who is to say, something might be here." Jackie was smooth, relaxed.

Gerri looked over her shoulder. "Better get back to my date. Good to see you."

"Good to see you, too."

Gerri left with the older man, she waved as she did.

The two watched the bar. It was a pickup place, but every now and then one of the girls would go to the ladies room then stop by a table with three younger men. Not for long. Then she'd rejoin the man at the bar with a big smile.

"Are you bored?" Jackie asked.

"Not so much bored as knowing people are being picked up. But what happens next? Wait, don't answer that. You know what I mean."

"I do." She raised her eyebrows.

They sat there for another half hour then got up to leave. As they walked out, the three young men at the table followed them, although Jude and Jackie didn't know this.

Halfway across the parking lot, two of the men jumped Jude and the third grabbed Jackie, who had her hand in her coat pocket. She pulled out her pistol, smashing him across the face. Teeth scattered.

Then she ran to Jude, hit one of the men on the back of the head. He crumpled, which gave Jude enough time to kick the other guy in the crotch. He doubled over. Jude brought his knee up under the man's chin. More teeth on the tarmac.

"Stay where you are." Jackie held her pistol on the two men on the ground, as the third one, standing and rubbing his jaw, didn't move. "You okay?" she asked Jude.

"Yeah."

Jude pulled out his pistol as Jackie called the city police. She knew the numbers by heart.

Within minutes a siren wailed, for a squad car had been over at the hospital.

Two uniformed city policemen got out. The two county law enforcement officers described being attacked. The three men were handcuffed and shoved into the back of a squad car. Their teeth stayed on the ground.

"Thanks." Jude rubbed his throat where his attacker had grabbed him. "Our first piece of evidence."

"Glad I have the city's numbers memorized. We'll press charges. I think what happened is, Gerri told the woman sitting next to her that we graduated from the same high school and I'm a cop. Can't prove it, but I think that's what happened. How that got to the three goons, I don't know, but we do have a start."

"And we work well with the city. I know for people moving here from out of state, it doesn't make sense for the city to have its own police force while the county has a sheriff's department, but in a way it does. Are you okay? I should have asked first thing. I'm sorry."

"Jude, you had two men on you. I'm okay. When we left the bar I heard the footsteps behind us. I didn't look back, I didn't really anticipate trouble, but something told me to hold my gun."

"Glad you did."

"I think our being incognito at bars is over." She laughed.

He nodded as they reached his car. He opened the door for her as she slid into the passenger seat. He got in and cranked the motor, turned on the heat.

"Let's sit a minute. We'll warm up." He took a deep breath. "We made a start. Someone else will need to check the bars."

"Maybe." She exhaled to relax. "We can grill those guys tomorrow. We're not working, but let's go to the city jail."

"Sure. Could be a warning. A group of girls and their thugs sending a warning."

"Well, we sent one, too, didn't we?"

"We did." Jude looked over at her and noticed for the first time how her profile glowed in the dim parking lot light.

"I'll call the sheriff." She turned to look at Jude looking at her.

Once Ben was on the phone, she gave a detailed description of events.

"Let me talk to him." Jude reached for the phone, and as they remained sitting in the parking lot, he spoke, informing Ben of Jackie being prepared.

"Good work." Ben complimented him. "Give me back to Jackie."

"Good work, Jackie. I'll see you all Monday. As I recall, you both actually have a weekend off."

"We do, but we'll go to the city jail tomorrow."

As she clicked off the phone, Jude drove out of the parking lot. More people had left the bar and gotten into their cars. Some alone, some in twos.

Jackie, back on the case, murmured, "If only we knew a bartender. It would be good to know what they look for, what really happens, including who waters drinks."

Jude laughed. "That would be the hardest information to get."

CHAPTER 29

December 2, 2023, Saturday

Corn left for silage often proved fertile grounds for scent, and today proved no exception. The fixture, small, abutted Beasley Hall, the new "old" estate Crawford Howard had built for himself and Marty, his wife, when they first moved to the area from Indiana. Later, when he bought Old Paradise, they considered moving to it after restoring a small outbuilding. Old Paradise itself, magnificent, allowed to fall into disrepair, would take a long time to bring back to glory. An outbuilding could be made livable quickly. They decided to stay where they were and keep Old Paradise as a historic estate for the enrichment of Virginia history. One of the great things about pots of money, proven by Crawford, hardly a subtle man, is one truly can do good deeds, spend chunks on history, endow hospitals, universities, etc.

Kingswood rested on the other side of a ridge, perhaps nine hundred feet high with Beasley Hall on the other side. A few other smaller estates—true farms, really—also were located on the "poor" side of the ridge.

Kingswood, a working farm, was well foxed. The day delighted everyone, for fox after fox would appear, disappear, run in circles, or dump the entire pack without anyone figuring out how the devil they did it. In two hours' time, they had pushed out four foxes, healthy, in lovely coats, and fast, fast, fast.

A brief break in the action gave horses, hounds, and humans a chance to catch their breath.

Sister patted Matador on his gleaming neck. Her youngest hunt horse, a Thoroughbred, at last, was coming into his own. He could still have a hot moment, but he was not bad-tempered and those high spirits delighted Sister, although she did realize she no longer thought quirky moments as funny as she once did. She could stick, but there were times when she felt some daylight under her saddle.

Weevil waited while his hounds drank from the creek. The day, cold, saw some icing on the borders of the water, but hounds had run hard, fast, and long. Most worked up a thirst. His hands were folded on Gunpowder's gray neck. Both Master and Huntsman rode grays today. A pretty sight, two staff members on matching horses. In the old days, some hunts had staff ride mounts of matching colors. The effect was beautiful.

Betty and Tootie also caught their breath.

A few snowflakes twirled down. Sister noticed but thought the light snow would enhance the hunting. They would soon stop, having been out for two and a half hours. Roads should be okay. No one likes to trailer in bad weather.

"All right, my lovelies," Weevil spoke to his pack.

"I'm ready." Dasher bragged a bit.

"So are we," the P youngsters sang out.

"Come along." Weevil walked toward an outbuilding at the base of the ridge. Stuffed full of good hay, nearing it even he could inhale the aroma. The back side of the building faced the northwest, which protected the hay from weather. The front of the building was open, making it easier to fetch the hay with a big tractor.

Also, it's cheaper to build a three-sided building than a four-sided one, where one has to contend with doors. Four sides does offer more protection, but three is good.

"Find your fox," Weevil directed them as they neared the hay shed.

Noses down, the pack fanned out. Barmaid, mind maturing wonderfully well for such a young hound, immediately trotted to the front of the hay shed. Giorgio accompanied her. About one-fourth of the hay had already been used or sold.

A touch of alfalfa gave the hay a distinct odor—fabulous, really. The space between the large round bales was nonexistent. They were crammed in there, but Giorgio, taking a deep breath, moved to the edge of the stack. A small, clear tunnel became visible. Scent was strong.

"Is he in there?" Barmaid joined the older hound.

"No." Giorgio checked out the hay bales in the front, which he could reach. *"He's not alone, but they're all out."*

"Let's go outside and check all around the shed," Barmaid sensibly said.

The two hounds left the big shed, noses down, and began to walk along one wall, then the back wall.

"Got 'em," Giorgio called out, and the other hounds came to the spot.

All opened, ran a tight circle, ran another around the shed, then shot straight up the ridge.

Weevil looked for a way up. He didn't know Kingswood that well, as it was rarely hunted, being a small fixture.

"Follow me." Betty on Outlaw headed up a narrow but clear path. Weevil galloped to her; she adeptly moved to the side so he could pass to be behind his hounds. Tootie, down below, hurried to where she knew another path existed. She also knew once they reached the top of the ridge, they would be on Crawford's land, and one had to be careful.

Sister knew the fixture, so she followed behind Weevil and Betty by thirty yards. She had taken the precaution of calling Crawford, who was fine about Jefferson Hunt being on the other side of the ridge. If they crossed over, so be it, but like anyone with horses in the field, he didn't want them fired up. Which meant if the fox shot across one of the pastures, hounds would follow, as would Weevil and the two whippers-in. The field, on the other hand, couldn't go flying about. Bad enough that Weevil and staff would be doing it, but they might need to turn hounds or call them back.

On top of the ridge, hounds lost the scent. Frustrated, they searched.

Slowly, hounds began to walk down on the Beasley Hall side. Still nothing.

Pansy and Pickens moved back up to the top of the ridge. The other hounds kept searching on Crawford's side of the ridge. Sister, now on the ridge herself, thought the falling snow looked like a Currier and Ives print as it fell over Crawford's lovely estate. She could even see the two large boar statues on the pillars to the entrance, maybe a half mile away. The boar was the symbol of Warwick the Kingmaker, Crawford's hero.

"Here!" Pickens bellowed.

Within a minute, the pack blasted to the spot and then roared down the ridge on the Kingswood side, a relief to the Master but tough to negotiate, as the incline, steep, meant one had to lean back. Leaning forward puts more stress on one's horse, plus one misstep and your balance would be shot. So she leaned back, her feet forward, her thighs gripping. Matador, excited, wanted to run down the ridge. She restrained him with effort.

Once down, Matador leapt forward. Sister bobbled a moment

then settled. He was game, this boy. Hounds flew across the frosty meadows, sprinkled white, then through the silage, which was clunky footing, onto a farm road, then toward an old corncrib. Around that, more speaking, then off again straight they ran.

Sister breathed hard. Her eyes watered from the pace and the slight wind picking up. Snow, still light, allowed her to see, but the flakes, wet and cold, dotted her cheeks. Matador, in his element, wanted to catch Weevil. Her arms ached from trying to rate the young fellow.

Sister could hear hooves behind her.

A few people came off riding down the incline. Poor Bobby Franklin, with Second Flight, had to stop, as the fallen humans littered the path. Ever the gentlemen, Bobby and Ben Sidell dismounted to help everyone. The rest of Second Flight was furious, but that's hunting. Everyone could hear the hounds in rapturous cry.

Pookah, in front with his sister, followed the hot scent up to an old farm manager's cottage. A den opening appeared at the side of the small, decent clapboard house. Now all the hounds surrounded this, with the younger hounds digging.

"I know you're in there," Taz shouted.

"Drop dead," came the robust reply, which infuriated the hounds.

Weevil laughed when he heard the fox bark, as did Sister, who, thanks to Matador's speed, now stood fifteen feet away.

Blowing "Gone to Ground," Weevil dismounted, patted each head. He also surveyed the effects of the digging, decided it wasn't all that bad, no need to repair it, mounted back up, and pulled the hounds away from the site.

As he did so, the rest of First Flight thundered up. Sister pointed to the house, then rode by them as she followed her Huntsman.

Second Flight was straggling down from the ridge, having missed a good show. Everyone mounted reached the end. The two flights stopped for a moment. The mud, visible on the backs of some of Second Flight, gave testimony to the reason for the delay.

Sister rode up to Weevil. "It's been a splendid day. We've run hard and the ridge takes a toll. Let's pick up hounds, shall we?"

"Yes, Master." He smiled, as this had been one of the best days of a rickety Season.

However, with the change in temperature, oncoming winter, perhaps the rest of the Season would be good. One can always hope.

People rode back to their trailers.

Betty felt her legs burn a tiny bit when she dismounted. "Tootie, how's your leg?"

"I have two," Tootie teased her.

"Smart-ass." Betty laughed at her. "Are you sore?"

"A little bit. Going down that incline at speed took effort."

"Makes me feel so much better. It's not just that I'm getting old." Betty exhaled.

"I would never think that of you." Tootie meant that.

Freddie, in charge of today's breakfast, remarked to Alida, her best friend, "I think this will be a fast breakfast. We can use the three-sided hay shed, can't we? There's enough room."

Alida nodded. "We always used it in the past. It will be cold, but out of the wind."

People hurried, changed coats, grabbed heavier scarves, and met in the shed. Walter and Bobby already had tables set up and most people carried potluck dishes. Chairs and upturned buckets provided seating. A few people hurried back to their trailer tack rooms for folding chairs. Given the exertion, anything that could be eaten was. It all tasted good.

Betty smiled as she shoved a piece of spoon bread into her mouth. "Hunger is the best spice."

"Whoever said that had to be either a cook or a starving person." Kasmir smiled as he, too, sampled the spoon bread.

Everyone recounted the runs, the number of foxes, foxes so bold they showed themselves.

As the hasty breakfast was drawing to a close, Sister reminded everyone: "Next Saturday, Bull Run. You don't have to braid, but staff will. Up to you."

"Is Bull Run fancy?" Yvonne, who had little experience with other hunts, asked Tootie.

"Proper. But everyone knows people often don't have the time to braid or can't find people to hire. That's why, Mom, we only braid now for the four big hunts, like Opening Hunt."

"Ah." Yvonne considered this. "Too bad, isn't it, for it's such a stunning look."

"It is, but it's kind of like sidesaddle. Who can ride that way anymore? Those that can are fabulous. They take fences, too."

"I've never seen that. I would love to see it," Yvonne remarked.

"Maybe one of the ladies next Saturday will ride sidesaddle. Bull Run, Deep Run, Middleburg, Orange, Piedmont, and sometimes even Old Dominion might have a lady or two in the field, but there really are fewer and fewer sidesaddle ladies. I'm sure I forgot some hunts. I tried it once. You're locked in. It's not so bad, Mom, you could do it. But I couldn't help leaning toward my leg on the horse. Anyway, braided manes and tails, sidesaddles, men in weazlebelly. Glamour. So much glamour."

"Yes, I can see that." Yvonne then noticed, "Here come our wheel whips. Is there any food left?"

"Don't worry, Mom. I'll take them plates. You know Aunt Daniella won't want to come out in the cold." Tootie left her mother to fill plates for Kathleen and Aunt Daniella.

Snow began to fall thicker. People wisely decided to pack it up.

Aunt Daniella and Kathleen ate in the car. Sister came over to give them a recap of the day. Finally, everyone was loading up.

By the time Sister reached her truck and trailer, Betty had

loaded their horses, sat in the passenger seat, luxuriating in the warmth. The window had been open a crack. Betty quickly closed it.

Sister pulled off her coat, gloves, and scarf, then sat behind the wheel. "You turned on the motor, you smart thing."

"I wasn't going to sit here in the cold. I wore myself out today."

Sister sniffed deeply. "Betty, you had the window open a crack." She sniffed again.

"What."

"You had a cigarette."

A long silence followed this accusation.

"Betty."

"Well, I needed a pickup. I really did wear myself out."

"Since when did cigarettes give you energy? I thought they were supposed to relax you."

"Both. They do both for me. If I have a cigarette, sit while I smoke it, I'm ready for the next chore. Not that I'm smoking a lot."

"Right," came the sarcastic reply.

"Don't pick on me. I'm sensitive," came the response, accompanied by a soulful look.

"Yes, dear." Sister smiled, for much as she feared smoking's effect, maybe that nicotine gave Betty a buzz.

Then again, who was she to tell someone how to live?

"Hell of a hunt." Betty beamed.

"Was."

Jackie Anstine sat in her parents' living room. She usually visited them on Sunday. Her mother often cooked her something. For Mrs. Anstine, food was love. Jackie watched herself because she could eat herself into another size in no time if she stayed too long or too often at home. She loved her parents and they had the great good sense to give her a lot of space. No "When are you going to get married?" stuff.

"Dad, I felt like such a fool." She wanted her father's advice.

"You weren't in uniform." He crossed one leg over the other. "So the girl at the bar or someone who knew you could have identified you and Jude as officers not in uniform, off duty."

"Yeah." She sighed. "We couldn't help ourselves. We went down to the city prison today. The three guys had been sprung, their bail paid."

"Did you see who paid the bail?"

"Actually, Dad, I did. Jocelyn Jarvis. I read it upside down. I found his address, questioned his girlfriend, who said he was in Richmond for a few weeks on a big construction job. She didn't know anything about three friends in jail."

"You've done your homework."

"Dad, that's why I'm mad. I should have considered they might be bailed out early."

"Don't be too hard on yourself. You both were roughed up."

"I'm afraid they'll jump bail."

"Possible. Always possible."

"I wanted to question them. See if I could trip them up. Someone put them up to it, Dad. Otherwise, why would they follow us out and jump us? I figured if I could talk to them I might be able to piece together bits of information. We would grill them individually, of course." She looked mournfully at her dad. "I bet I'll never see them again."

CHAPTER 30

December 3, 2023, Sunday

"The late-afternoon sun paints everything with gold." Betty loved this time of day.

"Even the snow on the ground is gold." Sister walked briskly. "Thought today's sermon was interesting. Reverend Taliaferro touched so many subjects, things we think and do. Funny, I have a hard time calling her *Sally,* even though she says that's fine."

"I don't. Titles can be barriers. I really don't know, as I don't have a title, but you do."

"Master?" Sister thought about this. "*Master Equitum.* Used in ancient Rome. We know Masters' names. Henry VIII's Master of Horse was Browne. It's a title that is as deep in our history as the title *king.*" She switched the subject. "Are your feet cold?"

"No. These work boots have Thinsulate in them. Your old boots are good in the snow, you won't slip, but you have to wear more socks."

Sister glanced down at her old L.L. Bean boots. "I've had these for over forty years. There's a testimony to a product."

"So many things are made to fall apart. Hate it." A puff of condensation escaped Betty's lips. "I need this walk. Get the kinks out. At least I don't have to walk off stuffing myself at Sam and Gray's."

"Thought I'd give them a break. They always have us over after church. Maybe I'll do that next Sunday."

"I should do it. You've had some hunt breakfasts and I haven't done a thing."

"Nobody expects you to do that. You're staff. The only way you and Bobby could host a breakfast would be to have it catered, and that can cost."

"Yeah, but once a year, not so bad. Can you believe we've walked this far?"

Sister looked toward the end of her property, near the two-lane state highway. "We're almost to the covered bridge. Sometimes I get talking or thinking and forget to pay attention. I paid attention to the sermon today on the Feast Day of Saint Francis Xavier, S.J. Got me thinking of missionary work. And the gospel reading is odd, to me anyway. Mark 13:33–37."

" 'Be alert! You do not know when the time will come.' " Betty had great recall. "Well, that's clear enough. The rest of it, oh, I don't know. Telling you about traveling abroad or leaving home but then be alert. I get that part."

"Maybe it's about trust." Sister kicked up a bit of fluffy snow, not deep. "Today is the day for people with disabilities. I sometimes think about that. If my son had survived the tractor accident, I think he would have been disabled for life. His neck was snapped, but what if his spinal cord was broken but he had lived? Would it have been a life?"

"There's no way to know. It sounds cruel but, Sister, sometimes death is a gift. Then I think about that torn-apart corpse at Bishop's Gate. That couldn't have been a gift."

"No. But when we think of severe harm or long, lingering, painful diseases, yes, a swift end is a gift. But I can't say I was thinking about RayRay at today's sermon. I was thinking about the Society of Jesus and missionary work. You have to have guts to do that."

"Saint Francis Xavier traveled to Japan, India and in the middle of the 1500s. Can you imagine walking, riding a donkey for miles, years. Good Lord. And it's amazing that he wasn't killed. How many of those places had seen a European?"

"Guts. You know what will be a bit of fun? When Father Mancusco and Reverend Taliaferro hunt this Tuesday, they'll compare sermons. It was the first Sunday of Advent. They'll have to talk about it. Those two are a blessing, really." Sister smiled.

"Maybe we can get Sally to give a sermon for Saint Roch on August 16." Betty thought ahead.

"Let's survive Christmas first." Sister had put on three pairs of socks, the first being silk, so her feet were holding up.

"I love Christmas. All the lights. The fragrance of the tree. I can't bear fake trees."

"It's easier for people, but I like a real one, too. Anyway, I never tire of Reverend Taliaferro's sermons. And in the old days, I quite liked politicians' speeches. So many were hopeful, correctly citing history. I felt I was learning something."

"Those days are gone." Betty frowned. "Well, want to turn around when we hit the covered bridge?"

"Yes, but I wouldn't mind sitting for a moment once inside. That little guardrail is about my butt size."

"Well, not mine." Betty giggled.

Sister returned to the sermon. "We both believe in the saints. I draw comfort from their lives and maybe someday the Rev. will focus on Saint Roch, the patron saint of dogs." Sister was back to Betty's idea. "Saint Roch was saved by a hunting dog who found him starving and wounded. Why he was wounded, I don't know, but the hound brought him bread every day and licked his wounds. Middle of the fourteenth century. I truly believe a hound did that."

"Me too. Here we are in the twenty-first century, where people live to disprove any form of faith, disparage the emotions and intelligence of other living creatures. We're living through an ugly time. Ugly," Betty emphasized.

"Maybe there was always uproar, personal attacks. And if we were in the fourteenth century, we'd be fighting over land and infidels. You get to kill people who aren't Christian. Remember, two popes at one time. The fourteenth century. Confusing."

Betty listened to their footsteps as they walked into the covered bridge leading to After All. "Blocks the wind. Not a strong wind, but wind wears me out."

"Me too." Sister, grateful, sat on the ledge.

Quiet for a few moments, Sister looked along the bridge. "What's that?"

Betty turned to look in the direction as Sister pointed to the After All end of the bridge. "Looks like a bag of some sort. I'll get it."

She walked down, lifted up a mid-sized leather bag, which was scuffed, then walked it back and opened it. "Huh?"

Sister peered into the bag. "Looks stuck."

"It's kind of wedged in the corner at the bottom, this little box." Betty worked at it, finally freeing it.

"A little squished on the one side," Sister noted as Betty wiggled the top off. "What the hell?"

Betty pulled out an Omega watch; one side of the bracelet crushed, but the watch itself looked fine.

"A popular watch. Nothing like the Rolex, but not cheap. Why would there be a watch here?"

"I have no idea." Betty handed the watch to Sister.

"Two watches. It could be a coincidence." Sister's eyebrows raised.

"Could. But if someone knew Soldier Road, it is more than possible they know this state road and the turnoff to After All. Everyone knows about the covered bridge. They're forever taking pictures."

"Betty, could a watch be a symbol?" Sister's mind tried to think of symbols a watch might represent.

"Sure. Time. 'Be alert! You do not know when the time will come.'" Betty repeated St. Francis of Xavier's quote.

Sister dropped the watch back into the bag. "Uncanny. That quote, and now we find another watch. Apart from telling the time, they cost money. At least this one cost a few thousand. The Rolex cost a lot more." She turned the bag inside out. A faded initial, "J," was written on the bottom inside.

"What?"

Sister handed Betty the bag. She could just make out the initial, J.

"His or her watch?" Sister said.

"Probably his but can't be certain. You wear a man's watch."

"Betty, why toss them? Or drop them or whatever? If something is valuable, you hang on to it or hide it somewhere you can access later. A bag inside the covered bridge doesn't count as hiding."

Betty agreed. "No, it doesn't. But whoever J is didn't care. Maybe he or she was afraid. They were in our hunt territory. Wonder if they knew that. I hate this. I want answers."

Sister put her hands on her thighs, then stood up. "We need to find a watch collector and we need to give this to Ben. An Omega is even more expensive than a Rolex. We certainly can't keep this one."

"So whatever this is about, that person or persons knows our area and both watches were disposed of in a hurry."

Sister stated, "Whoever did this wasn't worried about this bag being found."

As the two women walked back to Roughneck Farm, Ben, who worked this Sunday, was called into the morgue by Peter Bamberg.

"Same MO as Trevor Goodall." Peter pointed to the head wound on the young man on the slab. "Close to the same spot where Trevor was dumped, too. Found early this morning."

"So it was in the county, not the city." Ben needed to be careful about jurisdiction.

"He had his driver's license, his wallet, no money in it."

"Other than the bullet's entrance and exit of his head, it doesn't appear he was beat up."

"No. No ring, watch, necklace. Sometimes gang members will have a symbol on their necklace or a tattoo. Nothing."

"No one has called in concerning a missing person?" Ben noted the driver's license. "Twenty-nine. Trevor Goodall."

"Jocelyn Jarvis." Peter noted his name on the driver's license. "I checked. No record. I wanted you to see the body. I never think a photograph conveys as much information." He turned over the corpse's hand. "Rough. Hard labor. Maybe farmwork. Construction. He's in good shape. Whoever killed him either wanted him known, hence the driver's license, or didn't care."

"Right." Ben now had no doubt this murder was tied to Trevor's murder. "Peter, two murders close in time, two fairly young men. Jarvis was a bit older. Thirty-two." He looked at Peter. "My worry now is, will there be a third?"

CHAPTER 31

December 4, 2023, Monday

The news pronounced a possible serial killer, since two men had been killed and dumped in the same fashion, plus a corpse had been found at Bishop's Gate. Ben's office was besieged.

Jarvis's family lived in Charlottesville, he had graduated from Western Albemarle High, a promising football player who lasted two years at Clemson then left.

His parents, who had been questioned by Ben, had no idea why anyone would kill him. His mother insisted he worked construction jobs, other odd jobs to make money. He didn't talk much about his work. Her one fear was that he would turn into an alcoholic since he spent a lot of time in bars.

The department was on this. Detectives visited the bars his mother mentioned. Others questioned his high school friends still in the area, as well as his girlfriend, who was devastated.

The sun was dipping toward the horizon. Ben, Jude, and Jackie gathered in his office before leaving for the day.

"Clean record," Jude remarked.

Jackie had questioned Jocelyn's girlfriend, again being best suited for that job. "He and his girlfriend, Tommi, shared the rent. She said he never missed paying his half. He'd been tied down by the Richmond job. They were hoping to be together next weekend. She was in shock, really. I'll go back after the funeral. She should be better able to recall things. All she could do was sob."

"Apartment?" Jude asked.

"Over a garage in Ivy. Very nice. She works at Barnes and Noble in Barracks Road Shopping Center. What about you?" Jackie looked at Jude.

"A few of the bartenders recognized him. Got along. Nothing unusual. So they said. I asked was he dealing in contraband? Didn't have to be drugs? Everyone said no, which I would expect but apart from the people being surprised at his violent death, I didn't get the sense that whatever this was about, they were or are in on it. There'd be more twitching, I think."

"Possibly." Ben looked at his phone, lit up.

"I went to the precinct. He had bailed out our attackers. Then disappeared for a bit. Maybe he just stayed over the garage in Ivy. I keep coming up with zero. As to the three who attacked us, who Jarvis got out, paid their bail, no one knows them or admits it. Gone. Those guys are gone. And it seemed our victim was gone. Someone had to know where he was."

"My first call today was Birdie Goodall. She was composed but angry, maybe a bit frightened. She did know Jocelyn. Not well, but once or twice he accompanied Trevor when Trevor came by, either to mooch for money or he was in the money and had brought a present for Birdie to make up. She swore he really did pay back everything he had borrowed over the years. That's important to her, obviously."

"Does she believe those monies came from his jobs?" Jude was doubtful.

"I didn't ask. Whatever she believes isn't going to help us find his killer. I've gone over with her Trevor's jobs, various apartments, old cars he bought, the small facts of his life. She once again alluded to the fact that he had no steady girlfriend. She felt if he had, he would have settled down. In her words, he was 'unmoored.'"

"Jarvis owned an old Outback. That was about it." Ben had gotten information from the Department of Motor Vehicles. "So he wasn't throwing money around to impress girls."

Jackie shrugged. "The three men he freed might still be around. Maybe we can find them. We have their mug shots."

"Good idea." Jude nodded. "Two victims are identified. The woman, nothing. It's a terrible statistic how many murdered women are never identified, or worse, are missing and never found." Ben once again glanced at the phone.

"Nothing connects that victim to the other two." Jackie then said, "But it's not impossible. All three bodies were dumped. Two literally dumped. Hers was somewhat hidden. But they were probably passengers in someone's vehicle. We have the old delivery truck."

"If you blow somebody's brains out, part of their skull flies off the head, so brains and maybe a car window shatter when the bullet leaves the head. Could have gone through the car window." Jude kept trying to piece together things, but it was conjecture.

However, that was all they had.

"It's possible neither man was shot in a vehicle. They could have been shot elsewhere, put in the car, then pushed out. That might leave some blood and skull fragments. But it's also possible our driver pulled to the side of the road, put on the brakes, opened the passenger door or told the victim to do so, shot him, pushed him out." Jackie tried to picture it. "And even if a window was shattered, if this is some sort of organization, they would have someone to clean up a mess. But I think whoever is behind this is smart."

Ben checked his watch. "Let's meet here tomorrow. We can drive to where the male victims were dumped. Forensics have gone all over that. But let's have the three of us look and then, to satisfy curiosity, let's go back to Bishop's Gate in the afternoon."

As they left, Ben picked up his phone to make a call before getting all his messages. "Sister."

"Ben. I know you must be swamped. I am so sorry there's been another murder like Trevor's."

"The department is doing everything they can. I'm calling you because I was going to lead Second Flight tomorrow and I can't. I'm sorry to leave you with a slot to fill."

"Don't give it a second thought."

"And I have a request. I'm going to be at Bishop's Gate tomorrow with Jackie and Jude. Do you think you could meet us there if we showed up say at two?"

"Of course. Would you like other staff members there? We know the territory."

"Betty. You and Betty know it the best."

"Two o'clock."

CHAPTER 32

December 5, 2023, Tuesday

Every time anyone picked up their foot, you could hear a slurp, as the footing turned to mud. A welcome warming trend that started Monday night made a day in the high forties feel balmy.

Sister, Betty, Ben, Jude, and Jackie carefully walked through the graveyard. "The team does a good job." Ben noticed a tombstone with a small harp carved on it, dated 1819.

"Few people come back here unless we're hunting or they have an interest in the history of Catholicism in the county," Betty mentioned. "The action for this area, the real beauty, is back at the crossroads."

"It is beautiful," Ben agreed. "And the north and south roads are impressive. Chapel Cross West winds up at the mountains, but there is Old Paradise, which covers so much of that. But someone had to have known of this, and as I told you, there had been a disturbance at Beveridge Hundred."

"Back when the ground was too hard," Sister remembered.

"This would have been easy. Not many people. Not inviting." Betty shuddered to remember the site of the body.

"Like the abandoned truck. Not inviting," Sister added.

"But hunt people know the area," Ben declared.

"We do, but so do the deer hunters, the turkey hunters, bear. I wouldn't say Bishop's Gate was overrun, but occasionally during hunt season we'll bump into someone."

"Are they poaching? I should know that." Ben smiled.

"Not exactly. As you know, Yvonne bought all this to save it. She is Catholic. The history is important to her, but she hasn't set it off bounds to hunters. She hasn't owned it for that long. Two years, and most of her impressive energies have focused on Beveridge Hundred."

"I didn't know she was Catholic." Ben mused. "Not that I generally find out about people's religion, or lack thereof. Betty, when you rode back here, did you notice tire tracks?"

"No. I was too startled to think."

"It was still so dry. I did look. Whoever dispensed with the body literally covered their tracks, which had to have been easy, given the dryness," Ben told them.

Jude and Jackie carefully walked through the graveyard. They had done so after Forensics left. Sometimes a tiny thing can go undetected, a safety pin, a scrap of a gas receipt. Usually any piece of paper, cloth, Forensics found. Ben had great confidence in them.

"Come on. Let's go in the church. It's unlocked. I called Yvonne. She was fine with our being here." Sister led them to the front door, opened it to the clean, small vestibule. "Come on. Jude, pick up a few logs. Jackie, grab some papers. It's warming up a bit, but it will be raw in here."

The two did so, built a fire in the potbellied stove. Warmed up quickly, as those old Franklin stoves really threw out the heat.

They sat in pews. Jude and Jackie were in the corner of one, while

Sister, Betty, and Ben sat in the corner of the other, the glow from the stove illuminating everyone's face, for it was dark in the church.

"I assume you all crawled all over the church," Betty said.

"We did." Ben nodded. "They scoured the basement and Jude even went up in the belfry."

"I was surprised the bell is still there."

"Yvonne says if the church opens again, the first thing that will be done is the bell will ring to gather the faithful." Sister thought it a perfect idea.

"Clean. Even the basement is clean. No furnace obviously." Jude then added, "I went from up to down. Forensics had been all through it, but not the belfry. Funny. Guess they didn't think about it."

"*The Hunchback of Notre Dame.* How can anyone not think of a belfry?" Betty sounded astonished.

"Well, you find out who reads and who doesn't." Sister laughed, glad to be warming up, because although the mercury had slightly risen outside it remained cold, crept into one's bones. The temperatures outside hung in the low forties.

"I don't know if I'm allowed to ask, but any closer to finding the killer or killers?" Sister addressed Ben.

"We know a bit more, but I can't say we're closer. The two men, killed in the same manner, were killed by the same person, or the same organization. As to the woman left here, nothing to tie that murder in. That doesn't mean there isn't a tie, only that as of now nothing presents itself." Ben leaned back; even though the pew was hard, it felt good to lean back.

"May I ask, did the corpse have a watch on?" Betty then added, "Or any jewelry?"

"No," Ben replied. "Not a thing."

"What about Trevor and the other fellow, Jocelyn Jarvis? I think the news said his name was Jarvis?" Betty pushed a little more.

"No, nothing distinguishing on them, either. Why do you ask?"

Ben was amazed at how quickly the Franklin stove was warming their side of the church.

"Because jewelry is so personal. I believe it can tell you things about a person. Is someone wearing a pendant to ward off the evil eye? Is someone else wearing a cross? Stuff like that. And there's always signet rings."

"You're right," Jackie chimed in. "If I see what rings a woman is wearing, I have a bit of an idea about her personality. You know, is it showy? Is it a simple band with maybe one stone? Big stones or semi-precious. I always look."

Sister held out her hand. "Well, what do you see?"

"A plain gold wedding band and no engagement ring."

"Right. We hunted today and I don't wear my engagement ring."

"If the corpse had her jewelry, we might know more about her. I think everything was stripped off. Maybe that meant it was valuable." Jackie was thinking.

"True." Betty agreed with her. "Or if not valuable, something identifiable. Why leave her here? Why not leave her in a car or in an apartment? Why make the effort to put her body out here?"

"Maybe she was killed close by. It was easier to leave her here, especially if she was killed in the truck." Sister put that out there.

"She was killed in the truck. The DNA matches. Actually, she could have been killed elsewhere, then hauled in the truck." Ben stopped. "But given the blood splatter, it appears she was killed in a rage."

"And the truck was left on that rutted mess of a road." Sister watched the flames inside the Franklin stove.

The front had long rectangular openings, so one could see the fire inside.

"Wonder why whoever killed her didn't just leave the truck where it was, with the body?" Jude shrugged. "Putting the body here was a decent hiding place. Whoever did it didn't count on your hounds."

"If we hadn't picked up that line of scent, I doubt anyone would have known there was a body back here for another month. I added a month because we would be back at Tattenhall Station in a month and it would be possible to run a fox back this way. You never know." Sister looked at the stained-glass windows. "Too bad it isn't sunny. It's lovely to see the sun streaming through the windows. It's been strange weather." She looked from one face to another. "Actually, it's been strange period."

They sat in silence for a bit then Betty zipped open her work jacket, a heavy Carhartt coat. "Do you think the two men are revenge killings?"

"Maybe that depends on how you define *revenge*," Ben replied. "As both the victims were young, neither rich, revenge usually involves a love interest, a rejection. But neither seems to fit into those categories."

"Maybe they made loose money. Cash you pick up for doing illegal odds and ends." Jude, like Betty, opened his jacket.

"Could be they were stealing business. We've talked about that before." Jackie indicated Ben and Jude. "Let's say they were delivering illegal liquor. Maybe they stole a load or two."

"That's heavy stuff." Sister knew where to get a bottle or two of local waters—but then, most longtime residents did.

"Yeah. Be hard to hide, I would think," Jude replied.

"There's lighter things. Anything that can be melted down. Silver. Stuff like that. It seems to me that if you were selling a stolen anything you couldn't keep hitting up the same people." Betty then added, "So maybe what those two did was be part of a long-term operation. Something that wouldn't make the papers. That's why my first thought is always drugs. You never hear about it until someone is caught. If it's an auto theft ring, it would be reported each time there was a theft. But this doesn't look like drugs."

Ben enjoyed the warmth. "A crime that depends on fear, say fear of getting caught. Like you said, some crimes are reported while ongoing." He interrupted his train of thought. "You'd think most thieves fear getting caught, but many don't. They believe they are smarter than law enforcement or, sad to say, they've paid off some law enforcement people."

"Or law enforcement is in on the profits." Betty's wheels were turning. "I keep coming back to human trafficking, booze, maybe cigarettes, or jewelry, silver. People get a cut not to notice."

"True." Ben sighed.

"Well, you know it's not stolen vehicles. Right?" Betty asked.

"Right," Ben said. "There are stolen vehicles in the county, but not enough for someone to make a living off of it. Same with human trafficking. Someone would need international connections for that to be really profitable. Can you steal adolescents, Americans? You can, but photos are posted, missing person reports are filed. Yes, there are young women, mostly women, kidnapped or lured into prostitution here, but the big money is overseas women. We have no records of them. They can be smuggled across our borders, not just the border with Mexico but any state with a coastline where it's easy to land. And profitable as this is, I don't think that's what we're facing."

"Are most of those women Eastern European?" Betty wondered. "They are often so beautiful."

"The high-class girls?" Ben smiled, having seen a few through work. "They often have a sponsor. No need for a coastline. They sail through Customs, and the truly high-class girls, even if they don't know exactly what they are getting into, aren't kidnapped, blindfolded, or terrified. We get people from Africa, Asia, some from South America. Often the girls from South America will do anything to get out. It's a business." He exhaled. "Trafficking in human beings has been going on for thousands of years. Here it is the twenty-first century and we still can't stop it. But back to what may be driving the two murders, or even three. I think it's a steady flow of income.

"If the victims were in physical danger, they would or someone would in time report that. So we don't have a victimless crime but we have one where a person is willing to endure it. Something simple, like stealing a few cartons from a store, cigarettes. If you took all of them, that would be a problem. If a few disappeared from time to time, not so much, especially if whoever is behind the counter is in on it. I don't think that's our crime. Not big enough. You need to haul truckloads of the stuff across the Mason–Dixon Line to make thousands, and you will make thousands."

"You mentioned tobacco? What if a bale of tobacco, I don't know the correct term, was driven up to, say, Philadelphia once a week? Not cigarettes, but cured tobacco. There have to be a lot of Cubans in a big city, people who grew up with tobacco. Maybe I should cite other people, but I think of Cubans because of cigars. If you got the tobacco to them, they could make cigarettes out of it. Roll them, pack them. Be even cheaper than stealing what's already made. Who would be looking for a huge load of tobacco?" Betty thought out loud.

"You could smell it." Sister smiled. "Smells wonderful."

"It's possible. Very profitable. You'd need men to lift the bales or a forklift. But it is possible." Jude was too young to remember the tobacco warehouses down in Richmond, by the James River.

"I keep waiting for a break," Ben confessed. "So often it's a tiny thing. But my hunch is that Trevor and Jarvis trafficked the same goods. I doubt they would be working for rival organizations because we would have seen more friction, more violence between two competing organizations. This was killing on the lower end. I think, my hunch is, this really is a warning. They may have known each other. Worked together. Now, if we can find what is 'bringing in the profits.'"

Sister reached over and touched Betty's forearm. "This may not bring in the profits but it is strange. When Clytemnestra and Orestes got out and were on my side of Soldier Road we were walking hounds up on the ridge. Anyway, Tootie and I left the hounds with Betty and Weevil to get those damn cows back to Foxglove Farm. I tripped and found a Submariner Rolex." She then went on to tell Ben, Jude, and Jackie how they had looked for ads for a lost watch, and why they didn't post an ad for a found one.

"And Sunday we found a scratched-up leather bag inside the Bancrofts' covered bridge. It had an Omega in it; the bracelet was damaged. What are the chances of finding two watches? One expensive and the other affordable but not cheap." Betty filled this in. "The leather bag had the initial J on it. We saved it for you."

Jude simply said, "Could be *J* for *Jarvis*."

"Gray has worn the Rolex to see if anyone recognizes it. Nobody's said anything. And we've all touched it; I mean Betty, Gray, and Tootie. As to the Omega, maybe you can pick up fingerprints. That isn't to say they would match anyone, say in the Hunt Club."

"Doesn't hurt to look. If someone has a record, like Trevor, slight though it was, we have his prints. A search for someone with no record can take weeks or months, but if those prints are registered, we'll eventually find out." Ben frowned. "That doesn't mean any prints belong to a thief. But it is strange. Two watches. Tossed?"

"We don't know," Betty replied. "But they were found in odd places. My belief is the Rolex was tossed. As to the bag, who knows, but why there?"

Betty offered, "Once back at Sister's I can give you the bag and watch. I dropped it in the Bronco."

"Well, do we need to douse this fire?" Ben looked at the wood-burning stove.

"No, it's been allowed to burn out for over two centuries." Betty stood up. "Fading, but still throwing off warmth. Can you imagine getting up throughout the night to feed the fire when that was your only heat source? I hope people took turns."

"I hope they had hard wood. Lasts longer." Sister stood also.

After Ben, Jude, and Jackie left in the department SUV from Sister's, Betty and Sister sat at the kitchen table.

Raleigh, Rooster, Golly, and presumably J. Edgar, were happy to see them. Everyone got treats.

"I don't know if I'll ever want to be at Bishop's Gate." Betty rested her chin on her palm.

"I can understand that. I've been thinking that maybe Wolverhampton was useful to someone transporting stuff. No one was living there. Now it's open for reconstruction. No longer useful. How do we know someone wasn't actually living there? Who would know? It's far back. Just a thought. It's possible it was used to store whatever is making an illegal profit."

"We'd know. Too many trucks going in and out." Betty was positive about that.

"Maybe not. It's a private location. You can't see it from Chapel Cross Road North, the driveway back is a good mile. Anything could be going in and out especially if the goods weren't heavy. Maybe all you'd need would be one truck from time to time."

"People from Close Shave would see the smoke if a fire was built." Betty was sure about that.

"Again, if deliveries or pickups were irregular, you wouldn't need anything. We have no signs it was in use, but any hidden back houses or barns could harbor goods."

Betty looked at Sister. "True."

Sister suggested, "We should call Ben tomorrow and tell him to ask Veronica if he and his team can go over to Wolverhampton. It's possible there might be odd bits of evidence."

"That will really freak her out," Betty predicted. "If there was contraband there, that doesn't mean he'll find out who is behind it. We should go to Wolverhampton to see how the work has progressed, because we are interested if it is for sale. Better us first than Ben and his team."

CHAPTER 33

December 7, 2023, Thursday

Looking westward, the land resembled an accordion, long raised ridges close together, little vales between them. Viewing eastward, this unrolled enough to provide some good galloping country. The westward ridges had trees, brush on the sides and more at the top. This provided good cover if one could negotiate it. Heading east, the woods, less thick, still offered decent living conditions for foxes, gophers, weasels, and den dwellers.

This is called Billy Goat land in Virginia, and indeed that was the name of the fixture, a new one. The club spent part of the summer learning trails, building jumps in the fence line of the two pastures. The owners, from Chicago . . . Yvonne's stomping ground, knew little about farming. They bought the place for its impressive views of the mountains, plus there were two big pastures for two horses that they had. The jumps in each fence line were simple coops thrown up hastily. In time perhaps the club would do more, but this was a start.

Sister looked over the land, remembering where they had cut

trails. No main highways meant hunting without much concern, although she still needed her wheel whip.

Billy Goat would test you to see if you were tight in the tack.

Behind Sister, some forty people waited for the first cast. Numbers were climbing as the Season progressed. Forty was a good number for a weekday. Christmas either pumped up the fields or decimated them. Sister had a feeling this December would pump up the fields. Sport increased thanks to the fact that the male fox was looking for a mate. Like so many mammals, the males had to search. Then they had to impress the female. Sister had seen vixens with three male foxes sitting by her den, hoping to win her favor. In theory, mating should be easy. In fact, it took time, effort, and determination for males.

Those thoughts crossed Sister's mind fleetingly. What so often mystified her was why young women didn't realize they controlled mating. "Don't sell yourself short." Her mother had said that so many times. Irritated her. But the years proved her mother's wisdom. Don't sell yourself short. Look them over. Vixens certainly did.

The house, Federal, painted brick, a crisp white with Charleston green shutters, suited this place. The barn, new, was also made out of brick. Unusual but fit perfectly.

The owners had come out to greet them all then ducked back in, as the temperature hovered at forty degrees with four-mile-an-hour winds. Not terribly cold, but you needed layers.

She nodded to Weevil, who picked up his horn, gave a toot, then headed east. The field rode outside the fences, as Weevil headed for woods on the east side of the pastures.

Once there, he urged his hounds "Lieu in."

Eyes bright, tails up, they surged into the woods. A variety of competing scents assailed their nostrils: rabbit, gopher, deer, and cur dogs. Pushing forward, Tinsel snuffled, feathered. Sister noticed the young hound's tail slowly wag. Pansy came over, as did Audrey.

"Red," Pansy opened.

The pack, now running, sang out. The faster they ran, the less they sang.

The fox was close.

The speed woke up everyone, surprised at getting on terms with their quarry this fast on a new fixture.

The trail in the woods had been cut wide enough for a tractor, so no one was hitting low-hanging branches. They skidded to a stop. Hounds lost scent, then Aero hollered and the field reversed.

They now barreled back the way they came.

Sister knew they were close to their fox but she didn't see him. If she took the fence up ahead, in the fence line they would save a few steps, a bit of time, but those horses were not accustomed to hunting. A pasture full of flying horses could set off even veteran horses. And what if they jumped out to be with the field?

Sister headed to the outside of the fence line, followed it. Weevil, up ahead, had made the same judgment concerning the horses in the pasture. As it was, they were running about, snorting and bucking.

On the other side, the scorching run skidded down the side of a low forested ridge. The flatland between the ridges was a half a football field at the most, so they tore across that, only to climb up the far side.

Fortunately, the club had carved out trails up and down each ridge as well as along the top. Quite a lot of work, but if hounds ran along the top of a ridge then shot down, there would be no getting down for the riders. Sister watched as hounds veered off the trail.

She listened. She walked down the trail to the flatter land below.

She couldn't see Weevil, her whippers-in, or the hounds, but she heard them. They were maybe three hundred yards away, in thick cover. Four hundred at most for the sound was loud. The fox was shooting through the woods, racing through the vales.

The third ridge was higher. Sister trotted up, listening intently, reached the top, and saw the hounds now in the farther vale, following a creek bed, coming back in her direction, as was Weevil. Betty was on the ridge in front of Sister and Tootie was on the ridge behind. Weevil was right behind his hounds—who, while speaking, were slowing. The fox had used the creek to foil his scent.

A thick tree trunk had fallen over the creek, probably years ago. The weight of the trunk had kept it from being washed away in the few floods of each year. A small creek could become a raging torrent, but the tree held fast, although some branches had been ripped off.

Zane, now on the tree trunk, nose down, walked with balance as he kept on the line. Soon the trunk had a file of hounds crossing it.

Once on the other side, they opened again. Sister found a decent crossing, so they all got over, messy but over.

Again, they ran flat out, climbed the other ridge, which was becoming tiring. Hounds ran along the top of the ridge, reversed, ran back then down. Betty, already ahead on the next ridge, looked down as hounds slowed, moved through the flatland below.

A mass of fallen small trees created a pile.

"He's in here," Dasher announced.

The trees were heavy enough, but hounds could wriggle under most of them, climb over others. In the middle of this was a den opening. There were others, but this was all hounds could get to. The fox was in there, and no way were hounds going to get him out. They boo-hooed, a few dug, but it was hopeless.

Weevil blew "Gone to Ground," praised everyone, then swung back up in the saddle. The prospect of going up and down those ridges was not appealing, but if they didn't find game, at least they could walk it.

Hounds reversed, as did the field, to begin the walk back. While it wasn't long, the ridges, if flat, would cover about six miles. Given the speed, the music, no one realized how much ground they had covered.

A slight breeze rattled the dried leaves on the trees. Sister often wondered, Why did some trees lose their leaves but others dried out? She noticed to her left four deer watching them go by. They stood wary, immobile, fascinated by the parade of humans and hounds. Horse scent got them. At once they bolted off.

A few of the youngest hounds started after them on Tootie's side. Tootie peeled away, got in front of the young ones, and cracked her whip. They stopped.

Barrister turned back, as did Barmaid, Bachelor. Jethro hesitated. Tootie called their names. They blinked then listened.

Sister watched. Tootie did what a whipper-in should do. As for the young hounds, this was part of learning. A hound is born to run something. It would run a little red Volkswagen if need be. So they must be trained on what is legitimate quarry. Most learn quickly, but occasionally, blood up, they want to run anything. Just run.

"What did you think you were doing?" Cora reprimanded them.

They didn't answer but the other hounds grumbled, a few gave the youngsters the stink eye. Humiliated, and chastised, they moved into the middle of the pack, silently walking back, heads a bit down.

Betty observed, smiled. "There's so much to learn when one is young, regardless of species."

"I know," Barmaid whimpered.

Back at the trailers, everyone got a cookie, even the four naughty ones. Weevil felt they'd been taught a good lesson. And he loved them.

Kathleen and Aunt Daniella pulled up. The trailers had some protection from wind thanks to a line of Leland cypress, which blocked the breeze. The mercury was dipping. Cold. A good coat and scarf made standing around okay. As always, a few people brought out their folding chairs, others had old blankets they draped over their legs. The breakfast was pleasant.

Walter, off for the day, readily sank into a folding chair, plate in hand, after he had served Aunt Daniella while Sam took a plate to Kathleen, who decided to stay in the car with the older woman. Then Sam sat next to Yvonne. A few people left early, but twenty-four stayed, a goodly number. Lots of people to talk to. Those who knew hunting brought up the deer lesson. Others discussed Sunday's upcoming hunt in Bull Run territory.

Bobby checked the drinks then he sat next to Betty. The staff, usually scattered among the people, sat together today; not by de-sign, it just happened that way. Kasmir, Alida, Freddie, and Ronnie pulled their chairs up to staff.

"I hired Birdie back," Walter told them. "Really, the office needs her, and she needs to work, keep herself busy. It's good to be needed."

Betty, hungry, as always, said, "Did you have to convince her to come back?"

"No. She was glad of it," Walter replied.

Alida, who liked Birdie, most people did, said, "I would think her life would be better, maybe not happy but better, if Trevor's mur-derer could be found."

"Maybe it's a comfort to know, but it's a cold comfort." Kasmir sighed. "But if you don't know, you might wonder if you're on the list."

"That's an awful thought," Freddie said.

"It is but it's, well, most people would wonder." Sam agreed with Kasmir.

"We aren't going to solve it," Alida said with conviction. "But I bet we are all more vigilant than before. Or aware that no matter who you are or where you are, anything can happen."

"Yes, but that means anything good can happen as well." Sister smiled, changed the subject. "Veronica hasn't made up her mind about Wolverhampton. Maybe she will restore it. She certainly has the team. Were we to buy it, we couldn't afford to restore it as cheaply as she and her sister can." She paused. "I mean, should we form a syndicate to buy it?"

As this was the first time many of the group had heard this idea, a buzz started. Sister was heartily sorry she let it slip before true fund-raising was in progress. Everyone was talking at once.

Finally, Yvonne threw out, "We'll see Veronica and Sheila on Sunday. Let's call for permission, and those of us who are interested can go through Wolverhampton Friday. Tomorrow. That will give us all ideas. Maybe the Sherwoods will get ideas, too."

Everyone looked at Yvonne.

Sam smiled briefly. "See how smart she is?"

Once back home, horses groomed, blankets on, and tack cleaned—as Weevil and Tootie cared for the hounds—Sister and Betty batted Yvonne's idea around.

"I'll call Kathleen; she'll give me Veronica's number. I'll phone you with what she says."

Veronica, once reached, agreed to a group going through the big place tomorrow. She thought if she decided to sell—Sheila was pushing for that—a buyer might be in the group. Sister did not mention the word *syndicate*. She could hear Sheila in the background telling her sister to make sure all the fireplaces on the first floor of Wolverhampton would be in use, keep things warm.

After that call, Sister called Betty. They used the old phone-tree model. Everyone interested was contacted. They didn't want to email. Too public.

Tomorrow was going to be quite a day. Sister and Betty wondered what they would find.

CHAPTER 34

December 8, 2023, Friday

A small group gathered at Wolverhampton, a fine mist rolling across the meadows, engulfing the house. Sister, Betty, Yvonne, Alida, Freddie, Kathleen, and Tootie stood in the impressive front hall, meticulously cleaned since Sister had last been at the house. A fire roared in the huge fireplace in the hall. In the dining room another fire kept that room warm.

"They were expecting us," Betty whispered.

"Good thing," Yvonne remarked as the foreman—or in this case, forewoman—met the group.

"Ladies, welcome. I'm Paula Nordhoof, foreman. I'll show you around then you can wander at will, if you choose." She swept her arm in a circle. "The foyer, grand. The flooring is marble, as you can see. Easy to clean. A simple checkerboard pattern, of the time. The downstairs is social, for entertainment. The private space, like the library, was open to guests but well, come on. We go directly to the dining room. You'll see that each room has a fireplace. No other way to heat in the early eighteen hundreds. As many of you know, this was wild at the time. Mostly unsettled."

The hunting women obediently walked from room to room, some empty but cleaned for showing. As they walked toward the kitchen, they encountered workers. Everyone was busy. If Sister happened to catch a woman's eye, the worker smiled, but there was no chat. The workers all seemed to be under thirty, all attractive. The hallway was cool, but each downstairs room had a big fireplace filled with good hard logs, burning slowly.

Alida lingered, as she and Kasmir both admired eighteenth-century architecture and furniture. She'd then scurry to catch up. Yvonne noticed the triple sash windows, very practical because you could use them as a door to get in and out if need be.

The library glowed. Paula stepped back so the small group could fit in; the room was large but not huge. No furniture was in there but Sister imagined two wing chairs or perhaps club chairs at a later time, a desk or a secretary, but she thought desk. Perhaps a chair or two along a wall. This room was dedicated to reading and writing.

"Miss Nordhoof," Kathleen addressed her. "Were the books here when Veronica bought the house?"

"I don't know." She looked at the floor-to-ceiling-filled shelves. "But it would be quite a job to pack them up and move them. I think books are the best decoration." She smiled.

Paula Nordhoof turned out to be an engaging guide. The second floor was cold, no fires in the bedrooms and the one communal room, which was a novelty. The rooms were large, each had a good view back or front. The moldings were carved with a long, graceful wave.

Betty pointed it out to Sister. "Have you ever seen that?"

Sister shook her head. "No. It's fabulous. We are so accustomed to dental molding. There are other kinds, but they are symmetrical. This is so different. Starts in one end and ends in the face of the wave. That's how I'd put it."

"When I get back home I'm going to have to research ceilings, moldings." Betty would do as she said, given her curiosity.

Climbing to the third floor, the temperature dropped even more.

"The rooms to the right of the stairway were for the men. To the left, the women. You'll notice doorways for each hall. In theory, the proprieties were kept as these were the servants' quarters."

They peeked into each room. A small fireplace in each one.

Freddie shivered. "Even with a fire, I bet when you came up from work, your water in the pitcher was frozen. You'd be dog-tired and need to start a fire. Those people were tough."

"Yes, they were," Paula agreed.

At the end of the hall there was a back stairway; across from the stairs were two larger rooms. Better rooms. Bigger fireplaces. One was for the mistress's ladies' maid and the other was for the woman who ran the house, given orders by the mistress. Some mistresses liked running a house and often those two women became like business partners. Others actually ran the place but deferred to the mistress as though she did. It worked.

This was explained but the small group knew that, because wealthy people on either side of the Mason–Dixon Line lived good lives, surrounded by people to run the estate, the houses, the stock, the horses, everything. They were worlds unto themselves, whether the Van Rensselaers in Albany, New York, or the grand Randolphs in the Tidewater. Both had slaves, although that word was rarely used on the estates. The country was built on unpaid labor, be it those captured after losing a war in Africa or those born female.

This was running through Sister's mind. If you had resources, you lived well regardless of century or where you lived. Was it easier now? Yes, but she thought people knew one another in more intimate ways than today.

She whispered this to Betty as they walked down the corridor; Yvonne lengthened her stride to catch up with them.

"I'll be glad to get down to the first floor." The great beauty wrapped her coat tighter, shoving her hands in her pockets. "Can you imagine getting up in the morning, the fire hot ashes if you're lucky, splashing ice cold water on your face, pulling on your clothes and shoes, trying to tie up your hair?"

"I bet they doubled up in the rooms, so your roommate could do your hair and vice versa." Alida, right behind, chipped in.

Freddie, with Alida, said, "What if you didn't like your roommate?"

"You suffered." Alida laughed.

"In silence?" Betty threw that out there.

"Well, who is to say? As far as I know, humans have always gossiped, although women are the only ones accused of it."

"When men do it, it's called news." Yvonne laughed, her footfall reverberating as they walked down the back curving stairs, finally winding up in the kitchen, where there was a fire in that original huge cooking fireplace.

Mary Willard-Brooks, all five feet of her, was in the kitchen.

"Mary, what are you doing back here?" Alida grinned at the firefighter who had helped Kasmir and her make sure the old chimneys and fireplaces, wood-burning stoves, were sound at Tattenhall Station.

"Checking out stuff like I did for you. The county is getting tougher about eighteenth- and nineteenth-century stoves, chimneys."

"As long as they don't try to stop usage. When the power goes out, my fireplace saves me," Alida jumped in.

"It's surprising how well our ancestors built anything having to do with fire. Don't worry, Alida, a lot of us will fight the good fight."

"It's space heaters that get you." Betty joined them. "Or people leave their gas stoves on for heat."

"I see far too much of that. Part of this," Mary stepped back so a woman with a two-by-four could pass, "is people can't afford more, even to clean old chimneys. We haven't come up with ways to help the poor. And the house burns down."

"That's true," Freddie agreed. "I'm hopeful about the small-housing push. Oops, everyone is leaving me. Good to see you, Mary."

Tootie stopped to warm herself for a moment. "Ah."

"You were born in Chicago. You hunt in the cold. Thought you could take it," Kathleen teased her; she much liked the young woman.

"I can take it but I don't like it. And remember, we can move when we're hunting. That helps. Oh, this feels good."

Paula pointed out the kitchen, the pantry, the back door, the walk to the summer kitchen. She gave a good tour.

Then she led them to the drawing room, not called a living room then. They pulled folding chairs around that stupendous fireplace with a Carrara marble surround and caryatids on each side of the open hearth. The chairs had been brought in, possibly just bought for the ladies. The Sherwoods wished them to have a pleasant tour.

Warmed by the fire, they chatted. Paula sat with them for a bit to answer questions.

Yvonne got to the point. "Miss Nordhoof—"

"Please call me Paula, I'm just the foreman."

"Paula, I live down at Beveridge Hundred, so my curiosity is high. Of course, I want good people to live here and I know that the Sherwood sisters are thinking of abandoning this restoration. Selling."

"I am not close to them. I mean, I work for them so I have some sense of them. The murder and the abandoned body have scared them."

"Understandable," Freddie piped up. "How long have you worked for them?"

"Three years now. Most of the work I've done is on well-built ranchers, one or two Federal homes. And I give the Sherwoods credit. The more I learned, the more responsibilities they gave me. But I am not privy to their thoughts. This is actually the largest project I have worked on. The skills of those original builders is astonishing. I don't know if we could reproduce it today. Wait, let me amend that. Yes, there are some construction companies that specialize in this type of work, but it is exorbitantly expensive. That's why I am excited to be on this job, to learn. I didn't know what *Federal* meant when I started. I did know a rancher." She smiled.

"Gives you another string to your bow," Tootie, usually so quiet, remarked.

Paula nodded. "The sisters gave me a chance. I will forever be grateful. I'd made a mess of my life. I wound up in a women's center for wild women, which is how I describe it. People in there had been sex workers, sold drugs, got hooked. Others were alcoholics. Some had children dumped with their parents. You get the idea. The Sherwoods support women's groups. They selected some of us to learn construction, others to learn accounting, stuff like that. Trades are good work. Could I go to work at one of those fancy restoration companies? Maybe, but I owe the Sherwoods more time and I like working with women. I'd have a hard time working for or with men who don't know as much as I do now but would tell me what to do."

Freddie smiled. "That seems to be a common problem."

Everyone laughed.

Sister changed the subject. "Speaking of men and women, do you know the story of the caryatids?" She pointed to the exquisitely carved figures at the fireplace.

"Greek." Freddie threw up her hands.

Sister laughed. "Well, that's a start. The city-state of Caryae sided with the Persians during the Greek versus Persian Wars. When the Greeks won, they killed all the men and sold the women into slavery. The caryatids are to remind us of the consequences of our actions, and wherever you find them, they are always beautiful women."

"Never ends, does it?" Alida sunk back into her chair.

"War?" Freddie asked.

"That and using other people for your own ends. You may not own their bodies but you circumscribe their lives to enhance yours," Alida answered.

"That's an interesting way to put it." Sister was processing, mind racing.

"I get confused," Betty confessed. "You aren't supposed to say *slaves* anymore, you're supposed to say *enslaved peoples*."

Yvonne, with authority, said, "I can answer that. Verbiage changes. It is a way to signify where you belong; it's also a way to free people. Remember, we're on my fighting territory. If I told you some of the absurd, insulting crap I dealt with modeling, you'd be surprised. Then again, maybe you wouldn't. It wasn't the other models. Yes, one or two were bitches, but it was the men, the agents, the photographers, and never forget the designers, most of whom didn't really like women. Otherwise, why make us look so absurd? Why make clothing that actually hurts to wear? Point one. Point two, saying 'enslaved peoples' gives us the people back. Using the word *slaves* denies that, denies that human aspect. *Slave* is a term like *blacksmith*. But here's the thing, it also wipes out the brutality of it. That's where I get confused, Betty. I fight with myself over what term is most accurate."

"Tootie, you're the youngest. What do you think?" Sister smiled at the woman she had grown to love in a maternal fashion, not that she was competing with Yvonne.

"Enslaved peoples? Like other words. All the gender stuff. Words can really hurt people."

"Better words than bullets or not getting a job." Freddie was not one to mince words. She might be canceled, but that wouldn't stop her.

"True." Paula surprised them. "Look, ladies, I was a sex worker. You know the words for that. Am I ashamed of what I did? Sometimes, but it was all I knew to live. I was so loaded on drugs, I couldn't learn anything. It took getting thrown into jail for me to realize I was destroying my life. If you call me a whore, I won't like it, but I won't deny it. Consider this: I think most of those people in Congress, in government, are whores. The big difference is, at least I provided a service."

A shocked silence followed this, and then the women roared. Everyone talked at once. Tootie, sweet thing that she was, sitting next to Paula, reached over and took her hand.

Sister sat there and couldn't remember a gathering like this. If nothing else, it was honest.

Paula, feeling warmly toward this group, stood up. "I've had such a good time showing you the house, but I'd better get back to work. It is unusually quiet in the kitchen. I can't hear much. Oh, feel free to visit the outbuildings. Nothing has been done to them yet. I know the Sherwoods intend to restore everything should they keep this place."

As she rose, the others rose with her, some offering their hand, others a hug. Then they sat back down, surprised at the talk. Some surprised with themselves.

Yvonne looked at Sister. "You're a white woman of a certain age. Lovely to look at, I might add, married to a Black man. Do you all ever talk about this stuff?"

"You have a good idea, since we usually spend dinners with Aunt Dan on Sundays and you are now keeping company with his brother. When we first got together, the gossip was both fierce and foolish. We talked more about it. Yvonne, I have known Gray since he was a teenager, so we knew a great deal about each other before the romance knocked us off our feet. But I will tell you all a little story. He had driven home from a consulting job in Washington early in our relationship, and he was furious. He was also tired, so this came out. He had gone to an expensive men's store and the salesman kept an eye on him, and one of the younger salesmen literally followed him. I mean, my beloved blew up when he came home. Said it happens a lot and he is sick of it, just sick of it. Of course, I felt for him. Here is a man who advises senators and a cabinet officer or two. I got him a scotch, took him to the library. He felt better after his drink. So I then said to him, 'Honey, I don't believe in parallel wrongs, but I have wanted to explode as you did.'

"He looked at me. 'Why? If someone has insulted you or put a hand on you, tell me. I will bust his provoking head.' You can understand why I am wildly in love with this man." She grinned. "I shook my head. 'No, honey, what drives me wild is when a man talks to my breasts and not me.'"

The others laughed in recognition.

"My poor husband couldn't help it. He stared at my upper assets. So I put my hand under his chin and lifted his face to my eyes. We both fell apart laughing. Then I kissed him."

Tootie, taking all this in, remarked, "There are a lot of ways to be, uh, diminished."

"Yes, there are," Betty agreed. "You can either address them on the spot or just keep going."

"Depends on the insult," Yvonne added.

That set them all off again. Those women sat there for an hour. Tootie got up to throw another log on the fire. When the group finally broke up, Betty, passing through the library, stopped for a moment, saw the spine of *Memoirs of a Fox-Hunting Man* by Siegfried Sassoon, published in 1929, illustrated. She couldn't help herself. She pulled it off the jammed shelf, slipping it in her coat. She told herself she would bring it back after rereading it, as it had been years.

Driving back to Sister's, they reviewed the house, the work that had been done, and the work still to be done. Once at the house, they went into the kitchen, rapturously greeted by two dogs, one cat, and one turtle, perhaps not rapturous but still a greeting.

Betty hung her coat on the chair back. Sister noticed the book in the large inside pocket.

"Betty, what did you do?"

Betty lifted it out. "I pinched it, but only for a short time. I'll take it back."

Sister took the book out of her hand. "You'll read it and drop ashes on it. This is a valuable first edition. I love Sassoon."

Betty grabbed it back. "I won't smoke when I read it."

"You are smoking."

"I am not smoking in bed." Betty raised her voice. Then she flipped open the volume, stopped. "What?"

Sister stepped next to her. "What the hell?"

In the middle of the volume, cut so it didn't show on the side, was a square not quite the size of a whole page.

Both women looked at each other, befuddled. Sister took the book again from Betty's hand. She rubbed her forefinger on the cut section, done with a sharp knife, done well. She breathed deeply. A look crossed her face. She handed Betty the book.

"I'll be right back."

"Are you okay?"

"I'm fine. Put on tea. I'll be right back. I have an idea."

Minutes later Sister strode into the kitchen. "Open the book."

Betty did, and Sister dropped in the Submariner Rolex.

Neither said a word. Both sat down until the tea kettle whistled.

Finally, Betty said, "This makes no sense."

"Betty, I'm afraid it does."

C H A P T E R 3 5

December 9, 2023, Saturday

Betty, the book covered by her hunt coat, which she held tight, asked Lynn Pirozzoli, parked close to Sister's trailer, if she knew Veronica Sherwood's trailer.

Casting her eyes over the fifty trailers, Lynn picked out the new black gooseneck with gold pinstripes, way down the line.

"There it is. She bought it from Blue Ridge Trailers. Hired a professional painter to put the gold pinstripe plus her farm's name, *Constance Hall.* Blue Ridge could have managed that." Lynn lifted her eyebrows. "It does look good." She glanced at Betty, who unbuckled one of the straps on her horse blankets. "Has that feel, doesn't it?"

"Snow." Betty helped slide the blanket off. "Thanks. I need to drop something off to a friend."

Lynn grinned. "Feels like it's going to be a good hunt."

Walking down the line of trailers, Betty intently looked ahead, hoping to catch sight of Veronica. She did. Veronica was on the passenger side of her trailer, removing her horse's blanket. Betty, carefully, reached the driver's side, quietly opened the door, placing *Memoirs of a Fox-Hunting Man* on the driver's seat, on top of gloves.

She didn't completely close the door, fearing Veronica would hear the latch catch. Then she ducked behind another trailer in a second row to hurry back.

Tying the lead rope on the trailer, Veronica walked around the trailer. As she opened the driver's slightly unlatched door, she thought she had completely closed it. She opened it to grab her fleece-lined gloves. Sassoon's book rested on the gloves.

As Betty returned to the Roughneck Farm trailer, Sister asked, "Where were you?"

"Put the Sassoon book on Veronica's driver's seat."

"Why the hell did you do that?" Sister's eyes widened.

"See if it shakes her up."

"Betty, that's nuts. Why would she show her hand if she is shipping out stolen goods?"

"Maybe she will. Maybe she won't. She might seem fine today. But maybe it will eat at her."

"You should have discussed this with me, Betty. Baiting people is not a good idea."

"That's why I didn't discuss it with you."

"Well, here's what I think." Sister stepped on the mounting block to swing her leg over Matador. "Dammit to hell is what I think."

When Veronica picked it up she thought it was a gift. There should be a note inside. She opened it to find the copy from Wolverhampton, a watch advertisement filling the cutout square.

Immobile for a moment, face livid, she shut the book. The only people at the house where books were kept were workwomen, except for the visit she approved from Sister, Betty, Yvonne, Tootie, Kathleen, Freddie, and Alida. Whoever lifted the book had to have come from that group.

She walked back to the good horse she had rented for the Season. He was sensible and, as she walked to her mounting block, stood still while she swung up. Everyone at the trailers stood on hard plastic mounting blocks, usually two big steps, to throw their leg over.

She knew, fury rising, that one or more of those women knew. She would figure it out. She was reasonably sure not all of them knew. No matter, she'd find her moment and take care of this. She patted her thick frock coat, feeling the small handgun nestled in the inside pocket. She had taken Aunt Daniella's advice, carrying the gun everywhere.

Low clouds, gray, added to the cold. At least it seemed that way as the large number of people smartly turned out waited for Tim Michel, the Bull Run huntsman, to cast the pack. Weevil rode with him, which was good of Tim to invite him.

Sister rode up with Adrianna, Lynn just behind them. Betty with Lynn. Mike Long, also a master, rode in front of the ladies. He knew the territory better than anyone.

A light snow began to fall, adding to the beauty of the setting, soft rolling hills, flattish pastures, well-tended fences and jumps.

Veronica rode with Kasmir and Alida, all near the front. Gray was close behind.

Some ninety people gathered for the joint meet, which met at the spectacular stable at Locust Hill, Mike and Betty Long's farm. The stable, new, looked as though it was a fine example of late–nineteenth century architecture.

Betty so rarely rode in the field, she thought this would be a nice diversion. Bull Run's staff graciously asked her if she wished to whip-in. Given their territory and hard riding, she took that as a compliment, plus she wanted the luxury of looking around.

Outlaw, braided, handsome, quietly stood. A few horses in the field fussed, but when one has that many people, horses, it's bound to happen.

Adrianna turned her head to identify the disturbance.

"One of your regulars?" Sister smiled, speaking low.

"Yes. I will never comprehend why people buy horses they can't ride."

Sister studied the offending duo. "Well, the horse is gorgeous, the rider, shall we say, a man of a certain age?"

"Exactly." Adrianna smiled weakly. "His steel gray horse does get him quite a lot of attention. Gray seems to attract people."

"My observation is, even if the horse is stunning, what happens when you dismount?"

Adrianna laughed.

Betty, next to Lynn, leaned closer. "Good coverts?"

"Terrific. Occasionally we'll pick up coyotes, but mostly we find red foxes. It's a large fixture, which helps. If we get the tennis court fox to run, it will be fast. He could turn to Cedar Mountain. The battle of Cedar Mountain was three high hills, not quite mountains. The valleys saw punishing fighting."

Sister turned her head toward Cedar Mountain. Dark shadows passed over it and the ridges as the clouds ranged from lighter gray to darker. Snow was falling there, too. She then looked to the west, the direction from which the weather was coming. The clouds were boiling black. She hoped this would hold off. They had an hour and a half—if not more, given the traffic—to get home. The weather apps predicted a few flurries, but this looked ominous.

The Huntsman blew hounds off after Adrianna nodded to him. They walked down a slight hill, soon onto an expansive pasture. The farm manager's house rested to their right. The farm manager was Mike's son-in-law, a man in the prime of life, who loved family, running cattle, and hunting deer.

As the field passed, three cats—Charlie, George, both orange, and Henri, a gray—shamelessly disported themselves in the windows. Hounds ignored them, which provoked them more.

Then again, Charlie, George, and Henri regarded the well-matched pack as lower life-forms.

Sister noticed as they walked by. She stifled a laugh.

As hounds worked, the wheel whip followed at a distance on the farm road. Within minutes he steered onto the pasture.

Also following by car, a quarter mile behind, were Kathleen, Aunt Daniella, and Sheila Sherwood, who volunteered to drive them. The Jefferson Hunt "girls," as they referred to themselves, didn't want to assume they could drive behind the Bull Run wheel whip. Adrianna at first was going to just let them do it, but Lynn advised her maybe not. The territory, seemingly so straightforward to them, might not seem so straightforward to guests, plus once off road they'd be jostled. They approached Sheila—who had an accommodating SUV, a big Range Rover—would she be willing to give up a day's hunting? As she didn't hunt that hard, she was happy to be of some service. Also, it kept her out of the cold.

Sheila was soon to be entertained by Aunt Daniella, but at this moment she was creeping along with Magnum and Baxter, also the passengers. Kathleen sat behind the front and the two dogs were with her, which was fine.

The two visitors had heard the history of the retired foxhound and Baxter. Baxter's Jack Russell chatter sometimes drove Magnum crazy, but at least starting off Baxter allowed himself to nestle in Kathleen's lap, so he actually shut up. The foxhound stared out the window, thrilled to watch the pack in silence. Sheila opened the window a crack so hounds could be heard.

"There is a line of oaks and some conifers, sort of a pasture divider but a good covert as it's never been parked out," Sheila explained. "You can see the creek, moving fast."

Parked out meant underbrush had been cleared out, pleasing to the eye but sure wiped out places for animals to create dens, deer to find those thick underbrush areas they could curl in, their weight smushing the stuff down. High grass could also make a decent sleeping area in the summers, but in winter deer wanted more cover. They slept with the heaviest part of the brush to the west. Their backs would be hard up on this. Birds lived in the rafters of the many outbuildings. Den dwellers, fox, gophers, chipmunks often made homes inside. Chipmunks rarely got credit for their homebuilding skills, but it worked for them as well.

The women discussed all this as they crept along.

"Bear?" Aunt Daniella asked.

"Cycles," Sheila simply replied. "Ah. There we go."

Baxter considered barking, but Kathleen's lap was too comfortable. Magnum listened intently. He knew this part of the fixture. The fox might run and cross Route 15 or he'd go northwest. Fortunately, he zoomed northwest.

The field snapped from a leisurely walk to a hard gallop. Matador, Sister's flea-bitten gray Thoroughbred, in the prime of life, surged forward. He, and all her horses, were accustomed to leading. She had to rate him, which irritated him, but he did it. Matador was smart enough to know he wasn't in his territory, plus Adrianna's horse would brook no interference.

Betty and Lynn, close behind, felt the snowflakes hit their faces. The slight sting was because they were moving so fast. They could still see clearly, the snow slanting slightly as it fell. Hounds in full cry stayed in view, thanks to the flatter land. So did the fox.

The music thrilled everyone. Up ahead, a coop loomed. Adrianna slid over, followed by Sister. The jump, three feet, was well placed, but generally in a field this large there were involuntary dismounts, even at the first jump. Not this time. A happy miracle. The fox was now out of view. He'd put on the afterburners.

Four strides from the coop, a huge field awaited. Sister didn't look behind her but often one could figure out what was happening by sounds. As she was a field master, she was sensitive to it, as was Adrianna. But it's not the field master's job to make sure all keep up. The person who rides tail takes care of this, and often it is someone with medical expertise. In this case, it was one of the vets who hunted with Bull Run.

Dr. Siski, early sixties, the vet, was still back trying to get a rider over the coop. He motioned for the rider on the horse that refused to come back. It was a newer member who wanted to just put his horse to the jump again. Fortunately, the next person in line in the field yelled at him to go to the rear. As the field was so big, there were still people at the jump. The good doctor rode up closer, called a name, and the offending rider did go back, stung that he was chastised by the lady who blew right by him. He started to sputter to Dr. Siski.

"Travis, she was right. You would have backed up the line. Look how many people are out today. If your horse had refused again, it would be worse than a foul-up. Now I'll give you a lead. If he doesn't go over, I'll jump back and we'll try again. We've got to catch up. Fortunately this jump, well," he thought quickly and decided to take another tack. "The Jefferson Hunt people can ride. They have some airy jumps. So their horses have seen everything. Okay," Dr. Siski looked, "we're just about ready. You follow me and give him a hard squeeze." Dr. Siski resisted saying Mike Long would blow through Madison County into Culpeper.

"Okay." Travis Yount realized he had been wrong, and his horse, like so many horses, would follow. He jumped a bit crooked, his hind end drifting to the right because the animal was still insecure about the coop, but he did it. Travis was smart enough to pat him on the neck and then he and Dr. Siski ran faster than he had ever galloped in his life. They had a lot of ground to make up. Even the rear of the big field was far in front of them, fast receding.

Betty and Lynn tucked right behind the two masters.

Veronica, too, was riding hard. This belied her saying she couldn't ride well. All Veronica's senses were on overdrive.

They covered two fast miles in what seemed like the batting of an eye. The field splashed through a creek then thundered into another wide-open pasture. This was bound on higher ground by thick woods. The fox turned up, hounds followed into those woods. The field paused, waiting as the music stopped. Hounds searched but the fox reached his den.

The pack arrived, some hounds digging furiously at the den entrance. The Huntsman threw a leg over, easily hopped off his horse, Weevil holding the reins. Tim blew "Gone to Ground." Then he praised hounds by name, swung back up.

"Not a bad start." Tim called his pack to him.

Weevil, big smile, replied, "I'd take that start anyday."

They trotted toward the lower pasture then pushed into a wider pasture, a small pond ahead, past the pond and into narrow woods, which offered some respite from the snow.

Again hounds hit. This time they moved deliberately, pushing the line. They were at Quiet Shade. Sister realized how much ground they had covered, to her surprise. A tidy log jump gave the field the way out. Matador slipped a bit on the other side, quickly regained his footing. The ground wasn't bad, but there would be more slips here and there. The snow wasn't piling; rather, it was sticking to the ground. If the snowfall intensified another hour, you wouldn't see the ground. The field got over. Second Flight was taking the gates, so they were behind. Bobby rode with them and helped with the gates. He was so used to it.

The Second Flight leader was happy to have someone with him. It's always so much easier if people know what they're doing. Fortunately, the person riding tail for Bull Run knew every inch of the territory, which also gave the masters relief.

"This farm, we're now on Quiet Shade, is well foxed. The way it sits though means the winds can rake it. You find and then you lose," Sheila informed them as she drove Aunt Daniella and Kathleen on the farm roads. They were relieved to be back on a dirt road.

"Thought you said you weren't much of a rider," Kathleen piped up from the back.

"I'm not really but I'm observant. I'm one of those people who has to learn as much as I can. My sister just plunges ahead. That's why she's been divorced three times."

"Really?" Aunt Daniella's eyebrows rose.

"Just plunges ahead."

"Were they handsome?" the older woman wondered.

Sheila slowed for Second Flight. "Uh, to her they were."

The three women laughed as Magnum said, *"Getting some speaking."*

"He's very interested," Kathleen remarked as the foxhound's ears swept forward.

"He's a big old hound. I'm the brains here," Baxter bragged.

"You're mental." Magnum lifted the corner of his lip.

As the two canines insulted each other, hounds found. This was a teasing line, a good opportunity for Weevil to see again how they handled. Any pack looks great in full cry. Noses down, the pack moved along, speaking but not full-throated singing. Their huntsman kept his mouth shut. No need to encourage them, they were intent. Weevil watched, impressed as the line heated up. So did the pack. They ran closely together. He envied that because Jefferson hounds could get strung out. Sister never wanted to retire a hound if it could go, even if falling to the rear. She said they were born for this, let them do it. Well, yes, but there's nothing as impressive as a pack of hounds running so closely you could throw a blanket over them, as the old foxhunting expression goes.

The speed picked up. Yvonne, Tootie, and Sam rode together. Gray, Kasmir, Alida, Veronica, and Freddie rode in front of them, the

Bull Run people allowing them to ride close to the front. Within a few minutes, they were flying yet again. At first, there were no jumps, the field was huge. Then a fence line appeared, a coop, then a depression between those pastures. You had to be alert. People were popping off like toast because they'd take their leg off. And the grade was steeper than one realized. Jumps appeared exactly where you'd need them.

Fortunately, most of the Jefferson Hunt visitors made it over the jumps but a few others did not. Siski had his hands full. They had covered a lot of territory. The Field of Buttons lay ahead. So many had died there that souvenir collectors still found uniform buttons from eight states.

They blasted from Quiet Shade to the Field of Buttons and were turning again. Sister, with a good sense of direction, knew they were heading back toward Locust Hill, traveling now on low ground, not high. She had no idea how far they were.

Sheila, behind the wheel whip, remarked, "It's so much easier on a farm road. Maybe a cow will be out, but better a cow than being on a state road with impatient drivers."

"More traffic than even ten years ago. Just keeps growing," Aunt Daniella added. "Like everything else, population growth brings some benefits, along with problems. I wish people who move here would realize this is Virginia. We're going to do it our way. You need to go along to get along."

A roar sent the wheel whip down the dirt road, heading straight ahead. "True," Kathleen agreed.

The wind picked up. Snow made that tic, tic, tic sound as it hit the branches. Cedar Mountain, in the near distance, glowed like a sugar loaf in the dimming light, almost noctilucent.

A brief trot, trees ahead, hounds circled then lost the line. Sister heard a click. Matador threw a shoe, grazing a smallish rock protruding from the soil.

"Dammit," she cursed under her breath.

Adrianna looked at her. "What?"

"Sorry. My voice carries. Matador just threw a shoe. I'll go back to the trailers. I can find the way."

"I'll go with you."

"Please don't. Really I can find the way. You lead the field with Brio." She smiled.

Veronica, now closer, having moved up bit by bit, saw the shoe fly off. She came up near Adrianna.

"Master, I'll take her back. I confess to being a little tired."

"Fine." Sister, passing Betty, informed her, "Threw a shoe. I'll be fine. Finish the hunt so you can tell me about it."

No sooner than the words were out of Sister's mouth than the hounds opened. Off they ran, full cry. Sister had no desire to ride back with Veronica. But she thought if she balked after what Betty had done, it might be awkward, or worse.

Sheila, on the road, heard the hounds, so she crept along toward the mountain. They lost sight of hounds and the field, but when they reappeared, Kathleen, sharp-eyed, noticed Sister was missing.

"We've lost Sister," Kathleen worried.

"Bet she's heading back to the trailers," Aunt Dan said. "If it were a problem, others would be with her. Well, might be a small problem. Broken tack. That sort of thing."

"Sheila, can you slow down? Maybe we'll see her, or better yet, go back to the trailers," Kathleen said.

"Let's wait a minute in case she appears at the end of Second Flight. Then we can head back. I'll go over the fields. Shorter."

"You all are right. Better safe than sorry," Aunt Daniella concurred.

The field passed them. No Sister. Sheila turned toward the farm road a quarter mile back.

"*Rats,*" Magnum grumbled.

As Sister and Veronica rode over the fields, a parked out woods up ahead, Veronica asked, "Who put the Sassoon in my truck?"

"Not me."

"But you know about it." A silence followed this. "How did you figure it out?"

"I'm not sure 1 did, but when I saw the space inside the book, well, it was perfect for a watch or jewelry. The book was still heavy enough, it would not arouse suspicion in case someone thought the carton light for books." Sister did not mention Betty's name, to protect her.

"Ride toward those trees," Veronica ordered Sister. The farm road appeared below them.

Sister turned. "No."

Veronica pulled out her gun. "Yes. Tell me as we walk, why did you put the book in my truck?"

"I didn't."

"But you knew about it.

"The book?"

"Yes." Sister honestly answered.

"You realized I'm making money by unusual means." Veronica smiled sardonically.

"I hoped not. The death of Trevor, Jocelyn, and the unidentified woman made a few of us nervous, curious. Betty and I found two watches, one was very expensive. The other is worth a few thousand. When Betty took the book, which she swore she would return, then opened it, one big piece of the puzzle fell into place. I give you credit, it's a brilliant idea."

"We thought we were safe, Sheila and I, until those idiots figured they could get away with stealing from us. When our profits dropped by about ten thousand a month, we knew, well, we knew."

"Ten thousand is a small sum." Sister flattered her as she looked for a way out.

"It's money. But you're right. Considering what we usually pull in per month, it's peanuts. That's how I knew they were idiots."

"You noticed less time on the job or maybe expensive purchases?"

"I gave those girls a way out of scrambling, halfway houses, being beaten by pimps. They could keep any cash from the sex work. The watches, rings, came to us. Not every girl in construction was a looker. I divided up the hours. The less-than-attractive worked more at the reconstruction. The pretty girls more or less worked half days."

"Pretty, as in what men found attractive?"

"Yes. If you think about it, my fortune depended on the stupidity of men. I couldn't lose." Veronica laughed.

Sister ignored the bragging. "How did you know it was Trevor and the other fellow?"

"Took time. They wanted more money, more salary. My first clue. Trevor especially became close to some of the girls. Those he liked he coached as to who had money. He was born and raised here. He was useful. Jocelyn learned from him, too."

"What about the dead woman?"

"I don't know anything about her," Veronica lied.

"So killing them was a warning. Were they blackmailing you, too?"

"No. I give them credit for that. The diminishing profits forced my hand."

"Why?"

"If they got away with it, others would do it."

"Ah."

"You've asked a lot of questions. I answered because I like you, but now you have endangered Sheila, too."

"Leave me alone."

"Can't."

"One last question, how big is your business?"

"The mid-Atlantic. We've trained women in other states as well, and take a small percentage of their profit. Small. Two percent."

"And you're safe?" Sister's eyebrows raised.

"Honor among thieves." Veronica shrugged.

They both moved closer to the trailers, a half mile away, just as Sheila and Aunt Daniella and Kathleen turned onto the farm road. The car followers couldn't see them yet, but would in a few minutes. If Sheila picked up speed, sooner than that.

Veronica dropped behind Sister, took her crop, and smashed it across Matador's hindquarters. He leapt forward. Sister easily stayed on, but then Veronica rode up behind hitting him again. He surged. A low-hanging branch loomed immediately ahead. Blinded by arrogance and rage, Veronica figured if the branch didn't crack open Sister's head, she could dismount and smack her with the butt of her gun. That would buy her some time.

Matador swerved as Sister held on, hanging on his side, her left leg over the saddle. She finally dropped off and heard something crack. Enraged that the good rider hadn't smashed her head to bits on the low-hanging branch, Veronica rode up slowly. She knew Sister was still alive. She would need to get closer, dismount, and finish her off.

Staggering to her feet, Sister dropped again as Matador galloped away. She faced Veronica riding toward her. Realizing Veronica was beyond reason, she stood to defend herself as best she could. She couldn't run. She'd try to fight if the red-faced woman got close enough.

As the Range Rover turned the bend on the farm road, they saw Matador flying without Sister. Sheila drove faster.

"Stop," Aunt Daniella called. "She's staggering up there. See?"

"She is. She's hurt." Kathleen then warned, "Veronica's riding her down."

"Stop. I told you to stop." Aunt Daniella opened her purse, pulling out her gun.

Sheila didn't stop, so Aunt Daniella shot through the driver's window, which shocked Sheila, who then stopped. Aunt Daniella opened the door, hopped out, steadied her arm as Veronica heard the shot, turning to see the car. Without a second's hesitation, Aunt Daniella fired a thirty-yard shot. Veronica slid out of the saddle; her horse stopped and stood still.

The dogs jumped out of Aunt Daniella's opened door as Magnum squeezed over the center console. Little Baxter was off and running.

Sheila, stunned, started moving again. Aunt Daniella swung around to shoot her through the open door. Sheila, hit in her right arm, took her hands off the steering wheel, her foot slipping off the gas.

"Kathleen, reach around the seat and pull her over!"

Kathleen leaned forward, wrapped her arms around the bothersome headrest, pulling Sheila, screaming louder, onto the center console so her body was falling away from the wheel.

Aunt Daniella left them to hurry as fast as she could go to Sister. Kathleen, too, got out of the car. Being quite a bit younger, she ran past Aunt Daniella, toward the fallen women.

"I'll save you!" Baxter shot past the humans, Magnum close behind.

Sister had fallen down to one knee.

Magnum reached Sister, licking her face. "You'll be all right."

Baxter ran to Veronica. "Dead." He took a deep inhale. "Fresh blood smells so good. Not much of it."

Moving to Sister struggling on one knee, the sturdy foxhound stood next to the shaken woman to help her balance. Baxter ran in circles around them.

"Slow down, you nit." Magnum noticed the two humans coming up, Kathleen in the lead.

Baxter rushed to Kathleen and Aunt Daniella. *"Follow me."*

Sister was grateful for Magnum's attention. Baxter was now doing laps around them.

Kathleen reached her. "Thank God." She put her hands under Sister's arms, lifting her up.

Sister leaned over to pet Magnum then sagged on Kathleen. Aunt Daniella reached them.

Sheila still had one good arm. She managed to get herself back in the seat as she drove away back down the road.

"She won't get far with that window," Kathleen remarked.

Baxter announced, *"There's a dead person."*

Magnum curled his lip. *"Come on. We need to get these people to a safe place."*

"We'll have to walk, or perhaps if I fire three times someone will come to us," Aunt Daniella said.

"I cracked my ribs. Maybe broke some." Sister gasped. "I can walk but it will be slow. I hear hounds."

"I'm not afraid of anything," the Jack Russell bragged.

Kathleen had checked Veronica. "Dead. That was one hell of a shot." She looked at Aunt Daniella.

"Remember when I told you to always keep a small pistol in your purse? You never know. When one is old or female or both, one is considered weak. Just pulling this gun out of my purse saved me a few times and saved a few others. Well, no matter. You'll heal, my dear."

Sister kissed her on the cheek. She couldn't stop shaking as snow fell more heavily.

"I expect you'll tell us what this is about?" Aunt Daniella put her arm around Sister's waist while Kathleen did the same on her other side. Slowly, they began walking. Magnum led the way. Baxter calmed down slightly.

"Uh." Sister took a few steps then straightened up. "Come on. I can do it. She would have killed me. Thank God you showed up when you did."

"The good Lord was with us." Aunt Daniella felt the crackle in Sister's ribs when she straightened up. "That has got to hurt. Feels like your ribs. Luckily they heal quickly."

"I'll remember that." Sister breathed hard.

As they walked, Sister explained the found watches and the altered book that led Betty and her to believe Veronica and Sheila were stealing then selling expensive jewelry and watches.

"So odd. They helped other women." Kathleen was shocked.

"They helped other women that they knew would be beholden to them, especially women with criminal records who were good-looking. Many people won't hire ex-cons."

"Given Veronica's divorces, maybe there was an element of revenge toward men." Kathleen stopped as Sister did.

"Who knows. People do crazy things. And they always believe they'll get away with it," Aunt Daniella said.

"I'll tell you, if Veronica were still alive I'd be tempted to take your gun, Aunt Dan, and shoot her dead." Sister gasped.

Hoofbeats diverted their attention. Matador, in the woods, heard their voices. He came toward them, limping slightly, onto the pasture then onto the road where the women were walking.

"My baby." Sister couldn't lift her hand to pat him. "Come along."

"*Go slow,*" Magnum ordered the horse. "*Baxter, don't nip at his heels.*"

"*I have to keep him in line,*" Baxter sassed.

"Kathleen, take his reins and throw them over his neck. Let's stop a moment." She looked at his hoof. "Dammit. He's okay, but a little bit of hoof went with the shoe."

"Sister, let's get you taken care of first. Matador will be fine," Aunt Daniella, in a firm voice, ordered.

"I can't hear hounds anymore." Kathleen strained to listen. "You can probably fire, Aunt Dan."

"No." It was Sister's turn to order. "Matador's been through enough. If you fire, he might run off again. Same with Veronica's horse, who's standing over there. That's a good horse. It will take us time, but once we get to the top of the far hill, someone may see us. In fact, the field might be coming back to the trailers."

Matador, his big brown eyes so kind, reached across Kathleen to nuzzle his rider.

"It's all right, baby. You are a good boy."

"It's like he knows." Kathleen was amazed.

"He does," Sister replied. "Think what Abdul knows about you? Why would your horse, in this case my horse, be any different? He knows I'm hurt and he was hit hard across the hindquarters. Veronica was hoping I'd lose my balance and a low-hanging branch up ahead would literally knock my block off. He swerved. It unseated me, but he saved me. Not every horse would swerve. So many people don't understand. Let me stop again. Catch my breath."

"How do you know the trailers are close?" Kathleen held on to her.

"They are," Magnum tried to reassure her.

"She leads the field. She has a good sense of direction." Aunt Daniella was tiring, too. She walked a mile each day, but not up hills.

"Apart from wanting a doctor or someone to put my ribs back into place. I think I separated them as well as cracked them; what I really want to know is how much money the Sherwoods made. I doubt we'll find out soon."

"Once Sheila gets caught or she wrecks, she might talk." Aunt Daniella watched Sister's breathing.

"Sheila saw Sister drop but she doesn't know Veronica is dead. Maybe she will talk." Kathleen thought about it.

"Now that I've seen the panic and, in Veronica's case, the fury, I believe they would do anything to protect their cash cow. But you know, she tried to make getting rid of me look like an accident. Failing that, she would have smashed out my brains, then hoped to figure a way out. Thank God for you, Aunt Dan."

Aunt Dan hugged her with the arm around her. "Fate."

They finally reached the top of the hill, the trailers in the distance. Hounds were coming in, from another direction easily seen in the distance.

"Let's stand here. Someone will notice," Sister advised. "Going down will be harder than going up."

"There is that," Aunt Daniella agreed.

As First Flight hove into view, the three waved their arms. Magnum and Baxter barked. Adrianna, noticing them, peeled off, galloping up. Once there she, being highly practical, told them to wait. She'd find a car to come get them. She rode back to find Mike Long. They both galloped toward the big stable. Adrianna yelled at Lynn to keep everyone walking.

Gray, dismounted, handed Cardinal Wolsey's reins over to Betty, then began running toward the figures in the distance. He could clearly see his wife being supported by his aunt and Kathleen.

Gray hopped into Mike's Land Cruiser, which appeared. As the two men reached Sister, Gray shot out of the car as Mike stopped, hurrying out as well.

Everyone talked at once.

Mike, calmly, with Gray's help, placed Sister in the passenger seat.

Lynn, who hopped in her own car, drove up to a very excited Baxter.

Sister let out a yelp. "I'm sorry."

"Honey, no apologies." Gray kissed her cheek. "I'll walk Matador back."

"I will. You stay with your wife," Lynn declared.

Gray hesitated a moment while Lynn got out of her car, took

Matador's reins, opened her car window, dropped the reins through. Then she climbed back in, intending to drive slowly as Matador walked with her.

Baxter leapt into Lynn's lap while Magnum stepped up into the backseat of the car. Gray closed the car door.

"Sit with me," Aunt Daniella told Gray.

Mike, a master himself, took charge.

Everyone filled Gray in at once, while Mike carefully drove on the old road, avoiding as many ruts and potholes as possible.

Back at the trailers, everyone rushed up, Walter in the lead. He asked Sister questions, leading her into his trailer, Gray and Betty also squeezing in.

Weevil ran up the old road to take Matador. As they walked back, Kathleen gave him the details.

In the trailer, Sister tried not to cry out as Walter removed her coat, tie, vest, and shirt.

"I can push your ribs back right now. It will be ferocious pain but then over. As to the cracked ribs, I can wrap you up, I have enough bandages here. A cast might be useless. We'll know after an X-ray," Walter calmly explained.

"I know. I've cracked them before. Okay, just do it, and plug your ears. I know I'll scream."

Walter, a tall, powerful man, put one hand on her torso from behind, one on the front, and quickly moved them. She did scream, quickly sitting down on the ledge inside his trailer, where small items are stored.

"Honey, are you all right?" Gray was ashen.

Now sweating, she nodded. Walter pulled an ace bandage out of his hanging bag. He carried scalpels, scissors, bandages, meds, alcohol to clean wounds. He could handle emergencies.

"You'll need to stand."

"Right." She wobbled a bit.

As Walter wrapped her, Aunt Daniella was with Sam, Yvonne, and Tootie, who walked over. She was filling them in. Everyone wanted to know what happened.

"Oh, hearing her scream, that had to really hurt." Yvonne wished she could do something.

"She's a stoic, but I don't think any of us could be banged around and not holler." Sam put his arm around Aunt Daniella, guiding her to the truck.

"I'm fine."

"I know you are, but you have had a shock and you've had a long walk."

She allowed him to lift her up.

"Give me a minute." He turned back to Yvonne and Tootie. "I'll cut on the motor. She likes heat and it is getting cold."

Everyone's shoulders were white with snow.

"All right. We need to get home." Gray looked at Walter, who nodded in affirmation. "She needs to get home. It's snowing harder. The last thing we need is highway drama."

Adrianna waited outside the tack room. Hearing the scream, she grimaced, her hand on Magnum's head. Mike called the sheriff's department. Recognizing Sister's pain, he knew she needed to go home and she had Walter. The law enforcement people could question her tomorrow. Mike knew this was going to be a long day. Best to keep people calm and see to Sister's welfare.

Lynn, meanwhile, was trying to organize food to give to the guests, since most everyone would miss the breakfast, thanks to the weather and the extraordinary circumstances of what was a good hunt.

Walter, voice firm, said, "I'll get you an X-ray tomorrow. Just in case. I'll call Nick Hexham. He has an X-ray machine in his office." Then he smiled at a friend, a mentor, a person he loved. "You'll be fine. Thank the Lord."

He put her shirt then coat back on, one side hanging on her shoulder. Her arm in the other.

Adrianna, outside Walter's trailer, held up her hand for Sister to balance. "If there is anything I can do, anytime, don't hesitate to ask. I am so sorry."

"Thank you." Her spirits somewhat returning, the silver-haired Master smiled. "No one will ever forget this hunt." She added, "Magnum stuck right next to me."

Lynn and Bull Run members brought food in plastic containers for each Jefferson Hunt visitor. They ran to the trailers. No one protested. They were starved.

"*I saved her,*" Baxter barked.

Fortunately Lynn missed his loud brags.

In the chaos, the concern, Sister, Aunt Daniella, and Kathleen forgot to mention that Veronica was dead. The focus was on Sister's injuries.

Sister, Betty, Gray, and Bobby fit in the Dually with extended doors. Betty was beside herself that she didn't ride back with Sister. She felt guilty that she put the Sassoon in Veronica's truck.

"Pipe down, Betty. She would have tried to kill us both. You did nothing wrong," Sister said, hoping to console her.

As they drove past Cedar Mountain, the wind pumped up, making an eerie sound.

"The dead." Betty shivered.

When the Bull Run staff realized they had not asked about Veronica, they set out to return to where Sister described the situation. Adrianna, Lynn in tow, took the farm road where she had seen Sister, Aunt Daniella, and Kathleen. They drove over the hill, stayed up on the road, and saw Veronica's horse standing patiently. Stopping, they got out and found her on the ground, already covered in snow.

CHAPTER 36

December 13, 2023, Wednesday

Sitting in Aunt Daniella's living room, all eyes were on Ben. Sister, nestled on pillows, sat near the fire. She figured it would take three weeks to heal and she intended to ride whether healed or not. No one dared to puncture her hopefulness. Everyone knew she'd ride, pain or not.

Walter brought some diclofenac, a painkiller with some punch but no opioids. He and Gray had discussed how to woo her into taking it. Sister didn't like to take meds. Sam and Yvonne sat next to each other, as did Betty and Bobby. Kathleen, Abdul at her feet, sat with Ronnie. Kasmir, Alida, and Freddie were also together. Ronnie doted on Aunt Daniella, giving the brothers a break, although Gray was quick with the bourbon.

Ben took a deep breath. "Aunt Daniella, how good of you to host us."

"We're all eager to know what you found out." She smiled plus she liked entertaining.

"As you know, Sheila didn't make it to Orange with her smashed windshield. The Orange County Sheriff picked her up before she hit the town limits. Given that she had glass all over her, they took her to the hospital. Since I alerted them, they kept an officer with her. No one spoke of anything involving shooting, attempted murder, but once she was determined not to be in any danger and patched up, the officer at the hospital arrested her.

"She didn't put up any fight. No doubt too shocked and too exhausted."

Kathleen couldn't help it, she jumped in. "Did she know Veronica was dead?"

"No. She didn't learn that until booked and until she roused her lawyer to come to the jail. Given events, her lawyer felt she should stay in a safe place, as he put it, until she was strong enough to be released."

"Smart." Ronnie tilted his head. "The lawyer."

"He had a lot to juggle." Ben continued, "His client was not accused of murder but bail was set at one hundred thousand dollars. That's a huge amount for a county jail, so they suspected she would run if released. It was her lawyer who told her Veronica was dead. The shock somewhat loosened her tongue.

"She cried. She denied knowing what the problem with Sister was. She denied knowing anything about books carrying contraband. All she said was her sister was under great stress because of Wolverhampton. Veronica feared for her safety, as she spent so much time there and she feared for her employees."

"Did anyone find out anything?" Sam knew only too well how the system could drag out, plus how it often hampered the work of law enforcement officers. He'd been in the pokey, as he called it, plenty of times for being drunk in public or sleeping under the railroad bridge.

"My team and I went out to Wolverhampton. Since this didn't make the news until Monday night thanks to the storm, we made it there before news was out and to our surprise, found workers made it there as well. The woman in charge, Paula Nordhoof, sensed there was trouble, but she didn't know how much. How often do officers from the sheriff's department intrude on restoring a house? We told her Sheila was in jail and Veronica was dead. Surprised, she stayed in control. We asked her, did she know they were dealing in contraband? She said no. Did she know that her girls, for lack of a better word, were engaged in if not prostitution, then luring men out of the bars to steal from them? She said, 'No.' "

"Don't you think she was lying?" Betty burst out.

"Yes. I think she liked her bosses and much as she liked them she had no desire to be jailed for being part of criminal activity."

"So it is what we thought." Betty again spoke.

"Yes. But how can we prove it? If one of the girls talks, yes. I think someone will crack, maybe even today. Jackie is the one asking questions. She's at the Orange County jail. The murder took place in Orange County. The thefts, I think, are taking place in Central Virginia, if not even wider territory. But Orange County's sheriff's department has been helpful. A young woman might get further than an older male officer."

"So you start with thefts?" Kasmir asked.

"Yes. Wherever the sisters restored houses, it's possible the workers there packed up stolen goods and sent them off. Hiding items in the books was a brilliant idea. We'll be questioning employees and former employees for months. All we have right now is Sheila."

"Veronica seemed under control. Nor did Sheila seem emotional until she saw Veronica with Sister injured. What do you think? Aunt Daniella and Kathleen, you were in the car with her," Betty asked.

"Seemed fine," Kathleen remarked. "Until we got close. You could sense tension, even fear."

"When Weevil found the bloody truck, Veronica wanted to follow Kathleen. Granted, she appeared to want to know what was holding us up. However, what if she knew? I told her to stay put because
of hunting protocol, not because I thought she might be involved,"
Aunt Daniella replied.

"Obviously, I didn't think anything. And when we had a brief
exchange at Bishop's Gate, no reaction," Kathleen added to the
topic.

"That murder may have nothing to do with events, but I'm
pretty sure it did. Someone threatened to blow their cover. A worker?
Someone wanted more money." Alida spoke up. "Plus, who did the
killing?"

"The problem with a case such as this is there are victims, plenty
of victims. But they won't come forward. It's not like women even
twenty years ago and many today who won't come forward to press
charges for rape. Those women did nothing. The victims in cases
such as this are men who are stepping out, who can't afford to be
caught by wives, girlfriends, even their bosses, depending on their
professions." Ben paused. "No matter how hard we dig, I know no
man is going to come forward, admit to sleeping with one of the
pretty bar girls and having his watch, cash, rings lifted. It will never
happen. If a woman cites a name, he'll deny it. Her word against his.
No case. As to who actually did the killings, if Sheila cracks, we'll
know. I don't believe she herself killed anyone."

"Why do you think Veronica cracked?" Freddie wondered.

"Pressure. If she killed or had Trevor and Jarvis killed, that
would be great pressure. Do I think those two bartenders were not
reporting all their gain, all they managed to help the girls get, I do.
Again, if Shelia gives way, that can be answered. She can deny par-
ticipating but she'll talk if my team can find clear evidence or if one
of the girls blabs. That's why it helps to take them down to the station
to question them."

"Some of them had to be in jail before," Walter stated.

"Yes. That's why they went to the halfway houses and other places for women trying to rebuild their lives. Thank God for those places. Veronica and Sheila did give them a chance on one level. They agreed to learn construction and I'm sure they hinted at the other work during an interview. None of those girls would have a network to sell their goods." Ben took a swig of Aunt Daniella's bourbon, which she happily supplied to all. "But if they agreed to the seductions, they would benefit from the sisters' network plus they could keep what they might be paid by the man."

"How frustrating this must be for you." Yvonne smiled.

"It is," Ben agreed. "What is the most frustrating is after months or even years of work, you can finally put someone in the dock. An expensive lawyer gets them out. People who lie, cheat, steal, and kill often don't change. The two sisters were well educated, what my mother would call well-bred. If you consider just theft, well, it's bad but," he shrugged, "when you factor in murder. It's detestable."

"Sister, when Veronica tried to kill you, did you then think she was the killer?" Alida asked.

"Yes. What I saw as her mask slipped was pure rage directed at someone who could spoil her party. And I'm alive thanks to Matador and Aunt Daniella."

Ben added, "Aunt Daniella, did you have any idea?"

"No. But a good crook is one who can fit into whatever group they wish to fit into. They have the manners, the dress, the speech of, in a sense, their victim group."

"Are you going to charge my aunt for shooting Veronica?" Sam asked.

"No. There will be a further investigation, but it won't take long. We'll call it self-defense."

"Here's my prediction," Gray, deep voice, said quietly, "one of the workers will become frightened and tell what she knows. Maybe more than one. There will be enough evidence for thefts and robberies.

"As to the murders, if anyone knows and is again frightened, maybe. It's possible that Sheila will get off or receive a light sentence for stealing. She might be spending some time behind bars. And who is to say, that might not save her life? Who knows how many people are a part of this? People here who have something to hide? I would think those men who cheated on their wives will be nervous."

"It has to be lucrative. Very lucrative." Kasmir put that one out there.

"So it is one of the Seven Deadly Sins." Aunt Daniella nodded. "Greed."

"Is murder a seven deadly?" Yvonne wondered.

"No," Sam answered. "Murder is breaking one of the Ten Commandments. Actually, neither is good, is it? But strange to say sins are ranked and I would have to say the commandments are ranked in order. I think 'Thou Shalt Not Kill' is number six."

"I never thought of that," Betty confessed.

"Oh yes you have," Bobby contradicted her. "Divorce never, murder yes."

They all laughed.

"I wish I could tell you more. Bit by bit things will come out, but it's possible we will never have information about the murders. I wish I had an answer for Birdie. I can talk about the case now. Someone, a friend of Trevor's, Birdie didn't see him, assuming it's a him, left a roll of cash in her mailbox with a note that Trevor wanted her to have it. Fingerprinted it, but nothing. This is one of those cases that will go on and on. If Sheila would talk we'd have what we need. She's smart. Very smart." Ben had a tight smile. "Now you get an idea about real police work. Things don't tie up neatly. Often they don't tie up at all. People use false names, get fake IDs. Some disappear, only to reappear somewhere else as a new person. Criminals go free. You might know who they are, what they did, but you can't touch them. Issues that involve crime become politicized.

"This case will be difficult. One of the main suspects is dead. If I do my job, some people will attack me as being part of a repressive system. If I don't do my job, people get hurt, most often those without the resources to hire lawyers. I am frustrated. I am, but I'm not giving up." Ben's voice rose up a notch.

Kasmir smiled. "You're a glutton for punishment."

Alida thought out loud. "Well, maybe Sheila will sell Wolverhampton. That's a tiny bit of good."

"What she'll do is hire the best lawyer out there and fight every step of the way. I doubt she would sell Wolverhampton to any of us." Sam got up to refresh drinks.

"Maybe not. If she can make money, why not?" Gray thought if she put money first, which obviously she did, it might be possible. "People who steal love money. Much of what I saw in Washington was pure greed. You'd be amazed at how many people in government steal from the government. Then again, maybe you wouldn't. But for some, it's like an addiction. Money is the drug of choice."

Alida, still on Wolverhampton, said, "We can use a shill."

Yvonne pursed her lips. "Now there's an idea. She deserves it."

"Speaking of deserving it, Veronica's rented horse deserves a good home. He stayed calm, stood stock-still during gunfire, with his rider sliding off. Adrianna told me his owner. I bought him. He'll live a wonderful life," Sister announced.

"He is terrific. Can really jump." Freddie, behind Veronica in the hunt field, said, "You could rent him out."

"No. Though I would let you ride him. I'll ride him, but after a hunt he comes here, to my barn, to a big stall, good food, new equine friends, and big pastures."

"Lucky fellow." Sam knew Sister would always do right by horses, hounds, house pets, even a turtle. "What's his name?"

Sister smiled. "DeSoto."

"Now, there's a name. Great cars." Aunt Daniella lifted her glass for a refill, which Gray was swift to provide as Sam put more logs in the fire.

"Ben, you're frustrated, but are you disappointed? They're different," Sister asked.

"No. We know more than we did before. And I am glad you are all right. That was a close call, Master."

"Aunt Daniella saved me." Sister thanked her again. She could never thank her enough.

Aunt Daniella lifted her glass to the assembled. "Not bad for an old girl."

ACKNOWLEDGMENTS

The idea for *Time Will Tell* was provoked by Adrianna Waddy, MFH of Bull Run Hunt, along with Lynn Pirozzoli.

Mike Long, MFH of Bull Run Hunt, accompanied by Adrianna, hauled me over their history/blood-soaked Cedar Run territory. Apart from being well-foxed, every hound and hunter's dream, you don't know how many people sleep beneath your feet. Thousands died. Many of their horses died with them.

Did we learn anything?

Foxhunting is a rapturous passion, sweeping all before it. You are never so alive as when on the horse of your heart following a great pack of hounds chasing one of Nature's most beautiful, clever creatures.

Foxhunting has given me my happiest moments.

It has brought into my life wondrous people, hard-riding.

Thank you all.

I wish you an equivalent joy.

Up and Over,
Rita Mae

ABOUT THE AUTHOR

RITA MAE BROWN is the bestselling author of the Sneaky Pie Brown mysteries; the Sister Jane series; the Runnymede novels, including *Six of One* and *Cakewalk; A Nose for Justice; Murder Unleashed; Rubyfruit Jungle;* and *In Her Day,* as well as many other books. An Emmy-nominated screenwriter and a poet, Brown lives in Afton, Virginia, and is a Master of Foxhounds and the Huntsman.

ritamaebrownbooks.com

To inquire about booking Rita Mae Brown
for a speaking engagement, please contact the
Penguin Random House Speakers Bureau at
speakers@penguinrandomhouse.com.

ABOUT THE TYPE

This book was set in Baskerville, a typeface designed by John Baskerville (1706–75), an amateur printer and typefounder, and cut for him by John Handy in 1750. The type became popular again when the Lanston Monotype Corporation of London revived the classic roman face in 1923. The Mergenthaler Linotype Company in England and the United States cut a version of Baskerville in 1931, making it one of the most widely used typefaces today.